KU-593-706

KERRY GREENWOOD

QUEEN OF THE FLOWERS

A Phryne Fisher Mystery

Complete and Unabridged

LIBRARIES NI WITHDRAWN FROM STOCK

ULVERSCROFT
Leicester

First published in Great Britain in 2018 by
Constable
An imprint of Little, Brown Book Group
London

First Ulverscroft Edition
published 2018
by arrangement with
Little, Brown Book Group
An Hachette UK Company
London

The moral right of the author has been asserted

All characters and events in this publication, other
than those clearly in the public domain, are fictitious
and any resemblance to real persons, living or dead,
is purely coincidental.

Copyright © 2004 by Kerry Greenwood

Cover illustration © Tabitha King by arrangement
with Allen & Unwin Book Publishers
All rights reserved

A catalogue record for this book is available
from the British Library.

ISBN 978–1–4448–3846–6

Published by
F. A. Thorpe (Publishing)
Anstey, Leicestershire

Set by Words & Graphics Ltd.
Anstey, Leicestershire
Printed and bound in Great Britain by
T. J. International Ltd., Padstow, Cornwall

This book is printed on acid-free paper

This book is for Christine Day, a real
Queen of the flowers.

With thanks to Dennis Pryor, Mark Pryor
and Ben Pryor, David Greagg and Richard
Revill, the inimitable Jean 'I'm sure I can
find it somewhere, dear' Greenwood, Jenny
Pausacker, Joss Whedon, Edgar Allen Poe,
James 'Charlie' Ferrari, Adrian Munro, and
A.W. Greenwood, who taught me many
valuable things, including never, never to
draw to an inside straight.

Le bon Papa est capable du tout (the good father is capable of anything).

French proverb

CHAPTER ONE

And how Horatius held the bridge
In the brave days of yore.

> Thomas Babbington, Lord Macauley
> 'Horatius',
> *Lays of Ancient Rome*

The elephant was the last straw.

All day Mr Butler, strangely resembling Cerberus except for the number of heads, had kept the world at bay. The Hon. Miss Phryne Fisher was engaged in a solemn ritual and all visitors were to be refused, all tradesmen redirected and all trespassers prosecuted. The bell was not to ring and disturb the votaries' concentration. A holy hush must be maintained.

The household had been dispersed for this special occasion. Miss Ruth and Miss Jane had been banished to the moving pictures to see an improving newsreel and a cowboy adventure, have lunch at a suitable café and spend the afternoon blamelessly at the museum. The dog Molly had been muzzled with the femur of what must have been an ox, or possibly a mammoth. Mrs Butler had put on her good coat and gone hat shopping in the city, leaving a cold collation under a mist of muslin on the dining room table. Dorothy, Miss Phryne's maid and inseparable companion, had naturally joined the rites in attendance, as had the cat Ember. Three times Dot had crept down the stairs to tell Mr Butler that so far it was all going well.

And Mr Butler had kept the door, valiantly turning aside three hawkers (of infallible washing powders, fly repellents and an ingenious new form of mouse-trap), seven society visitors and a worried representative from the mayor's office, calling about another minor detail in the forthcoming Flower Parade. All of these he had awed into leaving cards and departing quietly, closing the gate silently behind them. He was just allowing himself to lean a little into the porch, mopping his brow and wondering how long this could possibly go on, when an elephant stepped easily over the front fence and stood face to face with him.

It was surprisingly large. It had small, wise eyes set into deep wrinkles and for a moment Mr Butler and the elephant stared at each other without moving or reacting. Mr Butler was so astonished that he could not think of anything to say except 'Shoo!' and he did not think that wise, in view of the newly planted dahlias.

They stood there, an interesting tableau out of an Anglo-Indian painting. Then the elephant, obviously feeling that the first move in this new friendship was up to her, lifted her trunk and gently took the handkerchief out of Mr Butler's nerveless hand. She patted delicately at his brow and made a small, absurd squeaking noise. It sounded sympathetic.

'Thank you,' said Mr Butler, a broken man.

'Phryne in?' enquired a voice, and Mr Butler

looked up into the eyes of a raddled, middle-aged woman with fiery red hair, seated astride the elephant's neck. 'Flossie's taken to you, I see. She's the nicest elephant I've ever had, I'll say that for her.'

Mr Butler gathered what wits he had left. 'Miss Fisher is engaged,' he said. 'She is not at home to visitors today.'

'Too bad,' said the woman. 'I'm Dulcie Fanshawe of Fanshawe's elephants. Well, you might have guessed, eh? Any chance of a bucket of water for Flossie? And a cup of tea for me? We've just got off the train and they're still setting up down by the beach.'

'If you can keep your animal ... er... Flossie, quiet, madam, that can be arranged,' said Mr Butler. Miss Dulcie Fanshawe's hair was definitely artificial and her trousers were scandalous but she had a genuine, charming smile. And Miss Phryne would never turn aside a person or even an elephant in need of sustenance.

'She won't give trouble,' said Dulcie. 'Elephants are very quiet beasts.'

'Just walk her along to the back, then,' said Mr Butler. 'The kitchen door is open. I have to keep the door until Miss Fisher's at liberty to receive guests.'

'What is she doing?' asked Miss Fanshawe, permitting Flossie to lift her down and taking hold of one large, flapping ear.

Mr Butler told her. Miss Fanshawe grinned. 'How long has she been at it, then?' she asked,

'Since nine this morning.' Mr Butler finally did allow himself to lean into the porch and Flossie mopped his brow again. He observed the delicate, fingered ends of her trunk and the fine control she had over her grasp. She smelt strongly of hay.

'Lord, you poor man! Now, Floss, give the nice man back his hankie and we'll get you a drink.'

Flossie returned Mr Butler's handkerchief, gave his hair a light caress, and followed Miss Fanshawe around the side of the house to the kitchen.

Mr Butler resumed his vigil. Time was elapsing. The cold collation had been eaten on the run, standing, while discussing and arguing. The girls would be back soon, as would Mrs Butler, who would need to get the dinner started and show Mr Butler her new hat. Miss Phryne had better get a wriggle on or she was going to have disturbances which Mr Butler could not prevent.

Just then he remembered that Molly and her dinosaur bone were in the back garden. How, he wondered, would the black and white mongrel react to Flossie?

Nothing he could do about it from here, he thought, and at last heard the long-anticipated sounds of women reassuming coats, putting on hats, packing up, and chattering their way down the hall to his closely guarded door. At last. He felt like a sentry who had been relieved of his post long after he had assumed himself forgotten.

The rite was concluded. Miss Fisher's new dress had been fitted. Mr Butler bowed out Madame Fleuri, a grim devotee of the mode, her two assistants and her three seamstresses. Miss Fisher and Dot waved them goodbye.

And Mr Butler shut the front door just as

Molly, waking from a deep post-prandial nap in the asparagus bed, encountered her first elephant and entirely lost her poise. Howling, she fled into the house and dived under Miss Fisher's chair. After a while a small black nose stuck out from under the fringe, quivering.

Miss Phryne Fisher was dressed in a bright red house gown. She had put it on and taken it off eighteen times. She had listened to long lectures about fashion and stood unmoving as swatches of cloth were draped, pinned, whipped off and on and pinned again. For seven hours. She had gulped down her lunch and was feeling hungry, thirsty and frayed. She did not need an irruption of hysterical dogs into her now-quiet house.

'Molly?' asked Phryne wearily. 'What is the matter?'

'I think it was meeting Flossie,' said Miss Fanshawe, escorted in by Mr Butler. 'All the circus dogs are used to elephants, I'd forgotten how a nice urban dog might react. Sorry to drop in on you like this when you've had such an exhausting day, Phryne, but I came looking for a drink for Flossie and remembered that you lived here.'

'Dulcie Fanshawe!' Phryne jumped up. Molly declined to move. Until someone came up with a reasonable explanation for elephants, she was staying where she was. 'Come in, sit down, have a drink, how are you? I haven't seen you since London!'

'Can't stop,' said Miss Fanshawe. 'Come and meet Flossie. I can't leave her in that pretty little garden for long. Far too many edible plants.'

Phryne followed Dulcie to the garden and

5

found that Flossie had not fancied any of the vegetation on offer but was sucking up a lot of water from a bucket, continuously replenished with the hose.

'I took her for a little constitutional down by the sea and she would keep tasting the foam,' explained Dulcie Fanshawe. 'Too much salt is very bad for elephants and they're setting up the show right by the sea, on the sand. There,' she said to the gurgling elephant, 'that feels better, I'll warrant. Poor old Floss! I bought her from a frightful little road show – filthy place – where they kept her chained all the time. See the scars around her ankles? She was dying from pneumonia and neglect and loneliness and I got her for a song and a threat to report the owner to the RSPCA. I reported him anyway. If I'd had my way we would have chained him by the leg in filthy straw for a few months to see how he liked it. Horrible man. Then I sat up with Flossie for a week until she started to recover and she took to Rani and Kali right away. But she's the nicest elephant I've ever met. And the worst treated. Humans.'

'I know, as a species we have nothing to recommend ourselves. How did you end up in Australia?' asked Phryne.

'Well, with the three elephants I had a show, and we were something of a hit,' said Miss Fanshawe modestly. 'And none of us like the cold. Flossie's got a weak chest, poor girl. So we took Wirth up on his offer and came out here. Nice place,' she said. 'Kali likes the beer and I like the climate.'

6

Mr Butler brought a tray of drinks into the garden. Flossie squeaked her pleasure at renewing their acquaintance and he unbent far enough to pat her trunk.

'A refreshing cocktail, Miss Fisher,' he said. 'In view of the day we have all had.'

Phryne sipped. 'Oh, lovely,' she said. It tasted of cherries. A bubbly, delicate, utterly refreshing mouthful of spring.

Miss Fanshawe took a deep gulp, blinked and said, 'Oh my! That's enough to make you want to go out and get all hot and tired over again!'

Mr Butler withdrew, pleased. The lady might not be out of the top drawer but she knew a good cocktail when she drank it. Mrs Butler had returned with her new hat and was seated at the kitchen table, peeling vegetables for a roast. The adoptive daughters of the house were helping, eating bread and butter to stay their stomachs until dinner. Thin blonde Jane and darker, plumper Ruth, Miss Phryne's strays. Mr Butler wanted to unbend and he couldn't do it with them there, even though they were good girls and no trouble at all, really.

'Go into the garden,' said Mr Butler to the two girls. 'There's an elephant.'

They dived for the door without a word.

His new cocktail had gone down well. The day had been long. Mr Butler sat down, undid his shirt collar, and poured himself a small glass of the butler's infallible restorative, a good port. Mrs Butler stopped peeling and laid down her potato severely.

'Now, Mr B, you know it isn't right to fib to the

girls,' she reproved. 'Just because you'd rather have their room than their company.'

Mr Butler gave her a smile which bordered on smug – he had had a very trying day – and said nothing. Mrs Butler surveyed him closely. They had been married for nearly forty years. She picked up the vegetable peeler again, obscurely worried by that smile. 'There isn't really an elephant in the garden, is there?' pressed Mrs Butler, peeling industriously.

'Yes, Mrs B,' he replied, allowing himself another vindicated sip. 'There is.'

Phryne Fisher looked at her household as they came down to dinner, correctly dressed, clean and shining. A credit to themselves, she thought. Dot in her favourite brown jumper suit. The girls in matching summer dresses. Herself in her red house gown. Ember, who had not twitched a whisker when he sighted an elephant through the kitchen window, slouching elegantly along after Mr Butler's silver salver, which was redolent of gravy. Molly, who had been coaxed out from under the chair and assured that the elephant was definitely gone, sitting nervously under the table hoping for titbits. Mr Butler, restored by port. And dinner.

Phryne had a healthy appetite and the money to indulge it. And lunch had been scanty and hurried. Time to taste a nice Bordeaux and allow the day to fold peacefully to its close.

'Where did you meet Miss Fanshawe?' asked Jane. 'And did you know that the rock hyrax is the elephant's nearest relative?'

'In London and no,' replied Phryne. 'What is a rock hyrax?'

'It's a little rabbity thing,' said Jane. 'Not at all like an elephant, which is – as we saw – big. And Miss Fanshawe said that Flossie isn't even a very big elephant.'

'She was a special act in a circus I went to see,' said Phryne. 'I have always loved circuses. And I was able to help in a little emergency they had, so they invited me backstage–'

'Hang on,' interrupted Jane. 'What little emergency?'

'It wasn't anything really,' temporised Phryne. Jane looked at her. So did Dot and Ruth. 'Oh well, they had a big cat act. I was sitting ringside when a black panther called Princess, who had clearly had a bad day, decided that sitting up on her pedestal and waving her paws in the air was too, too tedious and it would be more amusing to knock her trainer down with one swipe and then bite his head off. She was about to do that when I grabbed the ice-cream man's slop dish and threw it in her face.'

'That was quick thinking!' said Jane.

'I reasoned that she was a cat and cats hate water and they especially hate to appear anything less than entirely well groomed,' Phryne told Jane. 'With her whiskers full of partly melted ice cream she felt that she could not face her public and rushed off stage. The other beasts went too and the trainer wasn't badly hurt. I don't like seeing those beautiful cats made to do stupid tricks, anyway. It's undignified. If I had allowed the panther to continue with her program for the day they would have had to shoot her, and that wouldn't have done at all. Anyway, they asked me to come backstage and there I met Dulcie. First, I met Kali. Now she is a big elephant. Not friendly. I was picking my way over the waste ground to the caravans when a stupid dog came yapping and biting at this huge elephant – it clearly had a death wish – and her trunk shot out and – whack – the dog was thrown into the air. It hit the side of a tent with a noise like a drum and retired into private life, howling. I was just standing very still, trying not to attract Kali's attention, when Dulcie said, "It's the heat. It's making them nervous," and Kali picked me up and set me on her back as gently as a mother. It was an odd evening, all round,' concluded Phryne, taking another bite of roast beef.

'No, really,' said Dot with some irony.

'Kali is named after the Hindu Goddess of Death,' Jane informed the company. 'She's usually depicted with a bunch of skulls in one hand and a sword in the other, dancing on a pile of severed heads.'

'Nice name,' said Dot, exercising her irony again. 'Nice thing for a young lady to know.'

'Knowledge is power,' said Phryne approvingly. 'Dulcie and elephants just go together like toast and honey. In the way that some people are good with dogs or children, she's good with elephants. And she had such a conventional upbringing, too. Nice girl from a nice school with a retired vicar as a father. Still, you can never tell.'

'Fathers are important,' said Ruth unexpectedly.

'Yes,' agreed Phryne. 'I suppose they are. But

there are fathers and fathers, you know. Mine is an old grump.'

'Mine's all right,' said Dot, helping herself to another roast potato. 'A hard working honest man. Even goes to church when Mum nags him. Wants his dinner right on the dot of five, of course, but he works hard and he deserves it. Never used to yell at us or hit us.'

'I don't remember mine very well,' confessed Jane. 'I always lived with my grandma. She said that my parents were travelling folk but kind in their way. They just left me with her and wandered off, then they got killed in a farming accident when I was four.'

'And I don't remember my father at all,' said Ruth. 'I wonder what he was like?'

Phryne suppressed the comment that since he had not gone to the trouble of actually marrying Ruth's mother and had exited stage left before Ruth was born, not even putting his name on her birth certificate, he wasn't particularly relevant. This lack of a father was clearly bothering Ruth, though. The girl read far too many romances.

'He might have been a good man,' she said gently. 'But we'll never know. Think of him as a good man,' she suggested.

'Mum said he was a sailor,' said Ruth.

'There are good sailors,' said Phryne. 'Well, some good sailors. In a way they are ideal as husbands. They drop in every six months for a wild celebration, then they drop out again before one gets bored with their company or annoyed by their habits. However, speculation is always lame. Let's see what Mrs Butler has for dessert. Ah!

11

Fruit salad and ice cream. I wonder if elephants like ice cream?'

'It would need to be a very big dixie cup,' said Jane.

Everyone, after their busy day, was sleepy and disinclined to go out to the movies or indeed to do anything more active than play the gramophone and flick through a magazine. Phryne read a detective story, frequently going back because she suddenly found herself reading a conversation between two characters she had not met before – a sure sign that an early night was indicated. The girls played a quiet game of cards. Dot knitted. Molly, still obscurely worried that huge grey beasts might invade her domain, slept in the kitchen wedged in beside the stove with her tail to the wall.

Ember had already retired to a boudoir which was no longer filled with intrusive humans talking, arguing and flourishing pointed objects. He was curled up in a perfect black sphere when Phryne cast off her red gown, bathed sumptuously in a lily of the valley scented tub, and assumed a red silk nightgown and her own place in her moss green bedroom.

Mr and Mrs Butler made a milk drink and retired. Both girls went to their jazz-coloured room and got into their beds. By ten o'clock the whole house was breathing deeply in well-deserved slumber.

No one heard the side window slide open after midnight.

Miss Mavis Sutherland to Miss Anna Ross
21 August 1912

Dear Annie

I have your letter and it all sounds so exciting! Three sailors, one a piper, one a violinist and one a drummer, all staying in your mama's house! Which one of the three do you like the best? Mr James Murray the fiddler (he doesn't sound very Scotch, by the way)? Oh no, I see that you said he had red hair. Red hair is so unattractive on a man. Not like your own deep auburn tresses which could hardly be called red at all. So is it the drummer Mr Neil McLeod, who is fair, or the dark-eyed Mr Rory McCrimmon? Come, Annie, 'fess up. It must be unbearably exciting to have musicians in the house. Tell all. I am agog.

Here it is very tedious as always, the London house is closed for the summer but they will all be back soon, now that autumn is closing in. There was frost on the windows last night. It must be lovely to be in sunny Australia where it never snows. Along about February, when the snow closes in and it's so dark, I miss dear old Melbourne more than ever. Well, I had better finish this or I'll miss the post. With my respects to your mother and my dear love to you,

Your friend
Mavis

CHAPTER TWO

The struggling pangs of conscious truth to hide
To quench the blushes of ingenuous shame.

Thomas Gray
'Elegy Written in a Country Churchyard'

Phryne woke refreshed after a short but erotic dream about Lin Chung. Dreams about Lin Chung, her Chinese lover, were almost always erotic. He was everything one could want in a lover: skilled, passionate, beautiful, exotic, devoted, and firmly married to the charming Camellia. Phryne was always willing to make appointments for passion, but hadn't a second to spare for jealousy, scenes, or matrimony. Even her father had given up on finding a suitable husband for Phryne.

She sipped at the dangerous, inky-brown Hellenic beverage on which she relied to shock her into wakefulness, and surveyed the day's activities. Meeting with the Mayor's representative at ten. Lunch with her flower maidens at twelve. Meeting with Phryne's favourite salesman, Mr Xavier from Xavier's Cellars, at four. She was saving Mr Xavier for last, as he was her favourite vendor. What do vintners buy, she mused with Omar Khayyám, one-half so precious as that which they sell? He might even have managed to track down that shipment of Louis Roederer Cristal which had been ordered for the Russian court and which, tragically, the revolution had prevented them from drinking. It had last been seen heading for South America. Still, the Russians did have a sweet tooth and Phryne abominated sweet champagne.

She pottered gently through the routine of bathing and dressing and sat brushing her hair in front of her vine-wreathed mirror. The Hon. Miss Phryne Fisher looked at herself. Short black hair cut in a cap like a Dutch doll. A small, decided chin, cupid's bow lips, fine etched black eyebrows, piercingly green eyes which gave her her Chinese name of the Jade Lady. Very nice, she told her reflection.

Dot had laid out a forest green cardigan suit and ivory silk blouse, low-heeled shoes and a natural straw hat with a respectable brim. Dot was a reliable weather forecaster. If she had selected this hat, it meant no rain in prospect but a danger of sunburn. Phryne spared a moment to reflect on how very fortunate she was in her family, and went downstairs.

Where a riot appeared to have broken out. Phryne halted on the last step and tried to work out what was happening, with a view to taking the poker to an intruder or clipping a few ears, whichever seemed indicated. She listened.

Female voices only, it seemed. Three, in fact. Ruth and Jane, screaming at each other in the breakfast room. Well, well. And they ordinarily got on amiably enough. Dot was yelling at both of them to be quiet while Miss Phryne was having breakfast, and Molly was helping by barking hysterically. Mr Butler came out of the room, restrained only by the inflexible butlers' code from throwing up his hands in despair. Phryne stepped past him and said, 'Well,' and got instant silence.

Jane was flushed and angry, her blonde hair straggling out of its plait where she had tugged at it. Ruth looked down, mutinous and red. Dot collected herself enough to take a deep breath.

'Anyone like to tell me what this is about?' asked Phryne pleasantly. 'Jane?'

'No,' said Jane miserably.

'Ruth?'

'No!' said Ruth.

'Dot, do you know?'

'No,' said Dot, sounding both cross and surprised. 'We were just having a nice quiet breakfast when they both went mental.'

'Are you going to tell me what is happening?' asked Phryne. Both girls shook their heads. Phryne was very curious but it was going to be a busy day and she made her deployments in a manner which not only kept the combatants safely apart but gave the two of them jobs which they would find both hard and uncongenial.

'Then you will go and apologise to poor Mr Butler. He does not like upsets. Neither do I, especially in the morning. Jane will help Mrs Lin with the flowers. Ruth will sit in the small parlour and finish off the hems for all those aprons. I will be in here, talking to the Mayor's secretary, if anyone would like to confide. Fair?'

The girls nodded glumly. Jane hated the idea of

16

spending valuable thinking time designing something as foolish as flower arrangements. Ruth loathed plain sewing. They trailed off to make their apologies and Dot poured herself a fresh cup of tea.

'That was interesting,' said Phryne, sitting down and nibbling at a piece of French toast, abandoned as it fell from a combatant's nervous hand. Why had Jane called Ruth a fool? And why had Ruth called Jane a liar?

'I don't know what's come over them,' said Dot. 'I'm that sorry, Miss Phryne.'

'Dot, dear, young women are not your fault,' said Phryne. 'Thank God. I would like to know what that was all about. It sounded serious. But meanwhile we have Miss Jones coming at ten and I'm sure that will give us enough to think about. Poor woman! The problems of this Flower Festival appear to be proliferating like ants at a picnic.'

Dot regained her composure and finished her breakfast. Mr Butler came in to clear away. Mrs Lin arrived with a folio of flower drawings. Miss Jones arrived and was shown in and supplied with tea. The day got under way.

Miss Jones was the sort of person who is concealed, like the nun in the foundation, in every organisation which does Good Works. Patient, dogged, meticulous, vastly overworked, unpaid and completely unappreciated, she finds, files, calls, arranges, soothes and ameliorates papers, contracts, tradesmen, repairs, hurt feelings and Very Important People. No one notices her until God finally calls her home or she quits to look

17

after her aged parents, when the whole edifice instantly falls astonished to the ground. Repeated harassment usually greys her hair and causes her to lose her glasses, and pressure of work requires her to clothe herself in serviceable garments which are never decorated with anything more daring than a scarf and possibly a bluebird brooch. But Miss Jones' strength was as the strength of ten because her heart was pure and Phryne liked her very much.

Therefore she always provided Miss Jones with a good solid pot of really strong tea, a plate of Mrs Butler's excellent ginger biscuits, and ten minutes in which to gather her thoughts. Miss Jones appreciated Phryne, too. Even though she was reputed to be Fast. Miss Fisher had handed over a thumping cheque to the Lord Mayor's Appeal and with that money Miss Jones could do an awful lot of good in the way of layettes for poor women, refuges for unwed mothers and meals for hungry children. Miss Fisher deserved to be Queen of the Flowers in the parade that was the grand finale of the Flower Festival, and Miss Jones just knew she was going to look absolutely beautiful. And she had not only paid for her own dress but those of the four flower maidens, too. Also, her tea was just as Miss Jones liked it and the biscuits were her favourite. She prized small courtesies, because they were the only ones she ever received.

She put down her cup and sighed. Miss Fisher took the sheaf of papers which Miss Jones offered.

'The bazaar will be opened by the Lady Mayoress at one on Friday,' said Miss Jones. 'The church ladies will be offering tea and cakes. I've sorted out the big wheel and the lucky envelopes, there will be a bran-tub lucky dip, games for the children and of course, the sale of work.'

Miss Jones closed her eyes and intoned with great pleasure, 'We have pokerwork and barbola work and lampshades and tassels and ribbon work and lace. We have knitting and tatting and crochet and beading, we have the daintiest dressed dolls, very pretty, we have jewellery and pottery and leaded glass, we have dried flower pictures and chocolate paper pictures and–'

'Stop, stop, Miss Jones dear, you overwhelm me,' exclaimed Phryne, charmed by Miss Jones' enthusiasm.

'And watercolours, of course,' added Miss Jones. 'But not, perhaps, for your walls, Miss Fisher.'

'Perhaps not,' said Phryne. 'You never know.'

Miss Jones knew that Miss Fisher's invariable method of tackling bazaars was to inveigle all the gentlemen of her acquaintance into the venue and then require them to buy as many armloads of the more despised produce – wobbly coffee cups, off-centre beading, tangled tatting – as they could carry in payment for her smile. They seemed to think it was worth it. Miss Jones thought that it must be nice to have a smile that valuable.

'So if you will arrange for the flowers to be delivered early, the church ladies will do the Town Hall,' said Miss Jones.

'Already done,' said Phryne, handing over the waybill from Misses' Ireland, Eastern Market. 'Ireland's are also delivering the flowers for the nosegays to me on the Saturday morning. We will

19

dress here and go down to the float in the car. Strike the flowers from your list of things to worry about, Miss Jones.'

Miss Jones, with considerable relief, did so.

'And here is the program for the whole week. I think you will agree that we have something for everybody.'

'Indeed,' agreed Phryne, scanning rapidly. Yes, from Monday to Saturday there was something going on somewhere: a carnival and a circus, Luna Park (just for fun), lifesaving and swimming demonstrations, marching bands, gymnastic displays, recitations, community singing. Lantern lectures! The Holy Land, she was prepared to bet. Or Along the Nile. Both were present, and a lecture from someone called Professor Mercken reading 'The Golden Journey to Samarkand', with illustrative slides. 'Our camels sniff the evening and are glad.' Yes, that might be worth seeing.

Miss Jones was getting up, smoothing her grey serge skirt and finding her glasses. Phryne saw her out cordially. Mr Butler brought in the post. There was nothing unusual except for a playing card. It was the ace of clubs. Phryne turned it over and saw, written in very black ink at the bottom of the card, W 11:15, K 3:00.

Cryptic. Probably someone calculating their losses. She set it aside for later consideration. No sound from the parlour, where Ruth was angrily hemming. No sound from the salon, where Jane was listening to Camellia talk about flower designs. Molly was truffling in the garden bed just outside the window. Phryne closed her eyes, just for a moment, listening to the silence of a well-conducted household. When she awoke Mr Butler was at the door, intimating that the car was ready to take her to lunch.

Walking into Café Anatole always made Phryne feel alive. It was a perfect Parisian bistro – lots of zinc, bosomy girl, gold-lettered glass and white paper tablecloths – set down in St Kilda, run by Monsieur Anatole Bertrand *et sa famille*. Phryne was very fond of all of them and surrendered her light coat to Jean-Paul, today's Cheeky French Waiter Extraordinaire, with relief. The air was scented with herbs and onion and she was suddenly ravenous.

Four flower maidens stood up as Phryne was shown to their table. Anatole's had become a Suitable Place for unattached young women from the best of circles to lunch unaccompanied by a chaperone. Anatole, a bon bourgeois with a strong sense of what was, and what was not, *convenable*, ran accounts for their parents and the Young Ladies were indulged with beautiful food and slightly Bohemian company. Anatole would never let anything *inconvenable* happen to them, and real trouble would be averted by the strong arm of Cousin Henri. But 'going to Anatole's' was slightly daring all the same. And both Jean-Paul and his brother Jean-Jacques were such outrageous flirts. Only Phryne knew that it was part of their training. One did not become a Cheeky French Waiter with a delicate line in flattery – enough to amuse, never slipping over into offence – without careful instruction.

Phryne sat and greeted the young ladies. They had raised the most money for the Lord Mayor's

Appeal from their charitable efforts and their acquaintances. They were not distinguished in looks, except for being young and healthy, and had tried Madame's ingenuity in finding a style of costume which would complement everyone from Joannie Smythe's rosy plumpness and blonde curls to Diane Pridham's dark solidity, Marie Bernhoff's adolescent gawkiness and Rose Weston's premature bust. Madame had, at one point, almost accepted Phryne's suggestion of pink smocks and sun bonnets, a measure of the difficulty of her task. Miss Fisher's next suggestion – matching sugar sacks – had at least made Madame Fleuri laugh, which didn't happen very often.

'*Salut*,' said Phryne. 'Do sit down, ladies. I think we might venture on one glass of champagne, and I'm sure that Anatole has something charming for lunch.'

'Madame Bertrand is cooking today,' said Jean-Paul, materialising with glasses and a wrapped bottle. 'There are *hors d'oeuvres froids*, a little soup, a fine *poulet roti à la diva* with *haricots flageolets* and *pommes de terre fondantes*, and such beautiful ladies will of course enjoy Madame's famous *glace Alhambra* for dessert.'

He coaxed the cork from the bottle – no French waiter, however cheeky, will retain his position if he wastes good champagne in popping, a practice fit only for Englishmen and barbarians – and allowed a little golden wine to trickle into Phryne's glass. She inhaled. Perfect. Sprightly and a little sweet, a gentle introduction to wine being part of a young lady's education.

22

They sipped obediently. Diane made a face and put down the glass. She knew what she liked and so far she didn't like wine. Child of a wealthy biscuit manufacturer and stolid from the nursery, Phryne considered. Joannie gulped and choked lightly. Possibly because she knew that Jean-Paul would thus have to pat her on the back. Good-natured and fond of her own way – the same might be said of me, Phryne thought, except for the bit about 'good-natured' – and possibly more intelligent than her cream-fed looks might indicate to the casual observer. Thin gawky Marie took another small taste, swallowed, and tried again. That one might easily prove to have taste, thought Phryne. Not the first champagne in her life, I'll warrant. Her father was a famous orchestral musician and Marie had raised her money by putting on select *thé-dansants* for the flirting pairs amongst her class. She herself had played the viola in the chamber ensemble.

Rose raised her glass and drank fully half of it without taking a breath. Rather too practised for thirteen. Phryne didn't know Rose's family, the Westons. Reputed to be old and reputed, also, to be miserly. They were ruled over by an antique grandfather who had not the slightest idea of the cost of the modern world or the least intimation about when to die. He had made Rose Weston's father adopt the family surname. Rose always rather worried Phryne. The girl was far too wound up to be comfortable company. Her eyes were too bright, her speech too fast, and she never sat still. Even now, halfway through a glass of good champagne, her thin fingers were tapping on the table.

Jean-Paul raised an eyebrow, strictly for the edification of Madame Fisher, and retreated to bring out a series of cold hors d'oeuvres. The girls commented on their champagne.

'I don't like this stuff,' said Diane. 'Can I have some orangeade?'

'I am getting used to it,' said Marie. 'I like the sort of lemony taste.'

'I love the way the bubbles tickle,' giggled Joannie.

'I'll have yours, if you don't want it,' said Rose.

Phryne allowed them free range amongst the little savouries which Anatole's made so well. Anchovies with red peppers. Little barquettes with various fillings – egg, salmon mousse, chicken, foie gras and ham. Phryne selected the plate of vegetable hearts with Madame's mayonnaise, always an alchemical marvel.

'These are really little eggs,' said Diane, eating three. 'Must come from really titchy hens.'

'Plovers,' explained Phryne. 'You might like a barquette, this one's egg.'

'And these are really salty grapes!' objected Marie.

'Olives,' explained Phryne. 'Another acquired taste. Just spit it into your napkin.'

'This is nice of you, Miss Fisher,' said Joannie, embarrassed by her gauche friends. 'To take us out to lunch like this at Anatole's. I mean, you didn't have to do it. You just have to tell us where to sit and what to do and we'll obey. It's a tremendous honour to meet you, my mother says.'

'I like to know who I'm sharing a float with,'

said Phryne, awarding Joannie a mark for savoir-faire. 'And it should be fun. Do you like your dress, Joan?'

'I've never seen anything so beautiful,' said Joannie. 'I never thought that scary old lady would make anything fit for me to wear. She glared at me the whole time she was pinning me into it. I mean, I know I'm the wrong shape for 1928.'

'You would have been perfect for 1890,' Marie consoled her. 'And I would have looked like a toothpick.'

'Yes, but we're in 1928 and looking like a toothpick is all the rage,' said Joannie sadly. 'But the sweet pea dress – I've never looked so good in anything. And Marie looks good in it too.'

'Madame Fleuri is a genius,' Phryne pointed out. 'What about you, Diane?'

'It's a lovely dress,' said Diane, munching an anchovy. 'I thought it was going to be like it was when my sister got married. All bridesmaids have to look like a lump of wet lettuce, you know, in case the bride gets cross. You remember my wet lettuce dress, Rose?'

'Not going to make any new husband look away from the blushing bride,' agreed Rose. 'I thought it was more like spinach, actually. Old spinach. At least green suits you. My mother adores white on girls, so I have to wear white, and white does not suit me.'

This was true. As Jean-Paul removed the empty plates and brought small cups of chilled bouillon, Phryne wondered what would look good on the blooming young women. Rose had almost red hair, pale blue eyes and blotchy, irritable skin.

Severely plain box-cut linen confined her curves but did not conceal them. She seemed about to burst out of her seams, which was disconcertingly erotic and surely not what her mother had intended. White was definitely not Rose's colour. She needed, perhaps, to wear dark shades, perhaps even wine red or dark blue, which would leach some of the redness from her skin and hair and show up those surprising Scandinavian eyes. A good dusting of pearl powder and a sedative and she might be quite presentable.

Phryne suggested darker colours and Rose shrugged.

'That's what Madame Fleuri said, but I can't do anything about it. No one listens to me. Girls wore white in Grandpapa's time and in Mamma's time too, so I've got to wear it. Even if I never find a husband and have to wear white forever.'

'There are worse fates,' said Marie darkly. 'I don't want a husband. What would I want a husband bothering me for? I've got music to learn. A husband would want me to have dinner with him and have babies and things. I haven't got time for all that sort of thing.'

'Well,' said Diane, slowly, 'there might be a lot of fun in having a husband who wanted to do the same sorts of things as I do. You know. Holidays. Hiking? Skiing? He might turn out to be a jolly chap and quite a dear to have around. He might have his own plane. And he might let me fly it.'

'He might at that,' agreed Phryne. 'But you might also have your own plane and you could let him fly it.'

'That's true,' said Diane, thinking about it. 'You

26

can fly, can't you, Miss Fisher? My brother said you were a famous flier.'

'Only in a plane. It isn't as hard as driving a car, you know.'

'Only a bit further to fall if you make a mistake,' said Joannie, shuddering. 'Not for me! I like jolly things, like theatres and shopping and nice little dinners. And I'd have a house full of babies. I like babies.'

'Someone has to,' said Phryne.

'And books,' said Joannie. 'Lots of books. I could fill up a library with the books I want! When I'd read all the French ones I could learn Italian. And Spanish. But not German. It's a lumpy language. Ugly.'

Joannie looked up in surprise and blushed like a poppy as Jean-Paul gave her an approving smile – Jean-Paul had lived through the siege of Paris as a child and did not approve of Germanness in any shape or form. Rose giggled.

As Jean-Paul turned away, Rose said in a piercing whisper, 'Joannie! I'll tell your mother you were flirting with the waiter!'

'Rose, you mustn't! I wasn't!' gasped Joan.

'I'll tell!' threatened Rose, giggling again.

This was the outside of enough. Phryne had never approved of schoolgirl malice. 'Rose,' she said, 'I might mention that if you wish to wound your friend, you could manage to do it with greater propriety and a good deal more wit. And you can do it elsewhere. Now, here is roast chicken with beans and piped potatoes. Bon appetit!'

Rose did not blush but stared down at her plate in abject misery. Phryne felt annoyed. Had she had such tender and explosive feelings at that age? Probably. But she had had the advantage of a steely will, a firm intention of doing exactly as she wished, and better manners. Also, perhaps, a greater measure of cunning. And a good idea of what she wished. And she had done it. All of it. Some of it unwise and some of it perilous, but she had left her family, established herself, and now had just what she wanted. She tried not to feel smug and bent a forgiving smile on the wretched Rose.

Kind Joannie coaxed Rose into tasting the chicken and soon they were discussing futures again. Phryne ate well, declined another glass of champagne in case she should set a bad example, and listened as they talked quietly, wary of setting Rose off again. They were nice girls, she decided. Nice and ordinary and plain, destined for nice ordinary fates. Except the bone-thin, dedicated Marie, who would probably find her viola a more attractive partner than any man, unless he could engage her interest, possibly by standing between her and her music stand. Joannie would have her books and her babies. Diane would find a stout lad from one of the Public Schools who would take her hiking and skiing and eventually on a long walk down the aisle to the tune of the march from Lohengrin. She would then have strong, stocky children who would always have skinned knees and would grow up to be engineers. And Rose... Yes, what about Rose? Rose was a puzzle. Noisy, bright, intermittently hysterical, jumpy, over-endowed, ill advised. Used to alcohol, too. She hadn't even gasped at her second glass of champagne. Phryne did not know what would become of Rose. But if someone didn't step in to protect and educate her, it might be for the worst.

On that dark thought, dessert arrived. Jean-Paul laid it down with a flourish. Madame, who had been an apprentice in the Anatole kitchen, specialised in cold puddings. *Glace Alhambra* was a heavenly pile of strawberry mousse with cold sweet vanilla ice cream at its heart. All of her ice creams were superb. Phryne intended to spend the summer working her way through them, from *glace à l'abricot* to *glace aux poires* and all the *glaces composées*. Even Berthe, Anatole's very severe sister, thought that Elise Bertrand, nee Lizzie Chambers, made a promising *pouding froid*.

Champagne might have been a strange new experience but ice cream was not, and the girls fell on the glace with squeaks of delight. Phryne told them to eat all of it and excused herself to go to the kitchen and greet her ex-clients, Lizzie and Bunny Jenkins, aware that she might receive a flung ladle for her pains. Cooks at lunch peppered more than the soup.

Lizzie was floury and hot and gave Phryne a floury, hot, pleased hug. Mr Jenkins brushed her floured front. He was wearing a cook's overall and now looked like the White Rabbit happily exiled from Wonderland.

'Nice lunch?' asked Lizzie, a trifle anxiously.

'Beautiful lunch. Wonderful lunch. Pity about the company. I really don't have a lot of fellow-feeling for girls of that age.'

'Yes you do. Just not those girls. Who have you got?' Lizzie allowed herself a peep through the

29

swinging doors. 'Ah. Well, Diane lunches here once a week with her aunt, who is just like her. Solid. Marie comes here with her father. That man is such a good musician, and he flirts with his daughter all the time – no wonder she sticks to music. Joannie is a dear. You must have liked her. She's the one who found that starving kitten in the alley, persuaded Anatole – and he was in a mood, too, the oysters were late – to compound a special dish of fish for it, and carried it home in the bosom of a dress which must have cost her mother ten pounds. Of course, she does speak very good French, or she might have been donged with a pot, customer or not. Her children are going to be polyglots. So I suppose – oh dear, yes. Well, that's Rose for you. Poor girl.'

'What about Rose?' asked Phryne.

Jean-Paul slammed into the kitchen, sniffed at the sight of the cook leaning on the sink and gossiping in the middle of lunch, and slammed out with a tray full of soups. Mr Jenkins twitched his pink nose anxiously.

'You get on with the salads,' Lizzie told him. 'I can talk while I work. Most of the orders are in now, anyway. I just have to watch this *bifteck* on the charcoal grill. You know, Phryne, I'm so happy and I owe this all to you. *Mon cher mari* is the kindest of men and I get to cook as much as I like. I'm learning such a lot! And I'm going to be a very good dessert chef. But you're busy and it's nice of you to come in and say hello. You don't want to hear all this stuff. Look at me, gossiping like an old woman.'

'I've got a reason for asking,' said Phryne. Lizzie's strong wrists turned the steak, slapped it on the plate, cleaned the edges and spooned out the bearnaise sauce which had been keeping warm on the edge of the grill. Her movements were all decided, skilled and complete. The young woman was robust and alive with purpose – the very thing which Rose lacked.

'Oh well, it's just that she's been in here rather often. At night. With gentlemen. If you can call them gentlemen. I only say that because I met your friend Mr Bert at the Vic Market recently and pointed one of them out and he said that they were bad men, and he told me that their money's as good as anyone's if I didn't mind where it came from. Would you trust his opinion? He looked quite severely at me.'

'On bad men, Bert is an acknowledged expert,' Phryne confirmed.

'And you know, Phryne, I'm no good at clothes and things, but last time I saw Rose she wasn't wearing much. I mean, the dress had a sort of front and really hardly any back. Jean-Jacques had to relieve Jean-Paul of that table because he was so distracted. Jean-Jacques is married,' she explained.

'And she was drinking too much,' said Phryne.

'I didn't tell you that,' said Lizzie.

'No, you didn't,' said Phryne. 'I heard you not saying it. Never mind. I'll come back one night when you aren't cooking and take you – out to dinner,' she promised. She blew a kiss to Mr Jenkins and left the kitchen for the severe black coffee which Jean-Paul had deposited next to her place. The girls had polished off the *glace*. They all looked pleased. Except for Rose, who was tapping again. Her chewed fingernails danced across the white paper tablecloth.

What, indeed, would become of Rose?

Miss Anna Ross to Miss Mavis Sutherland
1 October 1912

Dear Mavis

Thank you for your letter. As to your questions, I blush as I write to tell you that there is no one in the world for me but Mr Rory McCrimmon the piper. He comes from Skye where the best pipers can lure the seals out of the sea. They say their ancestor married a seal, a selkie. He has beautiful brown eyes and his hair is dark and curls in the most darling way at the back of his neck. And when he speaks to me to say something like 'pass the salt' I melt, I grow short of breath, and my knees become unreliable.

Mama hasn't noticed because we are very busy. All she has said was to approve of me helping more in the house and reading fewer novels. I confess that novel reading is my principal vice but novel heroes cannot compare with Mr McCrimmon. In my own mind I call him Rory Dubh the way the others do. It means Rory the Black, because of his hair and his eyes, not his skin, which is fairer than mine. In fact he has an almost girlish complexion, with pink cheeks like a milkmaid.

Mr McLeod is a cold man, not interested in servants. He isn't rude, but he isn't conversable, either. Mr James Murray is perfectly agreeable and tells very good stories, apart from playing a wonderful

32

fiddle. One of his reels even made old Mrs Carter get up and dance. And she dances surprisingly well for someone of her age and bulk. I asked him the name of the tune which had dragged us up out of our chairs and he said it was 'Round the House and Mind the Dresser' and I don't know if he was only funning because he has a very straight face.

There, now I've run out of paper even though I've written it across as well. Wish me well, dear Mavis. Mama has said that I can go to the church dance with Rory McCrimmon and I'm all aflutter.

Your loving friend
Anna

CHAPTER THREE

I heard a voice within the tavern cry
'Awake, my Little ones, and fill the cup
Before Life's Liquor in its Cup be dry'.

Edward Fitzgerald
Rubáiyát of Omar Khayyám

Phryne saw the flower maidens on their way. Diane's aunt arrived to collect her. Joannie's father had sent a car which also took Marie. Rose gave a wave and walked off down Fitzroy Street toward the sea. Mr Butler, in the Hispano-Suiza, escorted Miss Fisher home.

'How are things in the house?' she asked him,

catching the sensible hat before it took off for King Island.

'Much better, Miss, quite quiet. The young ladies have completed their tasks and Miss Dot took them out for a brisk walk. The flowers are all settled and Mrs B thinks they are going to look very pretty. The aprons are all hemmed and ready to be delivered to the rectory. Oh, and Miss Jones left her reading glasses behind. Would you wish me to restore them to her?'

'If you please, Mr B. Poor woman, no wonder she loses things. I ought to buy her a nice handbag. One of those huge ones with steel bugle beads and bells and tassels, so she can't misplace it.'

'Where would you find a thing like that?' asked Mr Butler, honestly puzzled.

'Oh, I am sure that it will be found at the great bazaar,' said Phryne. Mr Butler had never read Flecker. This had not incommoded him in life so far. He did not expect it to hinder his further career, either. Mr Butler did not approve of poetry. He drove Miss Fisher home, sedately.

The brisk walk sounded like a good idea to Phryne, who had lunched well. She put on her walking shoes and made good time down to where the sideshows were set up, all along the sands outside Luna Park. The Catani Gardens were thronged with the gawping multitude and Phryne slipped through them like a knife through butter, gaining the pavement and slowing to a stroll. She took a deep sniff of that ozone which people went all the way to Skegness to inhale, and coughed on a lungful of what tasted like saccharine fog.

Ah, Turkey lolly. A child's delight and a diabetic's dark fantasy of spun, unnaturally pink sugar. Or unnaturally green. The choice was up to the client. Both were probably equally venomous. She could also smell animal dung, ice cream, wet canvas, diesel exhaust, fresh paint, a shock of orange peel and – yes, faintly, but there – the smell of the sea.

Voices clamoured around her. 'Three shots a tanner!' 'See the Wild Man from Borneo!' 'Toffee apples! Toffee apples!' It was like the street cries of Old London, without the 'Gardy-loo!' of falling ordure and the 'Stop thief!' which had enriched the originals. Phryne slowed, happy to walk off her lunch in such interesting environs. She halted by the ''ot pies! 'ot pies!' vendor to buy one for a thin, slavering child whom she judged had missed out on too many breakfasts.

The performers had set up rows of little ex-army tents to accommodate the extra staff and hangers-on, there for the festival, and from one of them, in the middle, someone was playing a tune on a violin. Not so much a violin as a fiddle and not so much a tune as a catch. Phryne had heard it before. A long time ago and far away – no Australian or even English connection – a very simple little tune. Very evocative of – what? Something emotional; the impact was the same as unexpectedly identifying the scent of a lost lover's hair in a dark room. She stood like a small, very fashionable statue in a sensible straw hat for several minutes, rummaging furiously in a mind which appeared to have entirely lost its card index.

And the unseen fiddler kept playing, the same

little tune, over and over, and still Phryne could not remember where she had heard it, or what it meant. Except it meant something to her.

She came out of her trance at a tug on her elbow. It was the thin boy for whom she had bought a pie. His eyes were alight with faith and his grubby hand was attached to her sleeve. A smaller version of the same child was kept at his side by main force.

'Miss? Miss?' the child was asking. 'Buy one for me brother too? Miss? Please?'

The violinist now swung into a sugary ragtime version of 'Swing Low, Sweet Chariot'. The strange trance melted. Phryne shook herself into order.

'What do you want?' she asked the child. Then she surveyed the hopeful look in the hungry brother and handed over a sixpence. The children of the poor. Here they were, the objects of the Lord Mayor's benevolence. Thin, whippy kids, hollow of eye and cheek, scrubby of hair, fast with a fallen apple or a misplaced penny, fleet on their hard little bare feet. Phryne refrained from patting either of them, but nodded, and they nodded back. Someone had taught these two that they could catch more flies with honey than with vinegar. This boded well for their future as sellers of bridges and proprietors of three-card tricks.

'Thanks, Miss, real nice of you,' said the elder boy, before he dived on the pie vendor and demanded produce.

Phryne looked at her watch, realised that the admirable Mr Xavier must be awaiting her, and hurried away.

What was that tune? And why had it the power to stop a self-possessed young woman in her tracks like that? She tried to hum, and then to sing it, as she walked as briskly as any Swedish exercise manual might require back to her own house. By the time she arrived at the door she was fairly sure that she had the tune, but it didn't resemble any song which she had consciously heard in the last few years.

She took off her hat and went into her own parlour. A young man rose easily to his feet as she entered.

Mr Xavier from Xavier's Cellars was always worth looking at. He was a tall, willowy young man with carefully tamed dark hair who was invariably dressed in faultless gentlemen's wear. His suit today was grey, his shirt would have put a snowdrift to shame and one could have shaved in the gloss on his shoes. His family owned a wine importing business which supplied both Phryne and most of the luxury hotels in Melbourne. Compared to the Windsor, her orders were minuscule and could easily have been done by telephone from a catalogue. But Xavier's Cellars sent Mr Xavier himself every three months to restock Miss Fisher's wines and spirits, and she appreciated this courtesy.

Besides, they had the best wine and Mr Xavier gave the best advice. He might have been almost too exquisite a young man if it wasn't for his infectious enthusiasm and unaffected love for his subject. As Phryne sat down he was already easing the cork from a bottle wrapped in a white cloth. Mr Butler was actually prepared to allow

Mr Xavier to open a bottle of wine in Miss Fisher's parlour (Mr Butler's own particular domain), a signal mark of favour.

'Do try this, Miss Fisher,' he urged. Phryne, like the virgin sturgeon, needed little encouragement to drink French wine. She took a refreshing sip. Ah, bliss. Oh, rich, golden, grapey, wonderful.

'A mouthful of summer,' she said, opening her eyes on his delighted smile. 'Whatever is it?'

'It's sauterne, as you can tell, of course, and it's the best I have ever tasted. Best my father has ever tasted, he says. The 1921, Miss Fisher, from Yquem. Take another sip. Just enough sharpness, not too sweet, but that honey scent...'

'Exquisite. Ten dozen.' Phryne paused to give a great wine its due. One could not rush a good sauterne. She noticed that Mr Butler had provided a large plate of salted nuts, sliced raw vegetables, water biscuits, cheese and sprigs of watercress. Mr Xavier set down his glass and wrote down the order.

'Our uncle in France has arranged the chateau bottled Bordeaux, as you requested, Miss Fisher. I entirely agree that there is all the difference in the world between mis à cave and exported in a tun. Terrible things happen to wine on its long voyage to Australia, Miss Fisher.' He took another sip of sauterne to comfort himself. 'Barrels get left in the sun in India. They get rolled into icy warehouses in Europe. They get forgotten in shanties in the tropics. They get loaded under salted fish in the North Sea. Not to mention the pilferage and the chance of shipwreck. I'm always amazed that we get anything drinkable out of France at all. And of course, times are hard in the Champagne, there were the riots in 1911, of course, and now both the Russian Revolution and that obscene American social experiment mean that the farmers are tearing down the vines to plant potatoes. In fine *terroir!* In Champagne earth! Potatoes!'

'Terrible,' said Phryne. Given his profession and his passion, Mr Xavier could not be expected to approve of Prohibition. Of course, if the farmers could not sell the grapes, they could at least eat the potatoes, but that was no comfort to someone watching a century's viniculture vanish behind the oxen and plough. Mr Xavier pulled himself together with the help of another sip of wine.

'I think it was twenty of the Chateaux Margaux? If you were thinking of giving a small card party, say?'

'Why would I do that?' asked Phryne. 'But a small party, yes. I have too small a house for large gatherings. I'll need, say, three dozen of the Lafite – or maybe Latour?'

'Both?' suggested Mr Xavier, and Phryne laughed and agreed. She was always a sucker for chutzpah. One could hardly be overstocked with good wine and it was not going to go off for about fifty years. Phryne could drink a lot of wine in fifty years and intended to do so. With relish. She nibbled a piece of raw carrot.

'Mr Butler will tell you all about the spirits. English gin, of course, the usual liqueurs. Whatever he wants. I never enquire into any trade's secrets. What were you telling me about a new cognac?'

Mr Xavier brightened and went so far as to lean forward, preserving the immaculate creases in his trousers without apparent effort. This was a young man who would be able to slide down a mud bank in his long johns and arise without a stain. Phryne suppressed a giggle.

'Oh, the ladies' cognac? It was made during the War, when the men were away and some of the usual ingredients could not be had. The women ran the distilleries themselves with whatever labour and fuel they could find so as not to waste the vintage.'

Phryne nodded. Winemakers would much rather spill their own blood – or someone else's, for preference – than their wine. And women did what women had always done when they were left with a farm or a vineyard or a castle to run. They did the best they could. And sometimes they found a better way, by the exercise of desperation and mother-wit.

'Rumour says that it may be something quite extraordinary. Perhaps an advance order? They should bottle it in about twenty years. And as for port, the 1878 Dow is absolutely excellent.'

'I leave the port to Mr Butler. But if he chooses something else, put in a bottle of the Dow. Oh, yes. Courvoisier & Curlier Freres, do you have any more of their Grande Fine Champagne cognac?'

'I may be able to find a bottle or so. For an especially favoured lady.'

This young man is definitely flirting with me, thought Phryne, and very nice too. Young men who said it with grande fine champagne cognac definitely had an edge over those who said it with mere chocolates.

'And if you are packing a picnic for an evening's pleasant gambling, Miss Fisher, you might like a case or so of the Pol Roger, a little less expensive and very palatable.'

'I don't gamble,' said Phryne. 'But I do have a picnic planned. Very well, the Pol, and if the guests don't like it they can bring their own. Thank you so much for coming, Mr Xavier. It has been a pleasure, as always.'

Mr Xavier got to his feet easily, bent over Miss Fisher's hand, and followed Mr Butler to the kitchen to discuss port.

Phryne was just slipping into an idle meditation on the sadness of having a whole open bottle of superb sauterne and no one to share it with when Mrs Butler showed Lin Chung into the room and the day improved markedly.

'Do have a glass of this wine, Lin dear, it is really good,' she said.

'Thank you.' Lin sank down onto the arm of Phryne's chair and sipped. 'Lovely!'

He leaned over and kissed her. His mouth tasted of wine. His lips were soft. Phryne pulled harder and Lin slipped from the chair onto the floor, where she could put both arms around his neck and kiss him properly.

Or rather, improperly. Lin came up for air a few minutes later completely dazed.

'If that is the effect which sauterne has on you, Jade Lady, I shall have to lay in a few thousand bottles.'

'You didn't even put down your glass,' complained Phryne.

'I was ambushed,' explained Lin. He put down the glass. 'I am now entirely at your ladyship's disposal.'

'Mmm,' said Phryne. Flirting with Mr Xavier was pleasant, but Lin Chung was ravishing. He was slim and well dressed and beautiful and skilled, and he kissed extremely well. Also, he smelt exotic. Lin Chung's skin always carried a faint hint of saffron and cinnamon as well as the Floris honeysuckle he wore to remind himself of Phryne. Phryne finally released him with a small nip to the throat, returned his glass, and allowed him to sit down in a chair.

'The girls will be home soon,' she explained.

'Where did this wonderful wine come from?' asked Lin, smoothing his ruffled hair. 'You wouldn't open a bottle this good just for yourself.'

'Mr Xavier brought it. From Xavier's Cellars. I have purchased a lot of it. But I was just hoping that someone would come along to drink it with me. Mr Xavier is in the kitchen with Mr Butler, discussing port. And he made the oddest error, Lin dear. This is a young man who is going to be a great salesman. That requires one to observe the customer, to know their likes and dislikes. He knows mine. But he twice suggested a wine to go with a gambling expedition. I never gamble.'

'Except on lovers,' suggested Lin.

'No, my dear, you were a sure thing from the very moment I saw you. I don't play cards – such a waste of time! I don't play bridge, because people have broken up thirty-year marriages over bridge. People have been shot over bridge games! Besides, you have to learn a lot of fiddling rules and then obey them.'

'And you have never been very good at that,' observed Lin, smiling.

Phryne went on, counting off her points on her fingers.

'I am happy to go to the races, but I seldom put money on horses and even then it's only five bob. I don't even buy raffle tickets! I just give the collector the money. I refused to let you teach me how to play mah-jong. I won't play fan-tan. Even for beans. And if I was stuck with a whole lot of people in a boring bookless house on a wet afternoon we could always dance.'

'And...?' asked Lin.

'How did that clever young man come to make such an odd mistake?' she wondered.

'Everyone makes them sometimes,' observed Lin, wondering if he could possibly decoy Phryne upstairs before her family claimed her attention.

'I suppose so,' said Phryne. 'I've had rather a disconcerting day, Lin dear. First those un-comfortable odd girls at lunch – one of whom is going to come to a very bad end fairly soon if something isn't done about her – and then I heard this little tune, played by a fiddler some-where in the carnival, and it positively nailed me to my place. I can't remember where I have heard it before and there are words to it, but I can't recall them.'

'Sing it for me,' requested Lin. Phryne obliged, then sang it again. The tune was firming in her head as she repeated it.

'I've never heard it before,' said Lin. 'Sorry. But

I've heard things rather like it.'

'You have? Where?'

'When I was in London last, the Folk Song and Dance Society had a concert. It sounds like one of their things.'

'I'm not a good singer,' confessed Phryne. 'But that's the first clue, Lin, thank you. A folk song? When would I have ever heard a folk song? And it's such a strange little crinkle of music. Come along,' she said to Lin, holding out her hand and picking up the bottle. He put his hand in hers, a hard narrow palm and long fingers.

'Where are we going?'

'You and me and the sauterne,' said Phryne, 'are going upstairs.'

Mrs Butler, exiled from her own kitchen by deep discussions on port, had gone into the garden with a sherry cobbler and her crocheting. It had fallen unhooked into her lap. She drowsed. It was late afternoon. The bees buzzed in the jasmine flowers. Mr Butler and Mr Xavier would be an hour yet. The preparations for dinner were all made. Miss Fisher had retired to her boudoir for what Mrs Butler very firmly thought of as an afternoon nap with Mr Lin for company. Her eyes closed.

She was awoken by two sharp, fierce female voices. Jane and Ruth were standing beside the pen in which Mrs Butler's chickens clucked and grumbled.

'I still say you're mental!' That was Jane.

'I have to know.' That was Ruth, a slightly deeper voice, ragged with pain.

'What does it matter? We're lucky, Ruthie. Miss

44

Phryne took us in and she's adopted us and we're going to be all right.'

'But...' objected Ruth.

Jane, ordinarily the most logical and calm of the pair, unexpectedly lost her temper. 'But? But what? My parents just strolled off and left me with Grandma, and then she died, and what would have become of me if Miss Phryne hadn't kept me? Your mother–'

'Don't you talk about my mother!' Ruth's voice rose.

'All right, I'm not saying it was her fault, I know she had TB. But where were you when they took her away? You were scrubbing your fingers to the bone and starving, Ruthie, you can't deny it. I know you were 'cos so was I. And if you go upsetting everyone about your father, what's Miss Phryne going to think? Ungrateful, that's what she'll think we are. And I'm not ungrateful.'

'I just want to go and see my mum. I won't make trouble.'

'You're already making trouble!' snarled Jane.

There was a pause in which Black Bob, the cock, gave an experimental crow. Then Jane spoke again.

'All right. I'll go with you to ask Miss Phryne to make the appointment at the sanatorium. Mr Butler can take us. That's not unreasonable. But if your mum can't tell you anything, then you drop it, right? You promise?'

Ruth muttered something. Mrs Butler waited until the girls had gone and then began to lever herself out of the deckchair. Oh dear. Girls. Never anything but trouble if there were girls in the

45

house, Mrs Butler's father had said, and he had been right. Mrs Butler finished her sherry cobbler, gathered her crocheting, and went inside. She heard Dot passing the kitchen door and called her in to the Butlers' own sitting room. Mrs Butler did not know how Miss Phryne was going to respond to Ruth wanting to see her mother, and she had always found Dot's predictions of domestic weather very reliable.

Dot was not pleased. She bit her lip as Mrs Butler explained what she had overheard.

'Where did she get the girls, anyway?' asked Dot rhetorically. 'Rescued poor little Jane out of the clutches of a ... a procurer and a mesmerist. Jane's an orphan. That nice Miss Jilly-the-solicitor couldn't find any relatives at all. The old hag the two of them were living with was no blood kin at all, just a...' Dot's mouth almost formed the term 'bitch' and reformed itself smartly around 'greedy old woman. She was working them to death. Mr Bert said the poor girls hardly had a rag between them and when we found Jane on the Ballarat train she was wearing a winceyette thing you wouldn't polish brass with.'

'What about Ruth, then?' asked Mrs Butler. 'She's got a mother?'

'Hopeless case of consumption,' said Dot. 'She's been in the sanatorium at Dandenong for years. She signed the adoption papers. She knows she'll never come out. And she didn't want to see Ruth when we offered to bring her, either. Said she had lost the girl so long ago that she didn't want to remember her now. Drat,' said Dot, allowing herself one of her rare expletives. 'Just when Miss Phryne doesn't need to be upset, too, what with this Flower Festival and all.'

'What about Ruth's father?' Mrs Butler pressed.

'He's not even on her birth certificate,' said Dot. 'That woman was no better than she ought to have been. God forgive me,' she added, mentally putting this harsh judgment on her confession list for Sunday.

'Is Miss Phryne going to be upset?' asked Mrs Butler.

'Probably not very,' said Dot. 'But it might be a good notion to be fast off the mark with the cocktails.'

'I'll tell Mr Butler,' said Mrs Butler, relieved. She disliked domestic disharmony. It gave people indigestion and then they didn't appreciate her food properly. She retreated to the kitchen, where Mr Butler was just showing Mr Xavier out. The air was pleasantly redolent of good port and concluded orders. Time to put on the dinner and stop worrying about the girls.

She did pass on Dot's recommendation about the cocktails, though. Better safe than sorry.

Phryne did not emerge to dine until the table was laid and the company seated. Lin handed her to her chair and Mr Butler filled a water glass to clear the palate and a wine glass with a robust red. Phryne was pleased with her household, her afternoon, and her lover. Dinner was a simple affair of cold collations and differing tastes and textures; the crunch of raw celery, the suave texture of cold roasted chicken, and the sharp, lemon-thyme tang of a veal galantine, bedded on lettuce and wreathed in parsley. Dessert was a cleansing sorbet. Phryne folded her napkin and smiled on the company.

'Miss Phryne, can you write for an appointment for me to see...' said Ruth, having waited for this moment.

'Yes?' asked Phryne, sated and blissful and ready to grant almost any request.

'...my mother?' squeaked Ruth.

There was a silence around the table. Mr Butler brought in Phryne's coffee and a tray of liqueurs. Without asking he poured Miss Fisher a small glass of green chartreuse.

Lin Chung, battle-scarred veteran of some of the most complex and carefully nurtured family feuds in the history of Victoria, took in a slow breath and inched his hand along the tablecloth, laying it on Phryne's very gently. He had been ravished out of his senses and now needed them back rather quickly. Phryne had rescued the girls from slavery at considerable trouble and expense, and he was desperately hoping that she would not be affronted by this request, which might be seen, in certain lights, as rank ingratitude.

'That sounds reasonable,' he said quietly.

There was another long silence. Phryne was still trying to remember where she had heard that fiddle tune. After a moment she came out of her brown study and found that her whole family was staring at her with held breath. Silly of them. What did they expect her to do, forbid Ruth to see her mother? She smiled into Ruth's anxious eyes.

'Yes,' said Phryne. 'Perfectly reasonable. I shall

write tomorrow – or rather, I shall telephone. Then Mr Butler shall take you to the Dandenongs. I really can't vanish in the middle of all this festivity, but I'm sure that Dot will go too, and would you like a nice ride in the country, Jane? Mrs B will pack a suitable picnic.'

'Thank you,' said Jane, weak with relief. 'Any day but Thursday. We have a history test.'

'Oh? On what?'

'Queen Elizabeth,' said Jane. 'I think she must have been rather like you, Miss Phryne.'

'Except for one thing,' said Lin Chung.

Everyone looked at him. Surely Lin Chung was not going to be so crude as to refer to the celebrated queen's virginity and Phryne's equally celebrated lack of it?

'Queen Elizabeth said that she had the heart and stomach of a man,' he said, a little surprised at their reaction. 'Phryne Fisher has the heart of a lion. And any other parts of it which she might want,' he added.

Everyone laughed.

Mr Rory McCrimmon to Miss Anna Ross, (undated) on a bunch of roses

No rose could be fairer than you.

CHAPTER FOUR

Awake! for Morning in the Bowl of Night
Has flung the Stone that puts the stars to Flight.

Edward Fitzgerald
Rubáiyát of Omar Khayyám

Phryne slept well until five am when she came utterly and obstinately awake and all attempts at persuading herself that it was still dark outside and there was no point in waking failed completely.

She rose, dressed in her male disguise, took up a flat cap, and left the house without waking anyone. It was not safe for an unaccompanied female of any description to promenade along the promenade at this hour. But no one noticed boys. Pre-dawn light was beginning to filter into the sky. The dead hour of night, when old people died and babies were born. On the turn of the tide.

Dressed in men's clothes, Phryne made a convincing boy if not too closely inspected. She had the unpolished boots, the old tweed trousers, the jacket which had belonged to a larger brother, the collarless shirt and the cap of a St Kilda boy; not too scrupulous with an unlocked door, perhaps, open to various offers in relation to a little shop-breaking or car theft, but unarmed and relatively harmless. There were thousands of them, wondering where tomorrow's dinner was coming from. More every day. She dropped into the proper slouch of someone who had slept rough and cold, jammed her cap on her head and wandered down to the seashore.

The carnival, of course, was guarded by dogs, and the circus was guarded by dogs and men. But the seashore was open to all and she paced along the wet sand, wondering how this quest of Ruth's would affect her own family. She was comfortable with the two girls, but what would she do with a stray sailor father, expecting – no doubt – to be accommodated and fed in exchange for allowing Phryne to adopt his daughter. And that was assuming he was presentable at all. Not a pleasant prospect. Neither was the prospect of Ruth yearning for her missing progenitor for years and possibly going into a decline like her mother. The sea hissed in and out in that special St Kilda way; shh, slop, pause. Shh, slop, pause. As though it was too tired to splash.

A couple of dogs barked at her as she passed the trucks and tents of the carnival. A baby cried in one of the caravans. A lion had clearly woken up grumpy and roared. Silence spread in pools like cold water. Phryne heard the hiss and scratch of a match and the pop of a primus as someone decided that since they were awake they might as well make a cup of tea.

Someone was watching her from the darkness. She could feel their eyes. But no one moved or spoke and she passed on like a shadow, kicking seaweed aside with her thick boots, scuffing the sand. Damn all fathers. They were nothing but trouble.

Then she heard drumming, felt it in the soles of her feet. Felt something like that before, Phryne thought. The sand was quivering underfoot. Drumming and the crack of a whip. Horses coming. A lot of horses coming very fast. Phryne heard a shout of warning. She turned and they were upon her.

A mob of circus horses, galloping flat out along the tideline, a frieze of bobbing heads and wild manes and flashing wet hooves. There was nowhere to run. Acting entirely on trained instinct – had she not fallen off a circus horse every day for weeks until she could stick on even if it did handstands? Phryne threw herself to one side, grabbed and sprang, and she was up and riding astride, intoxicatingly fast, horsehair cutting her fingers, the mob caught up in its own shared consciousness. Fast, breathed the mob. Run fast!

She laughed aloud, pressing close to the horse's neck, digging in with her knees to save her hands. The mob moved with one mind and Phryne was part of it, unthinking, dark maned, wild. They galloped along the shore as though there was no end to the race, no light except the morning of the world, no humans but the chance-met waif who had been transported by the wild hunt. Phryne laughed with joy as they leapt a small culvert and poured along the sand.

It could not last. Now there were whips behind, men yelling, detestable dogs barking. The tail of the mob slacked, the head was turned, expertly, until they were cantering straight out to sea, into the sunrise reflections on the water. The impetus snapped. The mob shifted and broke, strung out like beads scattering from a broken necklace. Their group mind was lost. Each beast felt the onrush of cold foam and drew back or turned aside. Phryne's mount snorted, picked up its feet and trotted back to the hard sand. There Phryne slid down and leaned briefly on the heaving side, weak at the knees from the access of sheer speed and power. She was jolted wholly out of her annoyance and wanted to laugh or sing.

And on cue she heard that strange little crinkle of music and at last knew the words. They were charming and obscene and she was beginning to remember who had taught them to her. She moved beyond the sandy edge and sang aloud: 'Aye the cuckoo, oh the cuckoo, aye the cuckoo's nest! Aye the cuckoo, oh the cuckoo, aye the cuckoo's nest. I'll give anyone a penny, and a bottle of the best, who will ruffle up the feathers in my cuckoo's nest!' she sang.

The horses drew away. Phryne stepped back against the bank and let them go, with their attendant dogs and men. No one noticed her in the half-dark but a startled fiddler, who stood up, playing the tune as bait, and stalked out of the carnival camp. He had heard that strong small soprano before. Long ago and very, very far away.

Surely the divine and never forgotten Phryne Fisher couldn't be here? In Australia? In St Kilda? It seemed exceptionally unlikely. Though, if he had expected to see her again, it might well have been in the middle of a rush of wild horses. Phryne, the fiddler remembered, always existed as a still, self-possessed point in a maelstrom. Usually she had created the maelstrom herself. He crept forward, playing the wild refrain to the cuckoo's nest, until he came out onto the strand itself.

And the singer had gone. Only the retreating thud of hooves and the churned, pock-marked sand gave evidence that anyone had been there at all. The fiddler cursed richly in three languages and went back to his camp. He still had a little whisky in the bottle and there would be no more sleep for him now day had broken.

Phryne Fisher! Here? Impossible. But he had had stranger encounters with people he hadn't seen for ten years. And on this very foreshore, this very day. Perhaps two glasses of the whisky. The fiddler was shaken.

Phryne walked back to her own house, elated. The wild rush of the horses had been the very thing to break her despondent mood. If Ruth's father was alive and became an embarrassment, he could either be (1) bought off or (2) scared off. If that didn't work she might ask her wharfie mates, Bert and Cec, to find a like-minded colleague to drop him off a suitable bridge. But for the moment Phryne was delighted. A little chafed in some private places, and with some horsehair cuts on her hands, in need of a bath and some ointment, but delighted. As she walked she whistled the rousing air of the cuckoo's nest. And she remembered Orkney.

Returned from the Great War with several medals and a French pension, her heart comprehensively broken by that rat René and minded to try the Home Counties for a while, she had been brushing her hair before her own mirror in her father's manor when he had tapped on the door. She bade him come in and he did, his bearing unusually meek and his voice like that of a sucking dove calling to another sucking dove which was sensitive about loud noises. Behind him came the butler, bearing a tray on which reposed brandy, soda and two glasses.

'I say, Phryne, I brought you a drink,' he said. Phryne put down her hairbrush. This was unprecedented.

'So you did,' she agreed. 'Just cognac, please, Harker. Cheers,' she added, raising the glass.

'So, are you comfortable in the old place, then, daughter?' asked her father, astonishing Phryne still further. This was not his usual manner at all. He must want something very badly. She decided to hurry the process along, although there was a certain mean pleasure to be got out of watching His Lordship attempt to remember how one persuaded someone to do something. Usually he just yelled at them, and if that didn't work, he yelled louder.

'Very grateful to be here,' she said. 'And delighted to assist if you have any small task you would like me to do, Father. Provided it does not involve matrimony. Or knitting.'

Totally impervious to irony in the way of the Old School, Phryne's father sat down heavily in her Sheraton chair, which creaked.

'No, nothing like that. I've got an old friend, and his son ... well, he's damaged, unsightly. Scarred.'

'Yes?' asked Phryne, who had seen many scarred men in her ambulance-driving days. Scarred men did not worry Phryne.

'He can't stay in England. He's too ashamed. And his people – well, they find him...'

'Yes?' prompted Phryne. His people found him uncomfortable to have around, she thought, seething lightly. He wasn't the pretty boy they had sent off to the war. He wasn't an eligible prospect for any suitable gel. So what did they mean to do with him?

'Not as though he's the eldest son or anything,' said Phryne's father, making things worse. 'You knew him once, though you wouldn't know him now,' he said, taking a deep gulp of his brandy-and-hardly-any-soda. 'Ian Hamilton.'

'I remember him,' said Phryne.

'He wants to go and live with his old nurse,' said His Lordship. 'She's gone home, to the Orkney Islands, right at the top of Scotland. Curse the woman, why couldn't she have gone to Brighton like all the other old biddies? A long journey and he can't do it alone, he can't see very well. And his father asked who he'd like to have with him, and he said you. It's a lot to ask, daughter, you'll be stared at the whole way, I don't doubt. And no young woman likes to be seen with such–'

Before her father could say something like 'monster' and cause her to lose her temper just when she was having the first civil conversation with him in years, Phryne laid her hand on his and said, 'I'll do it.'

'Hamilton will pay all your expenses, of course, first class all the way. I wouldn't ask but he's an old friend of mine and you're such a competent girl, self-possessed and all, and I expect you saw worse in France.'

'I probably did,' said Phryne, pouring herself another cognac.

'Good girl,' said His Lordship. 'We never got on, Phryne. Maybe because we are too alike. You've got the old Fisher spirit in you, all right. Leave Friday, is that what I can tell Hamilton?'

'Friday,' said Phryne, suppressing her own view on what she shared with her father: a taste for good cognac and that was all. 'Perfect.'

And she had gone, taking only a knapsack, and met Ian Hamilton at Paddington. He was just visible behind a mountain of luggage. Ian Hamilton's parents did not mean him to return from Orkney. He was wearing a loose casing of bandage over his face and the porter was finding it hard to understand him.

'Where was you going, sir?' the porter yelled. Phryne could hear him thinking: poor gent must be deaf as well as blind, and that snooty madam of a nurse had just abandoned the man here with all this stuff and no idea of where he was going. There ought to be a law.

'We are booked first class on the train to Edinburgh,' said Phryne. 'Here are the tickets. Two sleepers. You'll need another porter for all that stuff. Purchase some help and get a move on, there's a dear, time is wasting away.' She pressed five shillings into his hand.

The porter waved to a friend and the baggage vanished with all the celerity that five shillings might induce. And Phryne could take the blind man's hand at last and say, 'Hello, Ian. How nice to meet you again. Come along and we'll catch the train. You don't need to do anything, old dear, but come along with me.'

He had almost laughed when he said, 'That's what all the best policemen say,' but there was a catch in his voice. Phryne was worried about him. Ian Hamilton had been rather bookish, not bad at cricket, a very good dancer and, really, that was all she knew about him.

When they were enclosed in the otherwise empty first-class compartment, she said, 'Can you see at all?'

'All right out of one eye, nearly blind in the other. Do you know why I asked you to come?'

'No idea,' she said as the train got up steam, clanked portentously a few times, and began to move out of Paddington.

'Because I was betting that you wouldn't faint if you saw ... this.'

He unwound the bandages and there was Ian Hamilton. Or rather, half of him. One side of his face was almost unmarked. The other looked like a wax doll which some careless child had left too close to the fire. The flesh had melted off the bones, sagging in ugly purple folds. The eye on that side was milky and unfocused. Phryne felt no urge to faint or even retch. He was alive, and that was an improvement on most faces she had seen reduced to this.

'Phosphorous grenade,' she said calmly. 'You must have been awfully close to the shell when it blew.'

'It fell almost on top of me,' said Ian Hamilton,

58

a trifle taken aback at her lack of reaction. 'The fire ran along my back and legs; the scars there have stretched but no one's going to see them. Well, Miss Fisher? Aren't you going to cry? Aren't you going to pity me and say "poor boy"?'

'I will if you want me to,' said Phryne. 'Everyone else in the trench would have been killed, yes? And you survived because you fell into the mud, and the mud put out the fire in your flesh, and by the time you started to drown, the gas had blown away. Your lungs sound all right to me. Have a cigarette? And I believe that tea will be brought soon. Don't throw a tantrum at me, Ian dear. You wanted me because I can look you in the eye and not be sorry for you.'

He sighed, agreed, took the cigarette and resumed the bandages as the porter came in with tea. Gradually, as the train clicked and clacked through luncheon, afternoon tea and dinner, all taken in the private car, he thawed enough to talk about something other than his own pain and horror and his own terrible sense of exclusion. Phryne recalled that he had been good at quick translation, and said, 'I'll set you a poem, if you can't sleep. A full translation to be delivered to me with my breakfast tray at eight tomorrow as we roll into Edinburgh. You game?'

'I've been trying to read, but nothing holds my attention enough. All right. I'm sick of taking laudanum anyway. What's the poem?'

She had set him Gerard de Nerval's 'El Desdichado' – 'The Dispossessed'. Phryne believed that to be an effective nurse, you had to be prepared, and had copied it herself from the book. She rolled

59

herself into her own sleeper and slept well. Phryne always slept well on trains, and this one did not even have Hommes Quarante Cheveaux Huit – Forty men: Eight horses – on the door, a great improvement.

When the porter brought her tea, she unfolded a sheet on which someone had written, under the French *Je suis le ténébreux – le veuf – l'inconsolé:*

I am the shadow, the relict, the unconsoled
The Prince of Acquitaine at the ruined tower:
My only star is dead – and my lute is starred
With the radiant black sun of melancholy.

In the fallen night, it is you who comfort me,
Give to me Pausillipus and the Italian sea.
The flower that consoles my wounded heart
The vine and strong vine stock which cradles the
  rose.

Phryne began to have hopes of his recovery. The rest of the journey was a delight. They transferred from Edinburgh to the Highland and Island line and travelled through precious landscapes where each glen, struck by sudden sun, glowed like opal. A full crowned red deer sneered lightly as they passed Rannock Moor, a primeval black peat landscape where one would not have been surprised to see a dinosaur. Then further, up to Aberdeen, where the cruel wind cut across the endless wastes of grass and heather and tumbled crofts, and never stopped blowing.

Her patient gradually became more conversable. People in the train did not stare at him. No one asked intrusive questions. When he enquired of a sailor on the Caledonian McBrayne ferry which was to take them to Stromness if it was safe to sail, the man had replied 'Sir! Caledonian McBrayne does not have accidents!' and hadn't even twitched at the bandaged face.

Then they crossed the great confused pot of Scapa Flow and there was Stromness. A pensive seal greeted them from the harbour. There was a comfortable inn there called the Sailor's Rest, where Phryne was to meet Mrs Murray, Ian Hamilton's nurse.

Stromness sat down solidly under its slate roofs like a town which had seen the worst that North Sea gales could throw at it and had not been impressed. Bring on your blow, it seemed to say. There's whisky yet in the jar. And a good herring in oatmeal on the fire. Several sheep looked up as Phryne and the mountain of baggage were escorted ashore by taciturn young men who carried a trunk as though it was a minor inconvenience. The front parlour of the Sailor's Rest was decorated with a lot of *objets trouvés*: fishing nets and bright glass floats, shells and unusual bits of driftwood. The landlord's wife came out from behind the bar and said quietly, 'You'll be Miss Fisher, then? I'm Mrs Munro. Mrs Murray is on her way. She doesn't walk so fast as she did once. Her grandson James is here to arrange about the baggage. Will you be staying the night, then? Ferry will be leaving in an hour, that's time enough to get the poor young man settled.'

'Stay,' pleaded Ian, grasping Phryne's hand.

'Until tomorrow, then. Now, sit down, my dear,

61

and take off that bandage. You must start as you mean to go on,' said Phryne firmly. 'A little whisky, Mrs Munro? And what will you have, Mr Murray?'

'A *lot* of whisky,' grinned James Murray, an engaging man with red hair.

'The Highland Park?' asked Mrs Munro of James Murray. He nodded.

'Vin du pays,' he said with a rather good French accent. 'You will like it, Mr Hamilton. Take a tint of this, now,' he said, and offered Ian the glass. 'And let's see your face. We're Vikings, here,' he said as he gently unwound the bandage. 'Not them soft Scots Jessies. We've seen battle wounds before. And if you cover your mouth,' he continued, 'you can't drink and that would be the pity of the world with a bottle of Highland Park on the bar.'

Phryne was touched. James Murray's grandmother was being paid, probably very well, to hide this disfigured man from the civilised world. James had no need to be gentle, but he was: so gentle that the bandage was gone before Ian really noticed it. He looked around at the fishermen and the crofters. They looked back at him. No one seemed affected. Finally someone spoke.

'You'll still have the sight of that eye, then?' asked one gnarled old man. 'Welcome, Mr Hamilton. My son came back blind. And he's out on the boats with me. Ye must not despair.'

The conversation returned to a gentle murmur. Like all fishermen, they were not talking about fish. Phryne took a deep sip of the whisky, a single malt of great subtlety and strength. James

Murray refilled her glass.

'Good, eh? It's the water. Filtered through a lot of peat and then through a lot of rock. We've got a lot of rock, hereabouts. He'll be all right, your young man. Grandma won't let nothing happen to him.'

'He's not my young man,' said Phryne. 'He's a friend. Are you a fisherman, too?' she asked.

'No, I'm a teacher,' he said. 'Of music. And a fine fiddler. You must come tonight,' he added. 'We're having a dance.'

'Will anyone dance with Ian?' asked Phryne.

'Surely,' said James Murray. 'Unlike a lot of our young men, he's got both arms and both legs.'

And so it had proved. Mrs Murray was not a soft, cuddly nurse. She was an upright, thin, stern old lady who had borne five children and raised three, then gone off to be a wet nurse to a lot of Hamiltons. She had only left when the last of them was grown, and had brought her savings back to her own country, where they had bought her a house and would provide for her old age. Therefore she did not need to take Ian. It was, she explained to Phryne, her duty. And he was her favourite among the children, though she had never told him so.

She allowed Ian to take her arm up the cobbled street to her clean, warm house, where the kitchen stove never went out. He had a room of his own with a new feather mattress and Orkney woollen blankets. Behind them trailed half of the population of Stromness, most carrying some-thing to save their countenances and acquit them of nosiness. Mrs Murray threw them out when the goods were all stowed to her liking, with handfuls of boiled sweets for the children. When they were all gone she stared Ian straight in the eye. Her voice was not gentle but entirely sure.

'This is your chair,' she said to him, sitting him down. 'Here, before the stove. Here is your place, and you need never depart from it.'

And then she had left him to cry for ten minutes, after which she said, 'And here is your pup. She's a good lineage but she's no sheepdog with that broken leg which healed short. Isaac was minded to put her down, but I saved her for you.' She laid in his London tailored lap a scruffy puppy, barely weaned, black and white with a patch over one eye. Ian laughed as she licked his scarred face.

'Your name is Sally,' Ian whispered to the puppy.

Then old Mrs Murray looked at Phryne. 'He'll do,' she said sharply. 'Now James will take you back to the inn. You'll want a rest. This will have been a great strain. But I can see you are a good-hearted girl. Not like some these days.'

Phryne found herself out on the front step as the door closed with a soft thump.

'My mother thought Grandma Murray was a witch,' said James, amused. 'But she'll take good care of him. Back to the pub, eh? I'll play you to sleep.'

Phryne, with a mug of hot milk and whisky inside and a large down comforter outside, fell asleep to the sound of a violin playing a lullaby outside her window.

And then to the dance, where joy was relatively unconfined and the wild notes of the fiddle stung the feet into action. Ian Hamilton, as promised, danced with several Orkney girls. Phryne watched the fiddler. He was compelling. And when he wanted to, he could make stones dance.

With regret, Phryne left Orkney three days later. James had shown her some marvels. The Ring of Brogar by dawn light. The perfect chambered tomb of Maes Howe with its Viking graffiti: 'Ingeborg is the fairest of women. A great treasure lies in the south west: happy the man who finds it.' He had fed her Orkney lamb, which was pre-salé like the French delicacy because the sheep ate seaweed. He had shown her how to make oatcakes and he had lain down with her in a shed full of new-mown hay: a satisfying lover with enthusiasm and dash. James Murray. Where was James Murray now? She remembered the last conversation she had had with him, sitting on a hill watching the sea.

'Will you ever leave Orkney?' she asked.

'Oh, I have left Orkney many times. I was a sailor before father opened his school. I have been to many places. But I get homesick for the dark, for the cold and the smell of peat smoke.'

'I can understand that. There is no place like this anywhere in the world.'

'That is true,' he said comfortably. 'And I will see you again, my hinny, my blossom. I am sure that I will see you again. And I'll come down to the dock and play you away in the morning.'

And as the Cal-Mac ferry took Phryne away from Orkney, she heard the wild fiddle above the engines. Not a lullaby, this time. 'Aye the cuckoo, oh the cuckoo, aye the cuckoo's nest ... I'll give anyone a penny, and a bottle of the best, if they'll ruffle up the feathers in my cuckoo's nest!' Extraordinary how all those respectable scholars, Sabine Baring Gould amongst them, hadn't identified the cuckoo's nest as the female genitalia when they censored all the lock and key references out of their songs. So many people trying so hard to keep us from enjoying ourselves, thought Phryne as she approached her own front door.

Someone was coming out of the side gate. Phryne halted. The person was moving like a shadow. He was too far away to grab and the early dawn light cast the face into shadow. Probably a man. He was in the street now. Phryne yelled 'Hi!' and leapt and grabbed, but he was too far away and too fast. She landed ignominiously on her knees with only a handful of shirt to show for her effort, and the footsteps raced away like a very fast drum.

'Damn,' swore Phryne. She stuffed the cloth into her pocket and slid down the sideway. No windows open, no sign of damage. It was too early to rouse the house if nothing was wrong. She slid a little, picked up what she had stepped on, and returned to the street.

It was a small bunch of pink roses, tied up with a silver ribbon. Was some swain courting Ruth or Jane? She would have to get to the bottom of this. Suddenly Phryne longed for the days when she didn't have a household or things to sort out. But it was her duty, as old Mrs Murray had said.

She went inside and crept up the stairs without waking anyone. Fairly soon Mrs Butler would rise and put the kettle on and Phryne would be supplied with breakfast in due course. For the moment, however, she shed the boy's clothes, attended to her injuries, wrapped herself in a dressing gown and made coffee on her spirit stove. She opened her own tin of dark chocolates to go with it.

Orkney. What a strange place. Ian Hamilton had written to her for a while. She remembered receiving an invitation to his wedding and later an announcement about a son. That must have annoyed the Hamiltons. The eldest son had turned out to be a wastrel and a bounder. Oh, and redheaded, charming James Murray. She had almost forgotten him. And he was worth remembering.

She must have fallen into a doze, because she was startled out of it by frantic banging on the door.

Miss Anna Ross to Miss Mavis Sutherland
11 December 1912

I'm sad today because Rory and his friends are going to Sydney for a month. They have an engagement with the Folk Song Society playing them tunes and singing songs for them to record on these odd wax discs, called gramophone records. They are thick heavy things and very brittle, but – it's almost magic – they can give you back a voice or a tune. I had heard a gramophone before and Mama says that if we finish the year well we can buy a machine. The boarders will like it and they can play their own records, which will be a saving. You have to wind it up. The machine, I mean, not the boarders.

Rory has been courting me and he is so sweet and

gentlemanly and lovely that I am in a whirl. He gives me flowers and sings to me and everyone has noticed how particular his attentions are except Mama, who just scolds me for inattention. I don't think she knows that I exist except as another pair of hands, scrubbing, serving, washing, cooking. The house is full and Rory and his friends will pay a month's rent so their rooms will be kept while they are away. That also means that they plan to come back because oh, Mavis, Rory says he loves me, he loves me! And I love him so it cannot be wrong that when we met by chance – entirely by chance – at the top of the stairs, he clasped me in his arms and kissed me.

If I marry him I will go with him to his home in Skye and then perhaps I might see you again. Dearest Mavis, I miss you so much, especially now when I desperately want someone to talk to and there is no one.

Your loving friend Anna

CHAPTER FIVE

Something in her bosom wrings
For relief a sigh she brings
And O, her een, they spak sic things!

Robert Burns
'Duncan Gray'

Phryne tied her dressing gown and found her slippers and her little gun. She heard Mr Butler

68

get up and stamp along the hall, and she flew down the stairs to stand behind him as he opened the door. St Kilda was not a safe place – nowhere was a safe place, really, but St Kilda had all the problems to be expected in a seaport – and anything threatening Phryne's household this morning was going to be looking death in the eye. Phryne had been startled and she did not like that feeling.

On the doorstep was a frantic woman. Her hair straggled around her shoulders. She had a nightdress on under her coat and her feet had been thrust into someone's tartan slippers. But her voice was educated and there was a chauffeur waiting inside the big Daimler parked at the kerb.

'Oh, Miss Fisher, I'm so sorry to wake you, but it's Rose! Is she here?'

By now everyone had been roused by the noise. Phryne turned to her two daughters, who were clad in red woolly gowns and slippers and were looking apprehensive. Ruth was holding Molly by the collar. Phryne slipped the little Beretta into her pocket. This caller had already been scared enough, by the look of her.

'Girls?' Both heads shook, both sets of plaits bounced. 'Dot?'

'No, Miss Phryne,' said Dot, still half asleep.

Phryne addressed the woman on the steps. 'Sorry, no Rose. I haven't seen her since we had lunch at Anatole's. Would you like to come in?'

Mrs Butler would be in the kitchen already, putting on the kettle. Soon there would be tea. And coffee. And breakfast.

'No, there're still two places to try. I'm sorry,'

said the woman. 'I'm her mother. Mrs Weston. She hasn't been in all night and her bed hasn't been slept in and she said she admired you so much, Miss Fisher, I thought she might have run away again – I mean, I thought she might be here. I'll go,' said Mrs Weston, and she went, her tartan slippers sliding treacherously underfoot as she descended the steps. Phryne felt a pang of pure pity. It was not fair that she should be made ridiculous when her daughter was missing.

Mr Butler shut the door. The family looked at one another.

'Well, it's morning,' said Phryne. 'Barely. How about a nice cup of something and then perhaps an early breakfast, or perhaps we might be so sleepy that we can all go back to bed?' she asked hopefully.

'I'm not sleepy,' Jane piped up.

'Nor me,' added Ruth helpfully.

'Nice cuppa's what we need,' soothed Mr Butler. 'I'll just put on the electric heater in the parlour, Miss Fisher, and we'll be warm in a tick.'

Mr Butler retained his authority even when dressed in a brown woollen gown made to fit the larger than average bear. Presently he brought tea, coffee, a tin of biscuits and the paper. He promised breakfast in half an hour and Phryne decided that she might as well wake up properly, bathe and dress. Early morning was such a bleak time, she thought.

Dot, on the other hand, liked dawn. She murmured a prayer thanking God for having allowed her to live through the night as she went back to her own room for suitable clothes. The girls

70

scrambled into their garments and ate biscuits, discussing whether Molly should be allowed one biscuit or two for so long that Molly lost patience and stole three. This settled the matter to the satisfaction of all.

Breakfast was one of Mrs Butler's dozen-egg omelettes, crispy as yellow tide-foam without, and succulent within. Phryne found that she was hungry. The bacon was admirably crisp and there were mounds of toast. Phryne insisted on the Butlers sitting down with her at the breakfast room table.

'Please, Mr Butler, it's too early to argue,' she said, and the Butlers sat down. Mrs Butler was pleased. She liked to watch people eating her excellent food.

'What can have happened to Rose?' asked Jane.

'She might have just slipped out and gone to a dance and is late home,' said Phryne.

'But her parents are awfully strict,' protested Ruth. 'I heard Joannie talking about them when they were having all those fittings.'

'Which is why she might have slipped out the window,' said Phryne. 'Or she may have run away. You heard Mrs Weston say "she might have run away again". That means that she has done so before. Is there a boyfriend in evidence, girls, do you know?'

'They talked a lot about boys,' said Ruth, biting precise semicircles out of her toast and marmalade. 'Joannie is keen on this boy called Derek. And Diane said that Derek was an angel and Joannie said that he was ever so handsome and ... let's see ... Marie scolded them both for fools

71

and Rose just smiled.'

'No, she smirked,' argued Jane, who was pedantic. 'You remember, Ruthie, she said something like "I could have your Derek any time I wanted", and Diane got angry with her. Then Madame told them to pipe down.'

'I bet Madame never said that,' said Dot.

'No, she said *"Tais-toi,* Jeanne!" to Joannie and they all shut up.'

'Interesting,' said Phryne. 'In reference to yourselves, by the way, I found this bunch of flowers in the sideway, and almost caught the person who left them there. If you want to go to a dance or if someone is courting you, I would like to know about it. I am not unreasonable. But I don't like strangers around the house before dawn. Do you know anything about this? Jane? Ruth?'

Both plaits bounced again as they shook their heads in unison. Phryne, for some reason, did not believe them. Perhaps they might spill the beans if she questioned them separately. Phryne put the roses in a glass of water. No sense in wasting good flowers.

'But Miss Rose's mother is frantic,' said Dot censoriously. 'And when she finds her she won't get out again before Rose's hair turns grey. If she was going to slip out of a window, wouldn't she have arranged to get back before she was missed?'

'Something must have gone wrong,' said Phryne, shelving the matter of the roses for the moment. 'Perhaps her ride home fell through, or proved importunate, and she had to walk. She's a febrile young woman with quite a lot of brain, and that is a very dangerous combination. Do you know anything about the Weston family, Dot?'

'Nothing,' said Dot. 'Except that she was always dressed in a child's clothes which didn't fit her. And she was unhappy.'

'Very unhappy. She talked to us a lot when she was here,' said Jane. 'Her grandfather rules the house, she said, and no one can do anything unless he says so because he has all the money. He has a lot of political friends, too. Rose's father went missing.'

'In action?' asked Phryne.

'No, I think he just went away,' said Jane.

'With a cinema usherette,' said Ruth. 'Rose has to answer to her mother, who has some sort of nervous trouble, and her grandpa, whom she hates. She actually said that she hates him. Didn't she, Jane?'

'Yes,' Jane confirmed. 'We were a bit surprised by that. There's a lot of money in the family but it all belongs to Grandpa and the other relatives just do as he says.'

'Still, that's not too unusual in old families,' observed Mrs Butler.

'I heard about old Mr Weston,' said Mr Butler. 'From several friends. He can't keep servants because he's so testy. No gentleman will put up with having boots thrown at his head because they aren't shined to suit Mr Weston's pleasure. He can't keep a cook because he has fads. I remember when Mrs Butler heard from his cook, an old school friend of hers, about his food reform diets. I had to get her a glass of sherry.'

'It wouldn't be so bad if it was just food reform,' said Mrs Butler, leaning her elbows on the table and settling down to a good gossip. 'Food reform just means no cream, no meat, no butter and very little sugar; a good cook can get around that. No, it's because he changes all the time. And everyone in his house has to eat the latest diet. When he thought his granddaughter was getting too plump he put the whole household on a lemon juice and raw vegetable diet. It must be hard for the girl. She might have been all right while she was at boarding school but the general opinion is that old Mr Weston is too much to bear.'

'And therefore he can't keep his staff and even when they are allowed real food, it is indifferently cooked and badly served,' commented Mr Butler. 'Not a happy household, Miss Fisher.'

'Yet they want their daughter back very badly,' said Phryne. 'I wonder why?'

'The scandal,' said Dot. 'They might not like the girl but they won't allow her to go to the bad in their own suburb, where their friends might see her.'

'Dot dear, what a cynic you are to be sure,' said Phryne affectionately. 'Has Rose any siblings, girls?'

'A younger brother who's the apple of everyone's eye,' answered Ruth. 'He's only about three, so he hasn't got into any trouble yet. When he was born she says that her family sort of forgot about her.'

That was a sad thought to go missing on, Phryne considered. She put down her empty cup and saw that everyone else had finished eating.

'Thank you for such a delightful breakfast, Mrs

Butler, at such an hour, too,' said Phryne. 'Now I'm going to call the sanatorium and get ready for the trials of the day. I do hope that silly girl hasn't done anything really foolish,' she added.

'Sure to have,' said Dot darkly.

On her telephone application to the sanatorium, Phryne was told that there was no reason why the girls should not go to see Mrs Ross on that very Sunday, and Jane and Ruth took Molly outside to explain why they couldn't take her for a walk. Mrs Butler provided a picnic basket. Dot gathered up her crocheting and a variety of things which might be needed on a trip so far outside the confines of civilisation. Mr Butler put on the Assyrian panoply of his motoring garments, including his peaked cap. Phryne decided that she would take the importunate puppy on a promenade once everyone had left. If Molly didn't get her walk she tended to bark hysterically at all passers-by and trample the pelargoniums.

But just as Phryne was waving her family off and turning to go back inside, she was stopped at the gate by a well-dressed young gentleman. He appeared agitated. His clothes, though good, seemed to have been assumed in a hurry; his tie was badly tied and one of his pockets was inside out. His umbrella was bundled together, not rolled, and his bowler had not been brushed.

'Miss Fisher? Could you be Miss Fisher?' he gasped.

Phryne had had enough of shocks and startlement for one day. 'Yes, certainly I could be. Who are you?' she enquired abruptly.

He took off his hat. 'Sorry, sorry. I'm Pryles, Duncan Pryles, Mr Elijah Johnson's secretary.'

Phryne remained unenlightened. 'And Mr Johnson is...?'

The young man writhed with frustration. 'Oh, you must know him, Miss Fisher, he's on all the boards of directors for practically everything. Gives a lot of money to charities.'

'Oh yes, that Johnson. And what does he want with me?'

'He wants to consult with you,' said Mr Pryles, looking really unhappy. 'About ... a girl.'

Phryne closed the gate. 'If he wants a girl, there're plenty over there,' she said. 'Just follow Fitzroy Street.'

'No, Miss Fisher, please!' The young man tied himself into a rather impressive knot. 'The missing girl.' He leaned forward to whisper. 'Rose Weston.'

'Oh,' said Phryne. 'Ah. Well, ask him to come in. I can give him a few minutes.'

Having bidden farewell to all her household, except Mrs Butler, who was getting on with the washing up, Phryne escorted Mr Johnson into the small parlour and settled him with a large gin. He was a tallish, rather imposing man with carefully trimmed grey hair and a fruity aldermanic voice. He seemed nervous.

'Rose Weston is missing,' he said. 'I understand that you are a private detective, Miss Fisher. I want to retain you to find her.'

'And your interest in the matter is...'

'A family friend. I have known her since she was so high.' He held out a shaking hand some three feet from the carpet.

'I will see what I can do,' said Phryne. 'But you are aware that she was unhappy at home and may have had reasons for leaving.'

Mr Johnson jumped and spilled some of his gin down his waistcoat. 'Oh, surely not, Miss Fisher,' he began, and Phryne cut him short.

'I do investigations for my own reasons, Mr Johnson, as I am sure that you are aware,' she said sternly. 'And I can't do a thing if my client is lying to me. If you know the family, you know that Rose was unhappy. Those ridiculous clothes, for example. She may have found a boy and run away just to be free. Young people do such things, you know.'

'Well, yes, well, as you say, Miss Fisher,' said Mr Johnson, mopping his brow. 'She probably found home life a bit restrictive. And her clothes were absurd, I agree. But her mother is frantic. If you can find Rose, tell her that things will be better, that she can choose her own clothes and perhaps even go out – properly chaperoned, of course. If you could try to find her.'

'All right.' Phryne's curiosity was piqued. And she hadn't done a rummage through the houses of ill repute for a while. But Phryne had seen a fair number of lost girl cases and Mr Johnson wasn't saying the one thing that they all said. And now he was writing her a fat cheque, taking his hat, his secretary and his leave, and actually leaving, without saying it. However angry the parents, they always said: 'as long as she's all right.' Mr Johnson had not said that. Curious. Very curious indeed.

Phryne put a note on the front door, 'Miss

Fisher Is Not at Home Today, and shut it. Then, calling out an explanation to Mrs Butler, she went upstairs and put herself to bed for a short nap.

Now that she had managed to persuade everyone to go on this expedition, Ruth was having second, or even third, thoughts.

Not that it wasn't a nice day for a drive, as Mr Butler remarked to Dot. Dot liked being driven by Mr Butler, who never exceeded the speed limit or tried his luck on the comparative agility between the Hispano-Suiza and a milk-cart. They proceeded at a decorous twenty miles an hour, which was quite fast enough for Dot. And it was a nice day. The hot wind had changed to a cool breeze and the blue sky was dotted with fleecy clouds. There was an ample picnic basket in the back and this journey might put Ruth's restlessness at ease. Dot jammed her immovable cloche down further on her head and snuggled into her car rug, happy to enjoy the scenery.

'Oh, Jane, what have I done?' moaned Ruth.

Jane gave her ear a light clip. 'This was all your idea,' she reminded her adoptive sister mercilessly. 'And you nagged until we did it. Now the least you can do is enjoy the ride.'

'This is a very nice car,' agreed Ruth. 'So smooth. I never rode in a car before Miss Phryne came, did you, Jane?'

'I seem ... to remember cars. And the train, I remember the train. But not cars like this. What do you want your mother to tell you, Ruth?'

'Who my father was,' said Ruth.

78

'And then what?'

'What?' Ruth hadn't thought beyond the first fence.

'Are you going to try to find him?'

'I don't know. Perhaps.'

'He might have married again,' said Jane. 'He might not want another daughter.'

'I hadn't thought of that!' said Ruth, beginning to panic.

'Never mind,' said Jane, relenting. 'Let's play I spy. I spy, with my little eye, something beginning with c.'

'Clouds,' said Ruth.

'Car,' said Jane.

The mountains became clearer. Mount Dandenong, Jane informed the occupants of the car, was 2077 feet high. Ruth was not listening. What, now she came to it, *was* she going to say to her mother? She didn't remember her mother. And what would this sick woman have to say to her?

Dandenong Road flew past under the steadily turning wheels of the big touring car. Suburbs were left behind, the road began to rise, and by the time Jane had run out of things to spy with her little eye they were up in the blue Dandenongs and the car was running through tree shadow.

'What's the name of the sanatorium?' asked Mr Butler, slowing down to look for a turn-off.

'Hygeia,' said Dot. 'I believe – yes, there's the sign. It's at the top of the hill. For the breezes.'

Hygeia was a large, comfortable country house of three storeys. Each room opened onto a balcony, which ran around three sides of the building. Mr Butler took the gravelled carriage drive up to the front door, which had a Greek goddess in marble standing beside it and a large brass bell next to it on a stand, as in all the best fairytales.

The forest which wreathed the lower slopes of the hill breathed green scents as the girls scrambled out of the Hispano-Suiza. Once away from the car's own aroma of brass polish, heated exhaust and leather, the cold antiseptic smell of eucalypt and myrtle wafted up from the dense thickets below. Jane listened.

'I can hear water,' she said.

'Creek down in the gully, I'll bet,' said Dot, shivering. 'Cold up here, too. Come along, girls. Mr Butler, if you wouldn't mind?'

Mr Butler struck the brass bell with some force and the large door opened instantly, as though the person who now appeared had been hiding behind it.

'The Misses Fisher? And Miss Williams? You are expected. Do come in,' she said cordially. 'I am Miss Brown. If you would like to take the car around to the stables, driver, you can be accommodated in the kitchen.'

The speaker was a short, neat woman with restrained hair and a linen wrapper of strident pink. She had a bunch of boronia pinned on one shoulder and a huge collection of keys at her belt.

'This way, please. Now, have you brought anything for the patient?'

'Just some chocolates,' said Dot. 'A bottle of the good port, a few books, and some freshly made ginger biscuits.'

'Very good. We cannot allow spirits, of course, but a little port is allowable. Our physician considers it strengthening. We do our best, you know,' she said a little plaintively as she led the way along a corridor where the linoleum was polished to a neck-breaking gloss and the walls were painted spring green. 'But we cannot cure them yet, you see, and at best we are just a staging post between earth and heaven, as our minister so beautifully puts it. But at least here there is no noise except the bellbirds.'

'It's very peaceful,' said Dot approvingly. Miss Brown beamed on this commonplace remark.

'Most of my ladies are younger than Mrs Ross, of course,' she said. 'We have little dances and picnics when they are feeling up to it.'

'How is Mrs Ross?' asked Dot bluntly. Miss Brown paused and clasped her hands to her bosom.

'Fading,' she said. 'She's been fading for years. She used to talk, but lately she hasn't been able to rouse herself to any real effect. And in all the time I've been here she's never had any visitors except for the minister and the church ladies. I've consulted her case notes, since you said that you were coming, and it appears that her own mother and father are dead and her only relative was a daughter – is this she?'

'Yes, she was adopted by my Miss Fisher.'

'And she's quite healthy?' whispered Miss Brown.

'Quite,' affirmed Dot.

Ruth and Jane, who had been straying behind, caught up.

'Now, don't be afraid when you see her,' said Miss Brown, taking Ruth's hand as they walked along. 'She isn't infectious anymore. She's just very thin and very, very tired.

'Mrs Ross, dear? I've brought you a visitor,' fluted Miss Brown in a voice so laden with sugary good will as to irritate the calmest invalid. Jane and Ruth went inside.

Anna Ross was so thin that sunlight seemed to fall through her. She was dressed in a white woollen gown of severe cut and her wheeled chair had been turned so that she looked out onto the rolling green forest below the sanatorium. But she was not looking out. She was staring down into her cupped hands, as though she could grasp the sunlight which spilled into them. Her hair was white and cut short like a boy's.

'Hello,' ventured Ruth, far too loudly, and then whispered, 'Hello, Mother.'

'So you've come,' said Mrs Ross. Her voice was almost gone. Standing close to her mother Ruth could see all the tiny bones in her wrists and the cords in her neck which seemed to be the only things holding up the heavy head.

'I've come,' said Ruth, sitting down next to her mother and wondering whether she dared to touch her hand.

'I loved him so much,' mourned the tiny voice, breathy with oncoming death. 'But he went away. You don't look like him,' she said, raising a finger with immense effort to touch Ruth's blooming cheek.

'What was his name?' asked Ruth very gently.

'Hamish. Hamish McGregor. But it was my

darling that I loved. But he died. Rory Dubh died. What do you want with me? I died too, I died a long time ago.'

Tears rolled down her white cheeks, across the patches of bright red as carmine as clown make-up.

'I've brought you some things,' said Ruth, casting a desperate look at Dot. Miss Williams was a deathbed veteran. She took a corkscrew and briskly pulled the cork on the fine old port, filled a large tooth glass and held it to Mrs Ross's pale lips.

'Just sip,' she advised. 'You, Ruth, come and cradle her head for me, yes, like that.'

Under Ruth's shrinking fingers the white hair was as dry and brittle as straw. Dot watched as Mrs Ross gulped the port and then patted her tears away with a clean handkerchief.

'You've got a chance to say goodbye,' she said to the stricken woman. 'Not many people have that. This is your daughter Ruth, who has had a hard life. You might not see her again. Talk to her.'

The port had put a little animation into Mrs Ross. 'Ruth,' she said consideringly. 'That is a nice name. I'm sorry if I harmed you, Ruth. But I did love him so much. I've had time to think about it and I wouldn't have done it any differently if I had the time over again.'

'Where is he now?' asked Ruth. Tears streamed down her face and she sniffed.

'He's dead,' said her mother. 'His friend brought me word he was dead, when I had been here a few years. And Hamish ... I don't know about Hamish. Bring me the box which is by my bed.'

Jane found the box and brought it. Mrs Ross opened it. It was full of letters. She groped through it, searching for something.

'Here,' she said to Ruth. 'This is all I have to give you.' She folded Ruth's fingers over an object on a chain. 'I'm glad I had a chance to say goodbye. But I must sleep now. Are you afraid to kiss me?'

'No,' said Ruth. She bent and printed a kiss on the cold cheek.

'God bless you, my daughter,' said Anna Ross, and closed her eyes. For a moment Ruth was afraid that she was dead, but her breast rose and fell.

'Just asleep,' said Miss Brown. 'Well! Who would have thought of Mrs Ross as having a romantic past. There's no telling,' she said, blithely unaware of Dot's glare.

They left Hygeia and piled back into the car.

'Where to, ladies?' asked Mr Butler heartily. He could see that Ruth had been crying and wished to apply his universal panacea for all female ills: a nice cup of tea, as soon as possible.

'Down to the picnic ground, Mr B,' said Dot.

'We can boil the billy,' agreed Mr Butler. 'And the cook was telling me that there are tame lyrebirds there. Gave me some kitchen scraps for them. Partial to a bit of bacon rind, apparently.'

The picnic ground was well wooded, with tables and benches made of local timber. There was a gazebo in case it rained and ample fresh water. Mr Butler built a small fire and soon had the billy singing. Because it was a weekday they had the grounds to themselves. Under the influence of ham sandwiches, ginger biscuits and tea, Ruth began to revive. Jane allowed her a small victory on the subject of Wilfred Owen being a better war poet than Siegfried Sassoon, and the sun shone down with increasing authority.

Then, at the edge of the forest, the lyrebird appeared. Mr Butler threw out handfuls of the chopped kitchen scraps and the party held its collective breath.

Stalking on its long legs, dragging its tail like a dowager's train with a strange faint frou-frou, the bird pecked its way forward, busily locating and dispatching each fragment of food. Then, as though it was grateful, it stopped, elevated the lyre-shaped tail and sang a long, complex oratorio composed of other birds' songs copied with remarkable skill – coachwhip crack, magpie water-music, bellbird bell, kookaburra laugh – concluding with a medley of country noises: the clop of a car door, the crack of a tree branch, the ringing of an axe and the ting-ting of the Hygeia doorbell.

Ruth forgot herself and applauded. The lyre-bird took another, hurried gulp of bacon rind, panicked and raced for the scrub, long legs flashing, lyre fishtailing behind.

Even Ruth found herself laughing.

Miss Mavis Sutherland to Miss Anna Ross
15 January 1913

Dear Annie, I love to hear about your Rory. Will your Mama oppose the match? He's just a sailor and they never have enough money to set up a suitable establishment, and you do have all those grand relations. What would they think of you marrying a Jack Tar? Not that he isn't as handsome as you say, and as good, and as moral. But you are only eighteen and can't marry without her consent until you are twenty-one. How does she feel about Rory? Does she like him? I love him already from your description.

The London house is full now and we are all as busy as beavers. My young lady is getting married in June, and the noise and mess and confusion is very wearing. The old lord her father said that planning a wedding was worse than planning a major military campaign. He is worried, I think, about the war he says is coming between Germany and Britain. No one else believes it but he does and it makes me nervous. So nervous that Mrs Grainger, the housekeeper, gives me five drops of laudanum every night and tells me not to be a silly girl. But I've been dreaming of war and I don't like it. You remember that my mother used to dream true. I'm dreaming of blood spilled on the ground. It not nice. Mrs Grainger says that if I don't get better soon she'll send me to the Big House in the Highlands for a rest cure and that might be for the best. Everything feels dark in London now. I've made this lucky garter for your wedding. And this locket with my picture in which I hope you will wear in memory of your loving friend.

Mavis

CHAPTER SIX

There came and looked him in the face
An angel beautiful and bright
And that he knew it was a Fiend

Samuel Taylor Coleridge
'Love'

Phryne Fisher was preparing to perform her own detective sorcery and, like Circe, began by summoning her minions. How to find a girl like Rose Weston, an unstable, unfortunate young woman who had recently been keeping the worst of company and had run away before? Consult her very own experts on the worst of company, viz, Bert and Cec. They were good mates and had come, over the time they had known her, to trust Phryne even though she was (1) a sheila and (2) worse, a capitalist. Bert had warned Madame Anatole against Rose's companions. Phryne rang him and asked both Bert and Cec to tea.

And that appeared to be that until the adventurers got back. Phryne left Mrs Butler slumbering gently in her armchair in the kitchen, caught the importunate Molly and attached a lead to her collar (Molly would fling herself to the floor with all her paws in the air in ecstasy at the very thought of a walk, which made putting on her lead difficult) and let herself out.

The sands were a time-honoured place to walk dogs but not advisable at present, due to the number of strong-minded circus animals and their concomitant guards, so Phryne decided to proceed along Acland Street and purchase some cakes. While she was there she also bought a ticket for the 'Journey to Samarkand' lantern show from a girl with a rather come-hither eye. Phryne gave the young woman points for poise as she endured being thoroughly sniffed by Molly, who drank in her scent as if it were nectar.

'I'm so sorry – she has no manners at all,' apologised Phryne. 'Perhaps I'd better buy another ticket.'

'You can take six for two shillings,' said the young woman. 'The professor's got a lovely voice. Just like hot honey running down your back. Ooh!' she said, as Molly's questing cold nose goosed a sensitive spot, and Phryne paid up and moved on.

Molly emphatically did not take to the raffle ticket seller who accosted Phryne next. She was carrying a miniature poodle of whom Molly had grave suspicions. Phryne gave her three pennies and hauled the hound close to her ankles. The poodle did not help by uttering the nearest thing that Phryne had ever heard to a canine snigger as the raffle seller passed.

Phryne bought her cakes and continued down the street, Molly mostly remembering her training and trotting amiably at her heels. The sun came out. Phryne was stung for two tickets to a Folk Music Society concert, which she did not mind because she had intended to go anyway, and a lecture on the 'Evils of Drink', which she did not want but had to buy as the seller had tripped over Molly's lead. Another raffle seller caught her when she was off guard and so did a boy vending cold cream shampoo, which smelt very like Lifebuoy soap, cut into cubes and wrapped in silver paper. She only avoided the infallible-mouse-trap man by crossing the road. Poorer and somewhat cross, Phryne returned to her own house to find a good strong gin and tonic and some lunch. St Kilda was becoming very expensive these days.

The gin and tonic was excellent and so were the cheese and tomato sandwiches which Mrs Butler made. Phryne settled down to plot the movements of Rose Weston, last seen by Phryne walking down Fitzroy Street towards the sea. No one yet admitted to seeing her after that, but Phryne still had plenty of people to ask, although all of them were presently unavailable, out at the festival. Restless, she collected Lin Chung and his wife when they called at her house and walked out to see a demonstration of lifesaving. It was very well organised, as Lin admitted. And if one was cast adrift in the harbour it would be very pleasant to see those fine young lads running down the beach with their reel.

Phryne yielded to fate, and accompanied Lin Chung and Camellia to the flower show in the town hall. The scent was wonderful. Massed begonias and tuberoses in all shades from salmon pink to white stood in the centre of the space. On either side were wide flat dishes of waterlilies: blue, pink, white and even some tinged with yellow. They floated like stars.

'Real Nile lotus,' whispered Camellia. 'I've

89

never seen them with that delicate sunlight shading. How beautiful! Lin, we must ask Great Grand Uncle if we can make a lotus pond.'

'Indeed,' said Lin, who did not botanise but liked landscapes. 'I'm sure he will be happy as long as you do all the planning and supervise the construction and he can sit by the pond in a comfortable chair and drink tea.'

'Tea!' exclaimed Camellia. 'Yes, husband, that is a clever thought. There is something in the Classic of Tea about tea-leaves enclosed in lotus petals.' She stared at the floating jewels and sighed. 'Then again, perhaps the blue lotus would be better. I could plant the edge with blue-tinged grasses and perhaps some of those rich blue irises...'

'I leave it entirely in your capable hands,' said Lin diplomatically. 'Phryne, do you care for lotuses?'

'Only if Camellia does,' said Phryne. She liked Lin's cultivated, intelligent wife very much. Camellia had designed Phryne's own garden, transforming an urban wasteland of dustbins and chickens into a fairy grove of jasmine, bamboo and wisteria. Camellia greatly admired Phryne for her courage and elan. She had been told that Lin had a concubine, and was thankful that she was so agreeable, for Camellia would have had to endure her company, pleasant or unpleasant, secure only in the knowledge that she was the accredited wife, and Phryne was merely an amusement.

Phryne, fortunately, liked being an amusement. She strayed over to a stand stuffed with paeony roses, which were not as beautiful as those grown by Mrs Lin, and then to one selling every kind of crocus, hyacinth and spring bulb. Camellia made a note of the grower's name once she had sniffed his wares. The seller was a young man with 'get-ahead' practically branded on his brow, though Phryne suspected that the real gardener was the old man who was sitting at the back of the booth with a felt hat over his face and his gnarled hands loose on his knees. The young man entered into eager discussion with Mrs Lin about the necessity for storing some bulbs in an ice-chest so that they would germinate on time.

A string quartet was playing in the hall and some young people had got up an impromptu dance in the cleared space in front of the players. Phryne wandered that way, unable to contribute to a deep discussion on the nature and colouring of freesias. How much could one actually say about freesias? Quite a lot, it would seem.

Phryne noticed that the viola in this quartet was being played by Miss Marie Bernhoff, one of her flower maidens. Phryne leaned against a pillar and watched. They really were quite good. A little too fast and a little overenthusiastic, but they were used to playing together. As the dancers moved they stirred the scent of that over-scented room so that they seemed to be swimming in perfume.

Aha, thought Phryne as she sighted another flower maiden, Joannie, sitting on a spindly chair and fanning herself, and a third, Diane, dancing with one of the most beautiful young men that had ever gladdened Phryne's eye. He was the epitome of that fragile, evanescent maleness, that angelic beauty, which is only found in young men between the ages of about sixteen and twenty. Before that, they are gawky. After that, they grow beards and become commonplace. But at the height of their beauty they take the breath and Phryne's was duly taken. Greek poets would have swooned. Michelangelo would have groped for his chisel, among other things. Oscar Wilde would have dropped Bosie.

'Oh my,' breathed Lin into Phryne's susceptible ear. 'Who's the Adonis?'

'I don't know,' said Phryne. 'Isn't he a piece of pure quattrocento art? He'd make an annunciation angel.'

'Too pale?' said Lin. 'His hair is only just gold and he has – yes – pale skin and blue eyes. Perhaps he is more of a Botticelli. Or a Pre-Raphaelite.'

'The Knight in Quest for the Grail,' said Phryne. 'Yes. Pity it won't last. They are so beautiful for such a short time.'

'Like Camellia's freesias,' remarked Lin.

Phryne turned at the slightly acid tone of voice. 'Oh come, Lin dear, you aren't going to be tiresome, are you?' asked Phryne.

'No. There is an exact female equivalent. Gorgeous at sixteen. Slatterns at twenty-five.'

'So there is. Isn't it lucky we are neither of us affected?'

'Age cannot wither nor custom stale,' agreed Lin. Unseen by the dancing crowd, he slid a hand down the curve of Phryne's admirable buttock and felt her shiver agreeably.

'Still,' said Phryne, 'he is dancing with Diane, one of my flower maidens. There, she's seen me and is bringing the youth across.'

'Rather like a triumphant cat with a mouse,' said Lin.

'She isn't feline. More like a shopper at the sales who has somehow beat off the opposition to the only genuine model dress in the shop.'

'And the florid girl is yours, too?' asked Lin as Joannie joined Diane.

'Step back unless you want to be introduced and cooed over,' Phryne warned Lin. He faded into the panelling. When Joannie and Diane came up to her, she was alone.

'Miss Fisher! I thought it was you,' said Diane. 'I said so to Derek. When I was dancing with him. Derek Roscombe, this is the Hon. Miss Phryne Fisher.'

Derek blushed a little, took Phryne's hand and shook it, then didn't quite know what to do with it. Phryne repossessed herself of her digits. He was a stunning creature. He might be – indeed, she suspected that he was – utterly brainless, but who needed brains if you looked like an angel? He was slender and tall and completely fitted for life as an artist's model. Diane had him in a firm grip, although the music had stopped to allow the musicians a tea-break.

Joannie flanked Derek on his other side and put a hand on his arm. 'You promised me the next dance,' she said demurely. Diane shot her a furious look. Phryne smelt a scene coming on. Oh dear. Time to break this up. One should not have all the flower girls hurling bouquets at each other and, in any case, she wanted to ask them about the missing Rose Weston.

'I'm sure that Derek would be kind enough to fetch us an ice,' she said.

The young man, who still hadn't uttered a word, smiled complaisantly and went off to fight his way into the scrum surrounding the ice-cream stall. Phryne drew both girls to a small table and sat them down. They were still glaring at each other.

'Young ladies,' she said severely. The tone was enough to jolt them into an awareness of where they were. 'I might give you some advice about beautiful young men but I can't see it having the faintest effect and I don't like wasting my time. I need your help in another matter. Rose Weston is missing.'

'I know,' said Joannie, willing to be helpful. 'Mrs Weston knocked my house up at some dreadful hour looking for her. Such a fuss! The dog got out and started chasing a cat and Papa quite lost his temper and yelled at everybody.'

From the astonished tone, it was clear that Mr Smythe didn't usually act the domestic tyrant. Joannie went on: 'But I haven't seen Rose since yesterday when the car picked us up at Anatole's. I told Mrs Weston I hadn't seen her and she went off. Then Mama soothed Papa down and we corralled the dog and had an early breakfast, so no harm done really.'

'Mrs Weston came to our house, too,' said Diane flatly. 'Seemed in a real state. Really! Just like Rose!'

'What's just like Rose?' Phryne asked carefully.

'To mess things up,' snarled Diane. 'She did the same thing with the school play, you remember, Joannie?'

'Yes, but I don't think it's all her fault,' said Joannie placatingly. 'Don't be so fierce, Di! We were doing "A Midsummer Night's Dream",' she explained for Phryne's benefit. 'And Rose really wanted to be in it, and she really couldn't act, so we gave her a part as one of the rustics, and then just when we looked like we had the play ready – in fact, on the first night – Rose was nowhere to be found. If the Snug costume hadn't fitted me, I don't know what would have happened.'

'You weren't acting, then?' asked Phryne.

Joannie dimpled modestly. 'No. I'm not the right shape for a heroine. I was backstage and prompt and wardrobe,' said Joannie, naming three of the hardest jobs in the theatre. 'I've got a good memory and I'd been prompting all through the rehearsals so I knew the lines. I just had to say them. It wasn't difficult. Went off without a hitch.'

'And where was Rose?' asked Phryne.

'She came back after it was all over and said she couldn't face going onstage with all those people looking at her. That's what she's like,' said Joannie forgivingly. 'She has these enthusiasms and then once she's committed herself she finds she can't go through with it.'

'I see,' said Phryne, feeling a chill. Starts things which she can't finish. In certain circles that would not be a survival skill. Phryne concluded that she'd better find Rose as fast as possible.

'Here's Derek,' exclaimed Joannie dotingly.

The young man had managed not only to purchase four ice creams but had somehow found a tray, probably by smiling at a susceptible female (ie, one over the age of twelve). Phryne realised

95

that if he was the – so to speak – bone of contention amongst the girls, he must know Rose Weston as well. She needed to speak to him alone. To do that she would have to cut out both flower maidens without hurting their feelings.

The ice cream was quickly demolished. Phryne got to her feet as the music started again. A foxtrot. Perfect. She drew in a deep breath and let it out slowly. Then she gave the young man a twinkling, sidelong look which had him out of his chair and proposing a dance so fast that there was a faint whooshing noise. Phryne accepted and danced him out of earshot, pleasantly conscious that there were some charms which were not possessed by the young and blooming.

Derek Roscombe was tall, slim, and a good dancer. His tailoring was good but not out of the top drawer and he was lightly scented with good soap. Someone who loved him, probably his mother, had bought him that restrained tie.

'I say, Miss Fisher,' he whispered into Phryne's hair. 'You're a super dancer.'

'Thank you,' said Phryne. 'You're also a good dancer. Now, my dear, I have an ulterior motive for taking you away from the girls.'

'Them?' His voice was sweet, husky, only half-broken. 'They're jolly girls. But they aren't like you, Miss Fisher.'

Help, thought Phryne, the next time I use that look I must cut down the wattage considerably if the subject is younger than twenty-five.

'I am not under discussion,' she said. 'I'm trying to find Rose Weston. Can you help me?'

He stumbled a little, but picked up the rhythm

again. 'Is she ... missing?'

'Yes, she is.'

'I don't know where she is,' he said carefully. 'Rose ... well, she's a bit ... fast. She throws herself into things.'

'Indeed. You don't know where she is, but do you know where she was intending to be?'

'She said she'd meet me on the beach,' he said miserably. 'I didn't go. I don't ... I mean, I did think ... but I can't afford to get into trouble. Everyone knows that her family is not quite, you know, and...'

'What time and which beach? Come on, the dance is finishing,' hissed Phryne.

'Where the caravans are. At midnight. I sleep in the same room as my brother. I can't get out late at night. I think she knew that. I think she was ... playing some game in her head.'

'You are much brighter than I gave you credit for,' said Phryne, releasing him as the music stopped. 'Now, you may kiss my hand, yes, like that, and thank me for the dance, and go back to Joannie and Diane. They, my boy, are your chosen species, and if I were you I'd stick with them.'

The beautiful boy kissed her hand, thanked her for the dance, and fled. Joannie and Diane received him with cries of joy. So Rose Weston had gone to a tryst, and had been left like that unfortunate Cretan maiden Ariadne on Naxos. However much Phryne privately thought that anyone was better off without that bounder Theseus, she had been disconsolate. And Ariadne had been found by the Bacchic rout and Dionysos. Who had found Rose Weston? And

97

what had they done with her?

Lin returned. He smiled at Phryne. 'So you danced with the pretty boy,' he observed.

'So I did, and got some information out of him. Now I need to talk to one of the musicians and I need to do it now, because Bert and Cec are coming to afternoon tea. I don't suppose you play the viola, Lin dear? You have so many unexpected talents.'

'Not that one, I regret,' he said. Whatever small prickle of jealousy he might have been feeling – could anything male ever be that beautiful? – was assuaged by Phryne's matter-of-fact tone. She did not have a new lover on her mind at the moment. Just a new puzzle which seemed to have become urgent.

'Viola is doubling violin in this tune,' he said. 'You could extract her without harming the dance.'

'What a good ear you have,' said Phryne. 'And what a pity that I never learned the piano and Camellia never learned the moon guitar.'

Camellia giggled. Phryne's confession of complete musical inadequacy had been an instant bond between them. Camellia was very pleased with her new life. And she had never been so delighted with a flower show. Everything was so beautiful that she felt like a child in a sweet shop – a little dizzy and very greedy. Already she had ordered a collection of tulips which would make a remarkable display in Miss Fisher's little garden come spring.

Phryne beckoned Miss Marie Bernhoff out of the ensemble and she laid down her viola and came, wiping her brow and chin with a silk hand-kerchief.

'It's very hot up there,' she complained. Lin slipped away to get her a cool drink and Phryne drew her into a corner behind a pillar.

'You shall have lemonade,' she promised. 'Did you know that Rose Weston is missing?'

'Yes, Mrs Weston came to our house and my father was very cross with her. He told her that I was not to associate with her daughter anymore and called Rose several bad names, though luckily he did it in Czech and I don't think poor Mrs Weston understood him. My father hates to be woken up in the morning as it is.'

'Do you know where Rose might have gone?'

'Well, she rather made a fool of herself about that pretty boy there,' said Marie coolly. 'But I could say the same of Joannie and Diane – you'd think they had more sense,' she said without emotion.

'Why did your father say nasty things about Rose?' asked Phryne. Lin had returned with a tall frosted glass of lemonade and Marie thanked him politely before gulping half of it.

'Oh, that's saved my life. Very kind of you,' she said. She looked at this soigné Chinese gentle-man, and then she looked at Phryne. An intro-duction was in order.

'This is Mr Lin,' said Phryne. 'And his wife, Camellia. Might I introduce Miss Marie Bern-hoff?'

They shook hands.

'You play well,' said Lin judiciously. 'But this is just café music, of course. I should like to hear you in something complex – Bach, say.'

'Oh, there's no one like Bach,' said Marie enthusiastically.

'Hold on a moment. Tell me about Rose and then you can get back to Johann Sebastian,' Phryne said quickly. She knew conversations about Bach. Days could go past. Continents could drift. Fossils could form. Marie dragged her mind away from music.

'Father says he saw Rose at Anatole's very late and in bad company. Father is never wrong about that sort of thing. He says ... well, he called her a very bad name. That's all I know. Except Rose said she could take Derek away from those two idiots. Nice thing if she could. They're quite mad about him,' concluded Marie, with the air of having said her last word on the subject. 'Now Bach–'

'Did you see where she went yesterday?' demanded Phryne.

'Off down Fitzroy Street towards the sea, and that's the last I saw of her,' said Marie, and Phryne relented. Lin and Marie deserved a small indulgence in Bach.

'Come, Camellia, show me your new flowers,' she said. Phryne and Camellia, arm in arm, went off to look at an astounding array of orchids. They ranged from alarming purple-toothed trumpets which looked like they might creep out of the conservatory by night and eat the family, to the smallest and most attractive, pincushion sized plants with tiny flowers.

'Perhaps these might suit,' said a familiar voice.

'Detective Inspector Robinson, how nice to see you,' Phryne exclaimed. 'This is my favourite policeman, Camellia. May I introduce Mrs Lin? She designed and planted my garden.'

Detective Inspector 'Jack' Robinson lifted his hat with great respect. Miss Fisher's back yard had been transformed and here was the lady who had managed it. He hoped she spoke English.

'My own particular passion is orchids,' he said. 'But you've done a lovely job on that garden. So small and everything in its place.'

'I am also very fond of orchids,' said Camellia, looking down modestly. 'I was wondering which ones might be best for Miss Fisher, and now you are here, perhaps you would be so kind as to advise me.'

'Well, there's always the catteleyas,' he said, delighted to have found a fellow devotee. Such a neat little woman, too, excellent English, and very sound on flowering vines. 'They're pretty tough.'

'There is a north facing wall,' said Camellia. 'I believe it would support a trellis. But the pots have to be cared for, of course.'

'And I'm not the one to remember to water them,' said Phryne cheerfully. 'Jack dear, have you had a Rose Weston reported missing?'

'Not as far as I've heard,' he said. 'Why?'

'I'm trying to find her. I wondered if we were on the same track.'

Jack Robinson looked uncertain. His mind was still on orchids, their care and feeding.

'Nothing's come to me, but I only get them after ... sorry, Mrs Lin ... I mean, after...'

'Quite,' said Phryne. 'Jack dear, you are looking tired. Something up at the Homicide Squad?'

'No, more on the Home Front,' replied Jack Robinson. 'My sister's come to live with us. Her husband has left, curse him, and she's got three small children. I mean, glad to have her, always been fond of Syl, and it's not that the house isn't big enough. It's just – well, they make a lot of noise and Syl's very upset. I've sort of got out of the habit of kids now my own are growing up so fast.'

'Too bad. Poor woman. Poor you as well. Now, I'm going home, and I can leave you in Jack's capable hands, Camellia. Lin is over by the musicians talking about Bach. Detach him after about an hour and take him home. I've seen these fits of music before. Toodle-pip,' she said, and sailed out of the town hall, content that she had left her guests in excellent company, discoursing on their favourite topics.

Which didn't get her any closer to finding Rose Weston.

Mr Rory McCrimmon to Miss Anna Ross
20 January 1913

Sweet Anna, I think of you always. Today we three were playing our hearts out for the Folk Song folk and I thought, I would play the better if Anna was here listening to me, so I imagined that you were there, that I could see your sweet face before me, and I played better than I ever had before. Though it sounds a little strange when they play the music on that disc, it is us, the three of us, and me piping like a storm.

When we come back, Anna, I have something particular to say to you, my rose of all the world. Can you not guess what it is?

With all my love
Ruari Dubh

CHAPTER SEVEN

'Tis seven long years since he left this land
A ring he took from off his lily-white hand
One half of the ring is still here with me
And the other's rolling at the bottom of the sea.

Anon
'The Dark Eyed Sailor'

The arrival of Bert and Cec coincided with the return of the sanatorium party and it took some time before everyone was sorted out around the parlour table, each with their chosen refreshment in front of them, ready to tell their tale.

Phryne listened without comment to the reports of Mrs Ross's words and slid a notebook and pencil across the table to Jane.

'Write them down as carefully as you can,' she instructed. 'Then turn the book upside down and give it to Ruth to do the same. What was on the chain, Ruth?'

Ruth passed it over. Phryne examined it.

'It looks like half of a finger ring,' she said, puzzled. 'A nice ring. Made of entwined gold wire. I've never seen one like that before.'

'I have,' said Cec. He was tall and pale. His Scandinavian ancestors had given him his blue eyes, his tow-coloured hair and his fatalism. Bert said 'she'll be right'. Cec never believed it. He turned the trinket around in his strong fingers. 'Sailors used to make these,' he told Phryne. 'It's a knot called a great ocean plait. Then I suppose they just welded the ends in.'

'Yair,' agreed Bert. He was short and stout and inclined to be ruddy of complexion. 'I've seen sailors wear these. One sort falls to pieces when you take it off – them Indians wear them. So you can't pretend you ain't married, see? If you take it off you can't get it on again. But this is fixed and it's been cut in half with something like bolt cutters. Who'd want to do a thing like that?'

'A token, perhaps?' asked Dot. 'Like cutting a coin in half? My uncle did that when he went off to the war. My aunt's still got the two halves.'

'A token between lovers who have to part,' said Ruth. 'That's sad.'

'Yes, it is,' agreed Phryne briskly. 'But it's an old story now, and nearly at an end.'

Ruth took the notebook from Jane and began to scribble busily, her face averted.

'Now, I need to find Rose Weston,' said Phryne. 'I last saw her walking away down Fitzroy Street at about four o'clock yesterday. I don't know what happened to her after that, but she thought she had a tryst with a very pretty young man. Girls,' she said, conscious of her audience, 'some of this – in fact, most of it – is not going to be suitable for your ears. Dot, would you like to escort the young ladies out? I believe that there is ice cream,' she added, with low cunning. 'And Molly needs a walk.'

Ruth abandoned the notebook and complied. Jane cast a longing look at the symposium – there might be interesting anatomical details – and followed Ruth. Phryne waited until the door had closed behind them.

'Rose thought she had a meeting on the beach at midnight with a very desirable young man.'

'What does this young bloke say?' asked Bert.

'He never went,' said Phryne. 'He was scared of getting into trouble.'

'Boys have changed since my day,' grinned Bert. Then he stopped grinning. 'But that means the young cow left the girl on the beach...'

'At that hour,' said Phryne. 'Unprotected.'

'This isn't good,' Cec decided.

Phryne continued: 'No. Derek says she wanted him to meet her where the caravans are. I was there this morning – that seems like such a long time ago – and it was quiet. Some dogs and a rush of horses but pretty light on for humans.'

'Yair, but I bet you wasn't trailing along the beach in a dress,' said Bert. 'Wringing your hands and saying "I'm all alone". I bet you were in that boy's rig.'

'I was,' said Phryne. 'And it was after five. Even the most roisterous are usually tucked up in someone's bed by then.'

'But about midnight – the joint might have been jumping. We'll have to ask the carnies,' said Bert. 'And there's the Ace of Clubs, she comes in about then.'

'The Ace of Clubs?' asked Phryne. 'How odd.

Someone sent me an ace of clubs.' She collected it from the mantelpiece.

Bert chuckled. 'Someone doesn't know you very well,' he commented.

'Why?' asked Phryne.

'You don't gamble. It's a boat, a gambling boat. Comes in every night. Here to Williamstown. See, there are the times, written down at the bottom here. Assuming you're a rich capitalist with far too much money and time on your hands, you arrive at Willi or at the pier, you go on board, you waste the money which you've ground out of the labour of the starving poor, and then they take you back, you pick up the Rolls, and home you go, drunker and poorer but probably not sadder or wiser. Been going on for years, ever since baccarat arrived in town. Run by Mr Walker. Not a man to even think about crossing. Supposed to have good wine, but,' Bert added.

'Nice boat. Steam yacht. Mate of mine says that there isn't an inch of brass unpolished,' said Cec. 'Treats his crew well. Good wages and not a hard job. They lie up during the day, do a bit of painting or repairs, take on stores. Only three journeys a night. Mind you, it's a bit hard to leave Mr Walker if you know any of his secrets. Good idea to go somewhere else if you want to retire peaceful.'

'Like Africa,' said Bert. 'Or New Zealand. Nah, New Zealand's probably too close. South America, maybe.'

'When you say peaceful, Cec, do you mean without any bullet holes in important parts of the anatomy?' asked Phryne. Cec nodded.

'Oh,' said Phryne. 'Well, this Ace of Clubs token must be fairly well known in gambling circles. My wine merchant recognised the card and leapt to the wrong conclusion. That is comforting. I should not like to trust the opinion of a young man who made that sort of mistake.'

'Oh yair, everyone knows about it.'

'Including the cops?'

'Of course. But baccarat, see, it's a simple game. Raid the boat and what do you get? A lot of people innocently playing bridge. No roulette wheel, no little horses. Vice know all about Mr Walker. And he don't like trouble. He only accepts cash, no markers, no jewellery. If you win big you get taken home in his car with his boys so no one relieves you of that heavy wallet in the street or on the beach. Been a couple of blokes tried to muscle in on such a sweet racket. And who knows what happened to them? They might'a seen the error of their sinful ways and entered a monastery. But I don't think so,' said Bert with heavy emphasis.

'I see,' said Phryne. 'Well, Cec, can you ask your mate if they saw a stray girl on the beach this morning? That isn't a loaded question.'

'With Mr Walker you never know,' said Cec. 'But no harm in asking.'

'As the bishop said to the actress,' agreed Bert, 'that ain't all, is it?'

'No. Several things. You saw Madame Anatole at the market one morning and warned her about some men. Who were they?'

'Who's Madame Anatole when she's at home?' asked Bert, puzzled.

'Sorry. Lizzie Chambers as was, the disguised

mute boy that the girls tracked across the city one night – you remember? Finally ended up in Kew?'

Bert grinned and took another sip of beer. 'Oh yair. Lizzie. Nice girl. Married that Frog cook who burns a grouse steak, but. She always gives me a g'day when she sees me. And she works hard. We often sees her at the fish market, real early, picking up the best of the catch. Yair. I remember. Though that was at the Queen Vic one morning, have to be a coupl'a weeks ago. She says to me, do you know those men, Mr Bert – that's what she calls me – they are often at our bistro? And I looks and it was that mug lair Simonds, and his bloody awful mate Mongrel. Real bad men, Miss. You want to stay away from them.'

'They are the men with whom our missing girl has been dining,' said Phryne. Bert whistled. Cec pursed his lips.

'Then I reckon she's in a bit of trouble.'

'What's their main business?' asked Phryne.

'Bank jobs,' said Cec. 'And payrolls. They carry guns. And I heard a rumour that Mr Walker wasn't pleased with them for saying that he ran an illegal game.'

'Not nice company for a young lady,' said Cec.

'No,' said Phryne. 'Ask around about them. Discreetly, we don't want to attract any unpleasant attention. Also, I need to know who runs the nearest brothel. One which might see an unprotected girl and decide to snatch her.'

Bert choked on his beer. He had never got used to Miss Fisher's plain speaking.

'They'd be mad,' he opined after Cec had pounded his back. 'Stray girls are always trouble.

No well-run house'd risk her getting away and calling the jacks. Anyway, St Kilda's pretty busy these days. Most of the girls are out on the street. What do you think, Cec?'

'There's the University,' said Cec, obscurely.

'They'd never steal a stray girl,' objected Bert.

'No, but they might take one in,' said Cec. 'If she turned up on their doorstep.'

'We'll have a look around,' said Bert dubiously. 'If you like.'

Phryne let this pass. Bert and Cec often spoke in riddles. 'Right,' she said, rising. 'You do that, and I'm off to talk to her family. Not that I expect they'll tell me anything resembling the truth,' she added, allowing Bert to help her to her feet.

'Why not?' asked Cec.

'Because in all my experience,' said Phryne, 'such families never have.'

Families with missing daughters need a jolt to get them to spill. Phryne decided on an appearance *en grande tenue* at a really inconvenient time. She dressed in a very expensive suit and hat, called up Mr Butler for chauffeur duty again and descended, unannounced, on the bereaved household at five in the afternoon.

It was a very large house in Brighton. Phryne wondered what Camellia, so happily discussing orchids with Jack Robinson, would think of the garden. It was largely composed of box hedges. Gravel covered most expanses. Such grass as grew was clipped close. There were no flowers, no decoration, not even a little playful topiary. Just the looming hedges and the dense dark leaves.

Cold. Neat. Unpleasantly like a graveyard.

In fact, it was a graveyard. Phryne saw small tombstones – surely too small for a human? – in a neatly railed enclosure near the fence. She sat up straighter. This looked like being an interesting visit.

Mr Butler parked the car at the steps and escorted Miss Fisher to the door. The iron-coloured stone of the house boasted what had been a fine set of French windows. These had been covered with solid iron bars. Phryne had seen more cheerful prisons.

'I don't know about this place,' muttered Mr Butler, who had a sincere devotion to his excitable Miss Fisher.

'Onward and upward, Mr Butler dear,' said Phryne bracingly.

Mr Butler seized the large iron gargoyle knocker on the front door and slammed it three times. It made a hollow boom. Nothing happened.

Then Phryne heard a scattering of feet and the very big door creaked open to reveal a very small, very dirty girl in a smock. She paused to wipe her nose with the back of her hand. She bobbed a curtsey and said, 'Yes?'

'The Hon. Miss Phryne Fisher to see Mrs Weston,' announced Mr Butler.

At the sight of him in his blue uniform glittering with buttons, the child gave a squeak of alarm and fled down the hall, screaming, 'Missus! There's a jack!'

'Probably not a child of the household, then,' commented Mr Butler drily.

'Did you hear what she called you?' asked

110

Phryne, intrigued.

'A jack, Miss Fisher? I don't know the term.'

'It means a policeman, Mr Butler. And it isn't the sort of slang one expects to hear in Brighton. Hello?' she called into the house. 'I'll give them another couple of minutes and then I'll write a note.'

'Oh, Jesus, Mary and Joseph, it is a lady, like Mary said,' exclaimed the second child of the day. This one was taller and more articulate, though Irish, but she bobbed the same little bob. She looked about fourteen and she was pinned into an overlarge white nurse's wrapper down which some child had spilled cocoa quite recently.

'Please come in, m'lady, and I'll tell Mrs Weston you are here. And your man.'

Phryne followed the white uniform down a long dark corridor. It was swept clean, bare of carpet or picture, and lit only by meagre electric bulbs at long intervals. The small servant retained Mr Butler as Phryne was conducted into a parlour notable for the dimness of its light and the overstuffed nature of its furniture. It smelt musty, as though no window had been opened in a long time. On inspection, this proved to be because not only was the window nailed shut, it also had iron bars fastened very sternly across it.

This room, Phryne decided, listening to the sounds of domestic mayhem, had belonged to an old lady, and she and the room had got older and shabbier together. There were her flower pictures, her tapestry fire screen in Berlin wool (depicting Dido and Aeneas) in front of a fireplace which contained a fancily folded paper fan, her wedding bouquet under a glass dome, her footstool drawn close to the fire. Nothing had been changed or cleared away. Phryne opened a mother of pearl box and found a store of stale cachous, the same violet ones with which her own grandmother had always rewarded Phryne for sitting still in church and reciting the Collect correctly on her return. Phryne had loved her grandmother and liked violet cachous so she had mostly qualified for one.

Phryne sat down in the visitor's chair and listened. She heard a small child shrieking at the top of his voice: 'No! Want Biddy!' She heard a dish smash on a hard floor. She heard Mr Butler's voice, saying something soothing. The child stopped crying. Then an old man's voice rose above the background noise. 'If we do not have instant silence you are all going to be sleeping under a bridge tonight!'

Waspish, thought Phryne. The aged gentleman is not subtle in his control over his family. That bridge might be looking like a more and more attractive form of accommodation if this was the usual standard of household management. One does not expect a bridge to be comfortable, so one is not disappointed.

Phryne was getting restless. The spirit of the old lady was so strong in her room that Phryne fancied she could almost see her, sitting in her chair, which over the years had conformed itself to her contours. Folding her hands in her lap. Allowing her head to nod. Taking a little nap before dinner which had turned into the longest sleep of all.

Phryne glanced at her watch. Ten more minutes and she would leave.

Five minutes later the door slammed open and into the room came the small Irish girl, carrying an unpolished tray on which reposed unmatching glasses and a decanter of some dark, sinister fluid, a small, fat, choleric dog hauled along by a small, fat, choleric boy, and Mrs Weston, who looked like a tragedy queen who had been told very bad news while being dragged through four hedges backwards.

'Miss Fisher!' she gasped, sinking down into the old lady's chair. Phryne could almost see the ghost bridling. 'Do have a drink. Bridget, pour the wine.'

'Yes, Miss,' said Bridget, and did so very neatly. Especially considering that the small boy was dragging on her arm and demanding in a high, irritating whine that she come and play with him. Phryne's fingers itched for his ears.

'Go on, then, Bridget,' said Mrs Weston, and the door closed behind boy, maid and dog. The silence came back with a rush.

'It's so hard to get good servants these days,' sighed Mrs Weston. 'That girl will be off as soon as her little sister can go to school. She only works here because she can keep little Mary with her.'

'Very likely,' said Phryne coolly. Any young woman with a morsel of pride would hear the siren call of the pickle factory from what was doubtless a cold, hard, grudged bed, accompanied by bad food, sixteen hours' work a day, no privacy and a household ruled by a nasty old man. In the pickle factory you got wages in your

113

pocket, a fixed eight hours' work a day and they supplied pattens against the brine. It would be heaven compared to the Weston household.

'Do have a drink,' urged Mrs Weston, gulping. Phryne tasted it gingerly. It had once, perhaps, been a fine wine, but it had been hoarded long past its prime, and now in its senility there was only the ghost of what it once had been. But it wasn't actively poisonous and Phryne sipped. The glass in her hand was Waterford crystal. Mrs Weston was drinking from carnival ware. This place was a puzzle.

'I have been engaged to find your daughter Rose,' she told Mrs Weston. 'I know she has run away before. Do you know where she has gone on previous occasions?'

'No, she never...' Phryne stared Mrs Weston down. 'Yes, all right, she has been naughty before. But it was just a girlish prank. Girls have these fancies, you know, Miss Fisher.'

'I know,' said Phryne gently.

'She always came back after one day,' sobbed Mrs Weston. 'I never knew where she went. Her grandfather said he'd beat it out of her but she refused to speak and I stopped him after a while.'

Phryne felt a qualm of nausea and put down her glass. Mrs Weston refilled hers and knocked it back. Phryne supposed that it still had some alcohol content.

'She wasn't missing on the day you came looking for her,' said Phryne. 'How did you know she'd run away? Was there a note?'

Mrs Weston froze.

'If you want me to find her I really must have

the truth,' said Phryne in her snake charmer's voice. 'You do see that, don't you? Give me the note,' she said, holding out her hand. Mrs Weston dived a hand into her bosom and brought out a folded note. Phryne put it into her bag. 'Who lives here?' she asked in a more everyday manner.

'Myself, my father. My husband ... left ... last year.'

'Was Rose very attached to her father?'

'No, I would have said, no, not really. They were great chums when she was younger. He used to take her with him wherever he went. Then something happened and she seemed to draw away from him. She never really talked to him after she was about – twelve? And he went not long after.'

'And my client Mr Johnson was your husband's friend?'

'Oh no, Miss Fisher, he's Father's friend. Jacob, my husband, never liked him. Father has a lot of financial interests in common with Mr Johnson.'

'Did Rose like Mr Johnson?'

'I suppose so. Well enough. She was all right at school, you know. It's when Father said that the fees were too high to have her continue as a boarder and made her come home that she became ... uncontrollable.'

'Who else lives here?' asked Phryne, continuing her line of questioning.

'Well, my son Elijah, little 'Lije. You've met him. Bridget. Little Mary. A woman comes in to clean. A kitchen maid called Ethel. We haven't a cook at present. The last one left a week ago. I'm off to the employment agency again tomorrow.

They don't seem to have many people who would suit me on their books, I must say, even though the papers go on about unemployment being so bad.'

'I see. And your father, of course.'

'Yes, it's Father's house. Jacob wasn't a very good businessman. We had to sell our house to pay his debts. Then Father offered us a place here, provided I ran the house, and it seemed like a good idea.'

'I'm sure. Did Rose get on with her little brother?'

'No, she almost seemed not to like him. Unnatural girl! And he's such a sweet little boy.'

Phryne suppressed any comment. 'Did she talk to Ethel?'

'I shouldn't think so,' said Mrs Weston. 'Rose never tried to help in the house.'

'Right. Now, I need to see her room, if you please,' said Phryne, rising. Mrs Weston emptied the decanter into the carnival ware tumbler and tossed the contents off.

'It will be in a mess,' said Mrs Weston.

'I don't mind,' said Phryne relentlessly.

Mrs Weston led the way out of the room. Another mud-coloured corridor took her towards the noise of another domestic disaster, though under it Phryne could hear the girl Bridget singing 'She Moved Through the Fair' in a small, sweet, true voice, interspersed with commands and lamentations.

'Last night she came to me, my dead love came in. Ethel, take that knife away from 'Lije. Holy Mary Mother of Sorrows, we're never going to get this supper cooked, so we shan't. And so softly she entered, her feet made no din, and she put her hand on me, and to me she did say, Ah, but it will not be long, love, till our wedding day. Mary! Where's your handkerchief? There now. Blow!'

Mrs Weston led Phryne up an uncarpeted staircase to the first floor landing, where an old man pounced so suddenly out of the darkness that Phryne had to bite her lip to suppress a cry. This was the child-beating grandfather, was it? Drown them in honey, was Phryne's philosophy, the mean and cranky have no defence against the old oil poured upon them in sufficient quantity.

'Hello,' she said, gracious as a duchess receiving a tattered, damp bouquet from a snotty peasant's child. 'I'm Phryne Fisher. Mr Weston, is it? How very nice to meet you at last.'

The reflexes of courtesy were still there. Old Mr Weston, resplendent in what was probably the very last Jaeger suit in captivity and carpet slippers much worn at the heel, took Miss Fisher's hand and bent over it politely. It was too dark on the landing to get a good look at him. His face was very thin, nose sharpened like a pencil, his cheeks fallen in from lack of teeth. He had a few remaining hairs scraped unconvincingly across his scalp and he smelt, oddly, of methylated spirits, flour and water paste, sulphur and roses.

'Mr Weston's hobby is chemistry,' said Mrs Weston.

'How engrossing,' said Phryne. She would have thought necrophilia if it hadn't been for the roses. Why did he smell of roses? It was a perfectly clear

117

scent and Phryne had never had occasion to doubt her nose before.

'You gave us a fine wine,' she said, 'A Margaux, was it?'

'The last of the forty-eight,' said the old man creakily. 'Laid down by my grandfather. I fear that it is past its prime.'

There was a bright, malicious gleam in the old eyes. Phryne declined to pander to outright fibs.

'A little elderly,' she said. The eyes blinked. He had not been expecting a prompt and accurate reply. 'I have been engaged by your friend Mr Johnson to find Rose,' she told him, in no doubt that he already knew all there was to be known about the transaction. 'I am just going up to look at her room.'

'Yes, yes, she must be found,' he said, grasping her ungently by the hand. 'She must be found. Johnson is paying your fees. Spare no expense. Dinner is late,' he said severely to Mrs Weston.

'You discharged the cook, Father,' she said, with some unexpected spirit. 'You can't expect much out of Ethel and Bridget.'

'Eating, always eating. Filthy habit,' grumbled Mr Weston. He let go of Phryne's hand and limped down the stairs, muttering.

Mrs Weston led the way to the second floor and opened a door.

'This is Rose's room,' she said sullenly.

'Good. I won't be long, and perhaps you had better see what is happening in the kitchen,' urged Phryne. 'Off you go, now.'

Mrs Weston allowed herself to be ushered out. Phryne shut the door on her. It had, she noticed, no lock or even latch. The overhead light was predictably dim and Phryne wished she had brought a flashlight. However, she noticed some candlesticks on the mantel and by dint of lighting all of them, she got a reasonable look at Rose Weston's room.

It was a spare, plain, amazingly uncomfortable room. Furniture which was not used anymore but was too good to throw away had gravitated here. A dressing table with a cracked mirror. An unmatching stool. A canvas stretcher with one blanket. A table and unpadded wooden chair which might have come out of the kitchen. A wardrobe in a horrible fumed-oak finish. This was where Rose slept. But where did Rose live?

Half an hour later Phryne had searched the room thoroughly by the Pinkerton method and had found five paperback romances for railway reading, a secret hoard of cheap chocolates and an illicit flask of Woolworth's rose scent, leaking. So that was where the old man had picked up the scent of roses so foreign to his hobby of chemistry. He had been searching Rose's room. Hoping to find – what? Some clue to where she had gone? There were no letters or pictures. Her schoolbooks must have been at school. Her toiletries were spare and plain, her clothes and underclothes of the cheapest. There was no way of knowing if Rose had taken anything with her when she ran away, because she had so little to take. As she was leaving, Phryne felt a floorboard give a little under her louis heel. She knelt and found that the board had been neatly sawed so that a foot-long section could be lifted up. Phryne did so. Underneath was

119

a purse with ten pounds in it and a bound book which looked like a diary. Phryne put both in her bag and came downstairs.

When Phryne entered the kitchen she saw that Mr Butler had had his usual calming influence on the household. Elijah and little Mary were engaged in making toast. Hoping that they would drop some, the fat cross dog was in attendance. Ethel, a thin, middle-aged woman in a stained apron, had made, with Bridget's assistance, a creditable omelette with some stewed tomatoes and the remains of a rind of cheese. Dinner was ready and it was time for Phryne to take her leave.

She informed Mrs Weston in the hall that she would try to find Rose and left. Mr Butler accompanied her and closed the front door with a thud. 'Phew,' said Phryne as he handed her into the car. He started the Hispano-Suiza with the starting handle and allowed the big car to idle. He did this in so leisurely a fashion that Phryne smelt a rat.

'Mr B,' she said, 'for whom are we waiting?'

'She can't get her bag out in the daytime,' he replied, smiling. 'Won't be a moment, Miss Fisher.'

Running footsteps scattered the gravel. Ethel flung her bag into the back seat, threw herself after it, and said, 'Oh please, let's go!' in a high, tense voice.

Mr Butler swung the great car around, the headlights falling like searchlights on the iron grey house, and then they were out of the drive and into New Street, and Ethel started to cry with relief.

Phryne handed over a clean hanky and the car's

emergency flask of the good cognac and was rewarded with a sniff and a gulp.

'I can't believe it,' said Ethel. 'I'm actually away. I'm actually out of that pest hole! Can't thank you enough,' she said brokenly to Phryne and Mr Butler. 'They knew I couldn't afford to buy new clothes and things and they wouldn't let me get my bag if I left without notice and I couldn't stand it any longer, I really couldn't.'

'I know,' said Phryne soothingly. 'It's like being in the last few pages of *The Fall of the House of Usher*. I kept looking for a tarn, myself.'

Ethel had no idea what Phryne was talking about.

'Where shall we take you, Miss Ethel?' asked Mr Butler jovially. It was a pleasure to get anyone out of that house. He was only sorry that he couldn't take Bridget and little Mary as well.

'My mum lives in St Kilda. Just drop me at the station.'

'We're going to St Kilda,' said Mr Butler. 'Enjoy the ride.'

'Miss,' said Ethel, greatly daring. 'You wouldn't have an aspirin, would you? That old devil won't allow "drugs" in his house and I've got such a headache.'

'You'll need something to take it with. Stop at that grocer's, Mr B, and get Miss Ethel a bottle of – ginger beer?'

'Oh, yes please,' said Ethel. 'Ginger beer was another of them things he wouldn't have. I been a kitchen maid all me life and I never been in such a place, never. Well, I don't care what Mum says about pubs being low places. They want a cook at the pub and I reckon a pub is going to be real comfortable after what I've been through. And once Mum hears about it she'll agree with me. And I'll get me wages without being put off and put off and niggled and paid in old pennies which look like they've been dug out of a tomb.'

The car stopped. Phryne asked, 'How much do they owe you?'

'Almost six pounds,' confessed Ethel miserably.

Phryne produced her purse. 'Here we are. I'm being paid to find Rose and we shall just add it to the expenses. Don't argue with me, there's a dear. It's a mean way of hanging on to people, not paying them. I shall have it out of the old skinflint's hide, I promise you,' said Phryne. Ethel looked into her hard, jade eyes and believed her.

'And I didn't like leaving Bridie,' said Ethel, folding the notes and putting them into her corset. 'But she'll understand. She's a good girl. They're not really mean to her because that nasty kid Elijah dotes on her.'

'Leave Bridie to me,' said Phryne. 'Now, tell me all about Rose Weston.'

'She's a strange one,' said Ethel, faint with relief and recovered wages. She kept talking while Mr Butler started the car again, through the consumption of a bottle of ginger beer and two aspirins. Her headache, she knew, would soon fade. Wonderful how this big car just glided through the night. It was like riding in a cloud. 'Well, what could she be, in a place like that? She had some fight with her dad, and he did like her. Her mother dressed her and spoiled her until the boy was born and then sort of forgot about her.

She was all right at school but then the old miser said she had to come home and it's no home for a girl, no wireless, no dances, no pretty clothes, just old Mr Mean telling her not to waste electricity. She's run off before.'

'Do you know where she went?' asked Phryne.

'No,' said Ethel. She racked her brains, trying to be helpful. 'I heard her talking to one of those school girls, outside the door – she was never allowed to bring anyone in and she didn't want to, you saw what a shambles the place is – about Anatole's. And ... something about the carnival. Carnival wagons, was it? She wouldn't have been allowed to go near a place like that. That's where I'd look for her,' said Ethel. 'She's not a bad girl,' she added, somewhat to her own surprise. 'She'd give me a chocolate once in a way. Mister Weston didn't allow sugar in the house.'

'You're well out of there,' said Mr Butler. He drove Ethel to her mother's house and conducted Miss Fisher home. He thought about his own excellent working conditions, high wages and comfortable quarters, and felt a pang of contentment.

Phryne, inside her own house, looked around her sea-green parlour, drew a deep breath of pure pleasure, and climbed the stairs in search of copious hot water to wash the Weston house off her skin. She had been in houses which ran black with fleas. She had been in rural cottages where the soot gloved the beams and the vulcanised grease on the kitchen walls had been classified by the National Trust. But she had never felt quite this grimy, and she didn't like it.

Mr James Murray to Mr Aaron Murray
25 January 1913

Dear Father

It is always at this time of the year that I think of home, the dark and the cold, the peat fires and the tales, and me here in this garish light which burns the skin and dazzles the eyes. It is a good country, Australia, but I cannot bide here long. I and my music are foreign and even exotic here. My voice strikes strange on the Australian ear and I have to repeat myself. The beer is good and the food is lavish but I need to be back with my own folk. And how is that to be, you say, with herrings selling at threepence a pound? No man can get a living from the sea in Orkney now, I hear. But I have an engagement on a cruise ship. You were right to give me a fiddle when I was a child, rather than the pipes. A good fiddler is always in demand and although I am not the fabled one, I am good. Your teaching supported me, Father dear, and now I would support you. This cruise ship pays indecently well for a musician rather than a sailor and the journey is leisurely and safe – no one would pay to be made seasick and tippled into the cold sea. Seven Atlantic runs and we should have the capital to start that school that you always wanted. It will take me a few more years, Father, but it will be done.

Rory McCrimmon has fallen desperately in love with our landlady's daughter, a good girl. He will likely stay here and marry. Neil McLeod is pining to be home and can ship out on any tramp – he has all his certificates. Might even get a Master berth. And I will be playing a nice douce violin to the old ladies at the thé dansants, Father dear, and dreaming of oat-cakes and whisky and puffins on the cliff. Orkney. And home.

Your loving son
James

CHAPTER EIGHT

How sweet the answer Echo makes
To Music at night

Thomas Moore
'*Echoes*'

Phryne waited until after dinner and beckoned Dot into her boudoir.

'How are the girls?' she asked.

'All right,' said Dot slowly. 'Ruth's a bit upset and no wonder. Her mother was a sad sight, Miss. Even if you never knew her you could see she wasn't long for this world. A couple of weeks, maybe. I've said I'll take them to the carnival later. Perhaps you might like to come?'

'A good notion. Poor Ruth! Does she want to find her father?'

'I don't know. How did you get on with the Westons, Miss?'

'Remarkably like being inside the Castle of

125

Otranto without the giant hand, though it might have put in an appearance later. Gothic, my dear Dot, and horribly inefficient. Old Mr Weston is a miser and grumpy with it. The house is a mess and Mr B and I contrived the escape of the last kitchen maid. It was almost comic, but not quite. Here I have Rose's purse, her book and her note to her mother, and I would like your opinion of them. Take your time.'

'This is an expensive purse,' said Dot, turning it inside out and inspecting the stitching. 'Ten quid in notes, that's a lot of money. No coins. Looks like a gift, perhaps. A birthday present. Something like that. And this is a good bound book, maybe intended for a diary, though it isn't marked in days. Nice paper, cream laid. She's written in it, Miss, but just as she fancied. A commonplace book, that's what they used to call them. And this note says "When you read this I'll be gone I can't stand it anymore I'm going no matter what you say Rose". Not a lot to go on. Not good paper this time, Woolworth's lined block, tuppence a pad. Is this what you want me to say?' asked Dot.

'Yes,' said Phryne. 'Unusual choice of words for a final farewell, don't you think?'

'I suppose,' said Dot, considering this. 'And you wouldn't have thought that...'

'She'd leave ten quid behind,' agreed Phryne. 'We shall see. She must have somewhere else to put her things. Madame Anatole said that Rose was wearing a dress with very little front and hardly any back and she must have had shoes to match. We must find Rose's cache. Perhaps it is

126

at school. I'll check tomorrow. Now, let's wander over to the carnival and perhaps we can find Dulcie. I wonder if any of my carny friends are there. I used to know a strong man and a snake handler and a rather delicious mechanic called Alan Lee. Unfortunately the circus is Wirth's, so the only person I know there is Dulcie Fanshawe. Perhaps we can get an elephant ride.'

The carnival was magical after dark. In daylight it was tawdry, battered, and lacking in paint. The curvaceous ladies appeared shopworn and over forty and the fairground prizes did not glitter. But in the dark, with the scent of Turkey lolly, it was full of marvels.

The little canvas booths offered delights ranging from the Princess of the Amazon and her snake, genuine cultured pearls, penny-a-throw shooting galleries, fried fish and chips, infallible oyster openers, crayfish wrapped in newspaper as a late night snack and a Strong Man bending a poker between two fingers. There were three fortune-tellers. Jane tugged at Phryne's sleeve.

'Miss Phryne? Can you advance me three sixpences on the nosegay job?'

Phryne had promised payment for the construction of nosegays for the Queen of the Flowers float on Saturday.

'Certainly,' said Phryne, unpouching one and six. 'Why?'

'I'm going to all three of the fortune-tellers,' said Jane, the light of scientific enquiry in her eyes. 'If all of them tell me the same thing, then I might have to look at the phenomenon of precognition more carefully instead of dismissing it out of hand.'

'Never dismiss something out of hand just because it doesn't fit your personal beliefs,' chided Phryne. 'Even Croesus tested the oracles.'

'So he did,' said Jane, who read Herodotus in bed. 'The envoys asked "What is the King of Lydia doing at this moment?" And only Ephesus and Delphi got it right. Cooking a lamb and a tortoise in a bronze cauldron.'

'And Croesus was not a credulous person,' said Phryne. 'He practically invented money.'

'But his oracles didn't turn out too well,' said Jane thoughtfully.

'You have to examine oracles very carefully. Now, since this is a scientific experiment, I do not believe that it constitutes "fun" and therefore you need not take it out of the nosegay money. Your research project is my treat. You won't, of course, be rude to the fortune-telling ladies, will you, Jane? That is never a good plan. Or you might have to investigate the psychic phenomenon of ill-wishing. Which is not a fruitful field of research, I would add.'

'Manners maketh the lady,' said Jane, clearly quoting someone. She took the money and headed for the farthest tent, where Madame Sosostris proclaimed that she might learn the mysteries of Fate. Phryne chuckled at the thought of Madame Sosostris confronted with Jane's eager scientific curiosity, and then said to Ruth, 'Well, that's one and six I owe you, Ruth dear. What would you like to do with it?'

'Nothing scientific,' said Ruth. 'I like those

strings of beads, though.'

'No woman can ever have enough jewellery,' agreed Phryne. 'What about you, Dot?'

'I'll have one and six worth of wandering around,' said Dot. 'Let's go and look at the beads.'

The stall was carefully lit from underneath so that the loops and festoons of common glass beads glittered and gleamed like Aladdin's cave. Ruth ran them through her hands, consideringly. Little rainbows flicked across her intent face like butterflies. Phryne watched her. Ruth took everything so seriously. But there was no doubt that she was brave. She had cared for and supported Jane in a house fully as awful as the House of Weston, and she had never lost hope that one day she would fight her way out. Phryne realised that she did not know Ruth very well. Perhaps she would get another clue to the girl's character by her choice of beads.

There were blue, green, yellow and red strings of unclear, slightly misshapen glass; there were imitation pearls, badly made rhinestones, ersatz Venetian glass with silver foil inside and millefiore with fewer than a thousand flowers. Ruth examined all of them and then found, hidden in a tangle, a length of pure violet, clear as amethyst. They were of much better quality than the others and might even have been real Venetian glass. Ruth held them out. The stall holder scowled.

'They must have slipped in from the five bobs,' she said, taking hold of the beads.

'Well, that was a bit of luck for Ruth, wasn't it?' commented Phryne, stepping up beside the girl. 'They're in the one and sixes. One and six we have and the beads are ours. You don't want any trouble, do you?' asked Phryne amiably, and the stall holder glanced at Phryne's good clothes and assured air and clearly decided that she didn't. She looped the beads around Ruth's neck and managed a creditable smile.

'There,' she said. 'You look very pretty. Enjoy the carnival,' she added as they wandered away towards the shooting galleries and the booths.

'They were a good choice,' said Phryne to Ruth. 'You have a good eye.'

'I just caught sight of them in the middle of a tangle and they shone clear,' explained Ruth. 'They're so pretty! Thank you,' she said, and gave Phryne a quick hug.

'Ooh,' murmured Dot, 'look at the elephants!'

Wading slowly and majestically through the sea, three elephants manifested themselves. They seemed primeval in the darkness, bigger than any animal had a right to be. Phryne called 'Dulcie!' and waved. The lead elephant turned and stopped.

'Hullo-ullo-ullo!' exclaimed Dulcie's voice. 'Want to come up? We're just taking a little walk to settle our stomachs after the performance. Ladies, this is Phryne. And this is...'

'Ruth,' said Ruth, a little disconcerted by the size of the slab-side and enormous feet which were approaching her.

'And Dot,' said Dot, excitedly. She had never been this close to an elephant before. Her childhood excursions had not extended to visits to the zoo to ride the elephants.

'Better come up onto Kali, she's wearing a saddle,' suggested Miss Fanshawe, invisible in the darkness. 'Kali, lift these two ladies, if you would be so kind?'

The huge black beast paused long enough to convey that she was complying with a reasonable request of her own free will, not taking orders like lesser beasts. Then her long trunk curled around Ruth and swung her up onto a broad saddle. Dot followed a moment later, clutching her hat. Dot and Ruth found that they were sitting side-saddle an awful long way off the ground and Kali was beginning to walk away with them.

'Isn't this fun?' asked Phryne, perched on Flossie.

'It's lovely!' said Dot. Kali's trunk reached sideways and examined Dot, feeling gently over her face, testing the material of her hat and skirt, then moved on to Ruth, who giggled as the hay-scented breath woofled into her collar. Dot ventured to pat the trunk as it passed and was prepared to swear afterwards that Kali had squeezed her hand as affably as any Sunday afternoon clergyman.

'Kali approves of you,' observed Miss Fanshawe. 'That's good.'

Phryne wondered what would have happened if Kali had not approved of her riders and decided that she did not want to know. It was fine to be up so high on an animal which moved so smoothly. There was less bounce on Flossie's back than there would have been on even a cantering horse.

'If you like, we can stop and you can buy them all a toffee apple. They only get one, and only after the performance. Hello, Jack,' she added.

'Three apples, Miss Fanshawe?' asked a respectful sweet-seller, touching his cap. Phryne considered that having charge of three animals of several tons' weight and remarkable intelligence ready to obey your slightest whim would tend to command a certain respect.

'Thank you, and Miss Fisher is paying,' chuckled Dulcie. 'Just hand one each to the riders, will you, Jack?' Phryne handed down the money. 'We'll just walk along a bit,' Miss Fanshawe told Flossie, and the elephants swayed through the carnival. They were surrounded by people making noises, touching them, and the banging of the shooting galleries, and were as unperturbed as a cat entering a drawing room. The great feet were placed very carefully, printing the sand. The high strings of electric lights were just within reach from here, thought Ruth. This was as high as the top of a tram. It was wonderful.

'Now, ladies,' said Dulcie, as they came out on the bare shore again. 'Your apples come to you tonight courtesy of Phryne for Flossie.' Phryne allowed the clever trunk to pluck the toffee apple from her grasp. 'Dot, for Rani,' and Dot let her toffee apple drop into Rani's grasp, 'and Ruth for Kali,' said Miss Fanshawe. Ruth put the toffee apple into Kali's hold and the black trunk whipped away like a snake. Kali began making noises like a concrete mixer. A happy concrete mixer.

'You can't feed elephants too much sugar,' Dulcie told them, 'but a bit of what you fancy does you good. Now, Phryne, what would you like to see? The big cats?'

'No,' said Phryne. 'I don't like to see them in cages.'

'Then we'll walk you back to the carnival,' said Dulcie agreeably. 'This way, ladies.'

The elephants turned briskly and began to walk back down the beach.

'Dulcie, I'm looking for a missing girl. Were you about on the beach at around midnight?' asked Phryne hopefully.

'No, I was comfortably tucked up in my caravan in blameless solitude,' replied Miss Fanshawe. 'Hang on, though. There was a bit of a barney of some sort on the beach at about midnight. The lions woke up, and that always wakes me. Something about a roaring lion, you know.'

'Yes, it does attract attention,' agreed Phryne.

'Zips straight down the spine and reminds us of a common heritage as prey,' said Dulcie. 'Don't know any more about it, though. Tell you what, I'll ask around amongst the circus folk. You'll have to do the carnies. We don't speak. Foolish, but there it is. Is the girl in real trouble, Phryne?'

'I'd say so, yes.'

'Some of those carnies can be a bit uncivilised,' said Miss Fanshawe. 'Want me to lend you some muscle?'

'What did you have in mind?' asked Phryne, expecting a couple of big strong men.

'Bounce,' replied the elephant woman. 'She's my mastiff. Confidentially, she's a big soppy girl, but like most big dogs she's a great bluffer. Likes to remind people that she's one meal away from the wolf. She's about the size of the Hound of the Baskervilles. I got her as a puppy. She was destined to die in a pit, fighting. Men,' snarled Miss Fanshawe with bottomless scorn. 'And she took to the elephants right away. They like her because she's big enough to see properly. Elephants hate little things yapping around their feet. That's where people got the idea that they hate mice.'

'I'll keep Bounce in reserve,' said Phryne. 'But I think I might attract less attention on my own. Thanks for the lift,' she said. 'That was lovely, wasn't it?' she appealed to the others.

'Oh, yes,' said Dot. 'So high up! And so nice and safe!'

'Lovely,' agreed Ruth.

Kali put Ruth and Dot down and Flossie deposited Phryne on the sand.

'Good night,' said Miss Fanshawe. 'Do call again. We are always in,' she added, and the elephants walked away with surprising speed and quietness.

'Suddenly I feel earthbound,' said Phryne.

'And much shorter,' agreed Ruth. 'Can we have a go on the darts?'

'A good plan,' said Phryne.

The darts stall was alive with bobbing balloons. Break a balloon and you won a prize. Either the darts were very blunt or the balloons were very tough, for somehow the missiles slid off their targets and the row of kewpie dolls glittered un-claimed above the stall. Phryne watched as Ruth expended her three darts for a penny.

'Tell me,' she said to the stall holder, a slim young woman with very blonde hair. 'Are the Lees here?'

'Nah,' she replied. 'They're away with Farrell's. You a friend?'

'Of Doreen, and Samson and Alan,' said

Phryne. The darts girl grinned.

'That Alan Lee. He's got a lot of friends,' she said. 'I'm Bet. Come on. Have another go,' she said to Ruth, holding out a dart. 'For free. Have to do this once in a way, otherwise the punters get all suspicious. Might as well be a friend of Alan's.'

Phryne observed that this was a slightly different dart. Longer, for one thing. And sharper.

Ruth threw and the dart burst a balloon with a satisfactory bang.

'There you are,' said the girl. 'Pick a doll.'

'I'm looking for a missing girl,' said Phryne. 'Did you hear a disturbance on the beach at about midnight, Bet?'

'No, I was asleep. But they did say that something woke the lions. And you gotta understand, this is a campsite for all the performers and not just us carnies. We'd know if something bad was happening. But there's all these musicians, jazz men, dancers, all sorts of riffraff. Not what we've been used to at all. There's already been a couple of fights about what a carny girl means when she says "no". This isn't a good place for a stray girl to be wandering around.'

'I'd guessed that. Here's my card. If you hear anything about her – her name is Rose Weston – call me. There is a reward.'

Bet looked at the card. 'Prin Fisher?' she asked.

'Phryne, ph as in physician and Phryne to rhyme with briny,' said Phryne. 'But when I was with Farrell's circus they called me Fern.'

'Dancer?' asked Bet.

'Rider,' said Phryne.

'All right, I'll ask around. But she might have

left, you know. Been taken somewhere else.'

'That is my next line of enquiry,' said Phryne. 'What now, Ruth?'

'We'd better find Jane,' said Ruth, unhooking a kewpie doll on a cane from the roof of the stall. 'Can I have this one?'

Bet nodded. 'I don't like the idea of a stray girl loose in the carnival,' she said. 'Can only lead to trouble.'

'As the sparks fly upward,' agreed Phryne. 'Back to the street, Jane must have finished her experiment by now.'

'I'll wait for her,' offered Dot. 'There's a seat and I'm a bit tired.'

Phryne assented and she and Ruth strayed further into the carnival.

'My mother told me the name of my father,' said Ruth unexpectedly.

'Yes,' said Phryne.

'But I think she said he was dead,' Ruth continued. 'So he can't be alive now, can he?'

'No,' said Phryne. 'Why, do you think he might be?'

'I got...' began Ruth, and was swept aside by a rush of minstrels. Phryne was pushed against the side of a booth as banjos strummed and a rather strained tenor declaimed 'Ma-a-a-my! Ma-a-a-my! The sun shines east, the sun shines west, but I know where the sun shines best!' Teeth flashed white in blacked-up faces. Presumably they meant well. Phryne disbursed a coin into the hat and they passed on, bleating about their old Kentucky home.

When she rejoined Ruth she found the girl

examining her kewpie doll and disinclined to resume the conversation. Drat those minstrels, thought Phryne. That Stephen Foster had a lot to answer for.

At the edge of the carnival, where the electric lights ran out, there was an expanse of tents and lean-tos, the homes of those too poor to have a caravan. Occasional thin plumes of smoke showed where someone was cooking a late supper of fish over a small hot fire. Washing flapped on lines stretched between poles. Just so must the armies of the camp followers have appeared in the Peninsular War. Babies wailed. Somewhere two men were having a loud argument, punctuated by the smash of glass. A scatter of children dodged around Phryne and Ruth. There was a scent of humanity, frail and incidental and almost un-protected from the elements. And a fiddle playing sweetly in the gloom. Not a reel, not a ballad. He was playing a Bach étude with great accuracy and feeling. It was pure, precise music, stepping note by note up and down a celestial ladder. No one else could possibly be playing Bach in a carnival. It had to be him.

Phryne cupped her hands and called, 'James Murray!'

The fiddle stopped abruptly. A dog barked. Then, from the middle of the tents, someone called, 'And who would be wanting him?'

'Phryne Fisher,' announced Phryne.

'Och, there's no one here by that name,' said the voice unconvincingly.

'James, if you do not come out right now, I shall roust the whole camp,' threatened Phryne. There was a silence. Ruth was embarrassed. She tugged at Phryne's sleeve.

'Come away, Miss Phryne,' urged Ruth. 'Everyone's looking!'

'And they are welcome to look,' replied Phryne. 'James?'

'A wilful woman will have her way,' said the voice, and a man came out of the camp carrying his fiddle and bow. He looked Phryne up and down without a smile.

'It is you,' said Phryne. 'I knew no one else would be playing Bach in a carnival.'

'And you were right,' he informed her. 'James Murray, m'lady, at your service. I'd know you anywhere,' he said. 'You were on the beach this morning, were you not, singing along to the cuckoo's nest? But when I looked out I only saw the horses.'

'That was me. You're looking well,' she added. 'Are you here alone?'

'I am,' he said.

'Then come and have a drink with me. I owe you a whisky. This is Ruth, my daughter,' she added. James Murray took Ruth's hand. He had the most beautiful brown eyes, she thought. His hand was strong and warm.

'You might as well do as she says,' Ruth told him.

'Aye, so I might,' he agreed.

Phryne tucked a hand under James's unoccupied elbow in case he bolted. She was dying to know what had brought him to Australia.

Jane and Dot were waiting and she introduced her guest. 'I knew James a long time ago, in Orkney,' she told them. 'And now we are going home. How did the experiment go, Jane?'

'I'll have to write it all down,' said Jane. 'Most of it was very general. Madame Sosostris was the most specific. Which Orkney island?' she asked James. 'There are seventy, I believe.'

'Main island,' he replied. He was suffering from a serious case of Phryne Fisher. How could these girls be her daughters? Had she borne children before he met her? That seemed unlikely. And while one girl was a nice plump wee birdie, this blonde one was examining him as though he was an anatomical specimen she was minded to dissect. Not to mention the companion, Miss Williams, in the straw hat, who was giving him a very old-fashioned look. Time to shake off his puzzlement and exert some charm, because Phryne had captured him fair and square and there was no going back to his incognito.

'Main island it is,' he said to Jane. 'In the town of Stromness I was born. My father is a teacher and I am a fiddler. I teach music.'

'Then what are you doing here?' asked Jane. Phryne had tried to explain to her about the propriety of asking indirect questions but although Jane had understood the convention, she had no time for it. If Jane wanted to know, she asked. James Murray did not seem to be offended.

'The Folk Song Society,' he explained. 'I had taken a place on a cruise ship to earn a little extra – times are cruel in Orkney these days – and when I came into the port of Melbourne I looked them up. They have six concerts and they pay well. I can save money by camping on the sand and I've slept in far worse places. And in worse company, too.'

'The carnival is rough,' said Dot with distaste. She did not approve of Miss Phryne just picking people up out of that milieu. Even if they were old friends. What sort of old friend? And what would Mr Lin say if ... but that was not to be thought of, of course.

'It's a little rough, yes,' said James Murray easily. 'But I keep myself to myself. The circus don't mix with the carnival and the carnival look down on the performers and we, in turn, look down on the petty criminals, the thimble riggers and the three-card trick men. Just like the world outside. Everyone has someone to despise. I never thought to meet anyone I knew here, much less the remarkable Miss Fisher. What brought you to Australia, Phryne girl, of all places in the world?'

'I wanted to get as far away from my father as I could,' said Phryne. 'I came out here to investigate a prospective murder. And I liked it here and I stayed. I'm a private detective. This is my house. Do come in. Mr Butler? Mr Murray would like a little of the Highland Park whisky.'

'A lot,' responded James, and smiled.

In the light of her own parlour, Phryne could see that he had aged. The red hair was brown now, and greying at the temples. His face was tanned and lined. But the smile was the same slightly cynical James Murray smile and she was very pleased to see him.

'Sit down, dear man, let's catch up. By the way, I am looking for a missing girl. Did you see anything on the beach at midnight last night?'

'This wouldn't be a fair girl in a long gown?' he

asked. 'I saw one such go past my tent early this morning, just before you turned up and sang me out of my tent like a seal from the sea.'

'And you didn't try to speak to her?' demanded Phryne.

James shrugged. 'Why should I? She was with a man. Generally such ladies do not need assistance.'

'Oh. That sort of lady. Would you know her again?'

'Probably,' said James.

Phryne produced the picture of the four flower maidens. James shook his head.

'It was dark,' he said, 'It would be this one if it was any of them. But I really can't say, Phryne. I'm sorry.'

'No matter.' Phryne had not expected instant success. James had picked Rose's picture.

Mr Butler arrived with the good whisky and two glasses of orangeade for the girls and a sherry for Dot. He filled glasses. Phryne raised hers.

'To happy meetings,' she toasted, and James Murray, still bemused, drank.

Miss Anna Ross to Miss Mavis Sutherland
24 February 1913

Oh Mavis, I am so happy! Rory came back from Sydney and he said he had a question to ask me and I said what was it and he said you know what it is and I did, but I was blushing so hard that I couldn't speak, so he dropped to one knee and asked 'Will you marry me?' and I could hardly get my 'yes' past my lips I was so shaken. And then he kissed me, so

141

sweetly, and I went to do the upstairs rooms and he went to talk to my mother. His friend Mr McLeod sneered but Mr Murray wished that we should be very happy and that Rory had found him a bonny bride. That's all I can fit on this card. I'll write a proper letter later, your very, very happy friend Anna.

CHAPTER NINE

...Rapine, avarice, expense,
This is idolatry; and these we adore

William Wordsworth
'London MDCCII'

James Murray was a great success, though Dot still had doubts about him for the first ten minutes. But his manner was so easy and his voice so attractive and he played such a beautiful violin that eventually she was seduced into forgetting that he might have been one of Miss Phryne's lovers. And that his presence might disrupt her household.

Jane doted on him for his readiness to answer her every question about the Orkney Islands. Ruth sat at his feet and cried luxurious tears while he played her the lament for Archibald McLeish.

'Of course, that's what we play on the way to the funeral,' he explained. 'But on the way back, when he's safely buried and we have to go on with the business of living, we play this: it's called

'Archie's a stiff".'

And he launched into a jaunty, rollicking version of the lament which had everyone laughing. Then Ruth said, 'Isn't that a hard-hearted thing to do? Leaving him alone in his grave like that and laughing on the way home?'

'Poor old Archie's dead, hinny,' James Murray told her gently. 'There's nought we can do for him anymore but remember him kindly. But we have to live, see? And living, we may as well dance. Because we all come to it, my bird.'

Dot, of all people, agreed. She was onto her second sherry.

'The dead are with God,' she said firmly. 'God will look after them. That's what God does. And mourning too long is a sin, Father O'Reilly says. As though you don't trust God.'

'And even if you don't,' said James, perilously close to blasphemy, 'there's nothing to be done but get used to it. If it must be borne, my grandma used to say, then it should be borne gladly.'

'Is she still living?' asked Phryne. 'I remember her very well. And poor Ian Hamilton. How did he fare?'

'Grandma is still living,' he said. 'Ian Hamilton married Lettice Howell, and he has three sons now, fine boys. His family asked him to come back, the eldest son is a disappointment, apparently. But he would not. They sent him to Orkney, he said, and in Orkney he would stay, it was his home. He's bought into the distillery and is doing very well. As you see, our whisky travels well.'

'That's nice,' said Phryne.

'And you, m'lady – a lovely house, two lovely

143

daughters, there is no husband for you?'

'I do not need a husband,' said Phryne. 'But I do not lack for company.'

'You never would,' said James affectionately.

'Time to go to bed,' announced Dot abruptly, shepherding the two girls before her out of the parlour. 'Goodnight, Miss. Goodnight, Mr Murray.'

'Would you like to sleep here?' asked Phryne. Was there another kind of invitation in her smile? 'I've a spare room and you would be welcome.'

'I'll come tomorrow, if I may stretch your kindness,' he told her. 'Tonight I have an appointment, and also I can ask around about your missing girl. That camp is no place for her.'

'If she was there,' said Phryne. 'Try to find out about the fracas on the beach. Rose Weston thought she had an assignation with a pretty boy. He didn't come. But someone else may have improved the shining hour.'

'So they might, at that,' agreed James. 'I'll bid you goodnight, then,' he said, taking up Phryne's hand and kissing it.

When he had gone, Phryne finished the whisky, remembering Orkney, and put herself to bed. She fell asleep immediately and slept like a log all night.

Monday dawned drizzly and chill, with a little wind which searched out crevices in tents and jackets. James Murray's violin was dry and cosy in its padded case enclosed in oilskin. James himself was wrapped in a blanket that was reverting to felt under a tent which had forgotten about

144

its duty to be waterproof. He swore, unwound himself and lit his primus. Tonight he would sleep under a roof, which would be a welcome change, and perhaps he could get a bath and wash his shirt. Phryne Fisher, here, and as bright and sharp and beautiful as ever. Wonderful are the ways of the Lord, he thought, as the gas popped and went out. He lit another match. All he had to do was explain about Maggie.

And, of course, ask around about this missing girl. That might not be well received. The camp had a tendency to keep itself to itself and would not welcome any enquirer after wisdom asking inconvenient questions. This needed planning.

He made his tea and drank it and packed up his possessions. Someone tripped over his guy rope and cursed, landing with a thud.

'Want a drink of tea, friend?' he asked as the figure picked itself up. It was Little Jack, a stringy youth vaguely connected with the three-card trick men.

'All right,' agreed Little Jack. He sugared the tea heavily and drank it in one gulp.

'I heard some rumour,' said James easily, 'that someone had lost a girl in this camp. A good girl,' he added. 'With people looking for her. You seen anyone like that, boy?'

'Girls?' said Little Jack. 'There's lots.'

'This will be a stray one. Been here since some time in the morning yesterday. Probably cries a lot.' Little Jack looked shifty. Unfortunately, that was his usual expression. James went on: 'And unless she gets given back, I reckon the camp'll be swarming with police by tomorrow.'

145

Little Jack looked frightened. James let him go. Then he wandered out into the settlement to find another gossip. If he did this properly, the news of police invasion should reach the ears of whoever had the girl – and then, with luck, they would turn her loose and Phryne could retrieve her. James told Bet from the darts stall, a known gossip. She would cover the carnies. And then, greatly daring, he went into the confines of the circus and sought out a rigger who had once sailed with him on a nervous run across the Atlantic. Spending two weeks listening for the underwater thud of a torpedo and expecting death by water creates a bond which the circus class system cannot break.

'Come in and have some tea, Jamie,' said Scottie, who was not Scottish but an Australian called Allen Scott. 'Bloody cold morning.'

'Not as cold as that North Sea crossing,' said James, sitting down on a stool in the rigger's tent and lighting a cigarette.

'Bloody right,' said Scottie, pouring two mugs of tea with a judicious admixture of rum. 'So, what's the news from the outcasts?'

'I'm moving out of the camp,' said James. 'I've met an old friend.'

'What, another one?' asked Scottie. 'You were surprised enough about that Neil bloke.'

'I was, but this one is much more attractive.'

'A sheila,' said Scottie.

'You have the right of it,' said James. 'But there's a girl missing in the camp, did you hear? A well-connected girl from a good family. Make sure you get rid of anything illegal, Scottie. The place will be crawling with police by tomorrow.'

'Jacks! I hate them jacks. So who's got this girl?'

'Ah, there you have me,' murmured James. 'But whoever it is had better give her up soon, or there will be trouble for all of us.'

'Girls are always trouble,' said Scottie into his rum.

James agreed, drank up, then went back to his campsite. He folded his tent with thoughtless efficiency, hoisted the tent and knapsack to his shoulder, and walked whistling through the camp, violin in hand. He could almost hear the whispers running behind him. That ought to produce an effect, he thought.

Phryne had gone out to consult with Rose Weston's school when he arrived at the bijou Fisher residence. Dot and the girls were home and he gladly gave himself up to an unfamiliar but very pleasant sensation of being cared for. His dirty clothes were whisked away to the Chinese laundry. His coat was taken off and brushed. He was provided with carpet slippers while his boots were cleaned and dried. A large breakfast was cooked especially for him. He ate it while a small black and white dog slept determinedly on his feet and two children asked him questions. It was like coming home. James Murray was sinfully pleased with the world.

Bert said to Cec, 'I dunno about this. That Mongrel is a real mongrel.'

'Too right,' said Cec.

'And if he's got the girl I dunno how we're gunna make him give her back.'

'Too right,' said Cec.

'But we're gunna do it anyway,' said Bert resignedly.

'Too right,' said Cec.

They knocked on the door of a dilapidated house. St Kilda had been a great watering place once, like Brighton. As the rich people got motor cars and built themselves houses in Mount Eliza and Portsea for their dose of ozone, the houses had changed hands, always downwards. Most were now divided into flats, or even rooms. Mongrel and Simonds lived on the third floor.

'I reckon one match and this whole place'd go up like a torch,' observed Cec. The rickety stairs were shedding touchwood, the woodworms were fighting the borers for ascendancy and Cec had just put his fingers through the bannister.

'Don't tempt me,' growled Bert. He was heavier than Cec and was walking carefully at the edge of the stairs, where they joined the wall and might be a fraction more robust.

When they reached the door it was shut and no amount of banging produced any answer.

'Bugger,' said Bert. He thumped on the next door, behind which he could hear a baby screaming.

'What?' asked an unimaginably weary voice. A woman stood there with a child in her arms and a toddler hanging on her stained apron. Both children were shrieking. There was a rolling stench of urine and burned milk.

'Looking for your neighbours,' said Bert, holding out a shilling. The grimy, work-worn hand snatched and the coin vanished.

'They ain't in,' she said flatly. 'I heard you

148

bashing on the door. Woke the baby, you bastard.'

'Sorry,' said Bert, holding out another shilling. 'Any idea of where they went?'

'Got jobs down on the foreshore,' said the woman. 'Hope they don't come back,' she added, grabbing the second shilling and slamming the door.

'You're welcome,' said Bert to the peeling paint. 'Bugger,' he said again.

'What?' asked Cec.

'First, that puts them right on the spot when the girl vanished,' said Bert. 'And second, now I got to tiptoe down them stairs again. What was that you said about a match, Cec?'

'Not with all them people in it,' chided Cec. 'Besides, it's held together by the bedbugs linking arms.'

This was a long sentence for Cec. He hated dirt. They made it down the stairs in one piece and got into the street with sighs of relief.

'We'd better go and tell her,' said Bert.

'Too right,' said Cec.

The school was not pleased with Rose Weston, Phryne could tell. The ancient red-brick buildings had survived bad girls before, and unstable girls, and girls prone to nervous hysterics. But Rose's combination of insolence and intelligence was hard to characterise. The form teacher, Miss Ellis, who carried the master locker keys, tried to explain.

'You see, she could be very clever – suddenly. It was always a surprise. I was never sure what to say to her. She could fail to understand something really simple, however often it was explained. For instance, she still doesn't understand fractions. She would sit there and shake her head slowly from side to side, like a moron. Then she could flash out with a comment that meant she was a long way ahead of me.'

The teacher was a young woman in a neat suit, with neat hair and neat hands and a precise, neat voice. She would not have had a chance against Rose Weston's irrational intelligence and nervy irritability.

'She comes from a troubled household,' said Phryne.

'Yes, but so do others. There are girls here whose parents have died and whose families have been dealt similar blows. We can understand tears, and rebellions, and melancholy, and vapours, and passing bad behaviour.'

'But Rose had all of them.'

'Yes. I believe that the headmistress was going to ask her grandfather to find her another school. When she was a boarder, mind you, there were no complaints of her, just a few little naughtinesses. I fear that her home environment was not ideal.'

'You could safely say that,' said Phryne.

A bank of lockers appeared. 'This is the only place she had leave to keep things at this school,' said Miss Ellis worriedly. 'But it's not to say that she didn't have another cache. She knows the buildings, she used to board here.'

'Let's just see what's in the locker,' said Phryne.

The door opened. Phryne caught the expected avalanche of textbooks and handed them to the form teacher, one by one.

'Funny, my locker at school was just like this,' she said chattily. 'I used to shut the door very fast and duck when I opened it again. Now, what do we have here? Ink-stained texts. History, chemistry, French conversation – *"Bonjour, Monsieur Dubois, ça va? Ça va bien, merci."* Exercise book full of rather good little drawings.'

'Yes, she could draw, but she never had the patience to learn it properly, and then she didn't do art anymore, because it was an extra. The art mistress always said she'd be good if she tried.'

'Could be said of all of us. Now. Pencil case. Box of drawing implements. Sports bag containing a box pleated sports tunic and a pair of soft shoes and – aha.'

Phryne drew out a pair of very unsuitable shoes. They were of purple kid with rhinestones in the heels.

'I gather that these are not school issue?' she asked. Miss Ellis's eyes had widened.

'I've never seen shoes like that before.'

'No,' said Phryne ambiguously. She shook the bag. Out fell a rolled-up dress. It was of artificial silk. Phryne held it up against Miss Ellis. It was scandalously short, hideously purple and lacking in both front and back. Tinkling onto the floor went a pair of rhinestone earrings. The bag was now empty. Phryne stuffed the sports clothes back into it and kept the exercise books, the dress and shoes and the earrings.

'I'll return these to the family when I have finished with them,' she told the appalled Miss Ellis, loading the locker with the rest of the things.

151

'Has something happened to Rose?' asked Miss Ellis.

'Yes,' said Phryne.

'We'd have her back,' said Miss Ellis. 'If she could board again. I felt very sorry for her even while she was driving me demented. Tell her family. When you find her,' she said, her brow creasing.

'If I find her,' said Phryne.

Returning to her own house, Phryne found James Murray ensconced in the small parlour like a pearl in an oyster, playing the fiddle to an enraptured audience. Dot tore herself away.

'I've given him the bigger guest room,' she told Phryne. 'Sent his clothes out to wash. He was almost in rags. I've lent him your gentleman's shirt to wear after his bath. What have you got there?'

'Some of the most horrible garments you might ever wish not to see,' said Phryne. 'Let's go up to my boudoir. I want your opinion and we need to go through these books to see if she has left any clue at all.'

'Oh, and Miss Jones called,' said Dot as she preceded Phryne up the stairs. 'She has heard that Rose is missing. She wants to know – oh, it seems very heartless – she wants to know if she should...'

'Find another flower maiden? Can't be helped, Dot dear. I think she should. As a stand-by, just in case we don't find Rose.'

'Or we don't find her alive,' said Dot.

'Yes.'

'Mr Murray says he's told all the gossips in the carnival and the circus and the camp about the missing girl and predicted that the cops would be coming tomorrow. He says that ought to flush her out if she's there.'

'Or get her killed,' said Phryne, stopping on the landing. 'That's not what I would have done.'

'No, but he's a man,' said Dot.

'Yes, he is, isn't he?' said Phryne and continued into her own rooms. She dumped the armload of impedimenta on her bed. 'What do you think of the clothes, Dot?'

Dot grimaced. 'Pretty awful. Twelve and six-penny art silk from Foy and Gibson, altered by someone who can't sew. See where they've just cut this neckline and tucked it in? Not even tacked. And the shoes are five bob from somewhere like Treadways. Cheap, nasty and badly made. I reckon the rhinestones were glued on later. With art gum, not cobbler's glue – see, they're falling off.'

Phyrne stared at the pitiful masquerade clothes and felt very sorry for Rose Weston. Where was the girl?

Dot sat down in a good light and began to examine the exercise books. They were a study. If Rose didn't like a subject, her work was full of blots and the facing pages were covered in caricatures, dragons, mice, faces, castles. She seemed to really like turrets. If she liked the subject the work was neat, clean, fairly written and accurate. Dot read through an English essay on 'Stories from the Lives of Noble Women' and one on the reign of Alfred the Great and found them well done and unexciting.

Phryne was leafing through the commonplace

book. She moved an electric lamp closer. The writing was hurried and in various media: lead, what looked like crayon, red ink, black ink, and the purple of indelible pencil. There were notes on colours like 'New beech leaves are so soft that you can curl them around your finger and are the tenderest of spring greens, almost gold', to 'I hate this place I hate it I hate it' in red ink. There was a very good cartoon of little Elijah as a pig – the child did have porcine qualities, Phryne had to admit – and her mother as a witch with warts, peaked hat and broomstick. But there was nothing in the book which might give a clue to her other life – no picture of Mongrel and his friend Simonds, for instance, no mention of Anatole's.

Phryne was about to set the book aside when she saw, where she had bent the hot globe close to the paper, spidery light brown lines of handwriting beginning to magically appear. Invisible writing. Lemon juice. Heat would bring it out. And each page which had invisible writing on it would have, she guessed, some misdirections in crayon or pencil, nothing that would blot. Calling Dot over, Phryne took a fountain pen and a clean sheet of paper and began to copy the evanescent script as it appeared and Dot read it aloud.

Time passed. Dot went downstairs for a magnifying glass to make sure that they had not missed anything. The violin was silent. Mr Murray and the girls were drinking tea. Jane had the big atlas on the parlour table and was asking questions about the Horn of Africa.

Dot ran lightly upstairs again. The method of reading and copying was working well enough, though even Phryne's hand faltered occasionally at what she was writing and Dot frequently choked on the reading.

After an hour they had copied out the commonplace book and were staring at each other with a wild surmise.

'I reckon we get that nice Mr Jack Robinson onto it,' said Dot. 'No wonder they want her back!'

'I'm wondering if they want her dead,' said Phryne. 'Yes, Jack Robinson by all means. Let's have a drink, Dot. We could do with one.'

'Yes,' said the abstemious Dot and rang the bell. When Mr Butler came, she sent him for the bottle of cognac and two glasses. And when she had a brandy, she swallowed it in two mouthfuls.

Dot believed firmly in the devil. She had no doubt of his power and influence, that he walked about to and fro upon the earth, seeking whom he would devour. She had seldom seen better proof of malefic presence than in Rose Weston's diary.

'Biddy!' said Dot, coming out of her cold horror. 'We can't leave her there!'

Phryne gulped brandy and flexed her writing fingers. 'No, they need Biddy, the little boy dotes on her and won't mind anyone else. And Bridget, I have no doubt, is a good girl who would rather die. Also, she is not as attractive as Rose Weston was – is. Plus, if we extract her now, it might warn them that we know. Tell you what. Call on the local priest tomorrow, Dot dear, and find out about Biddy's home situation. If we can slide her out sideways – for instance, her mother needs her at home, something like that – then we can get her out now. If not, we'll keep an eye on her and get her out as soon as we can. For, Dot dear, this cannot be borne. As Malvolio said in an entirely different context, "I'll be revenged on the whole pack of them!" and so I shall, you mark my words.'

Phryne's eyes were as hard as emeralds and her mouth was a thin red line. Dot believed her.

Bert and Cec came in just as lunch was finishing. James Murray sighed and excused himself to take a nap as he had a performance that night. The girls retreated to the kitchen to corral Molly and take her for a walk. Dot and Phryne supplied Bert with beer and Cec with raki and listened to their story.

'Not good,' said Bert. 'Them mongrels are in that camp somewhere. The girl might easily be with them.'

'And we need to get her back, not only because they are not nice company, but because she needs to make a statement to the police,' said Phryne. 'She has been outrageously used. I know now why Mr Johnson hired me to find her, and when we do find her we are going to have to hide her. She's a time bomb.'

'Not gonna be easy,' said Bert.

'No,' said Phryne. 'But it's going to be done.'

Miss Mavis Sutherland to Miss Anna Ross
19 March 1913

Anna I am so glad to hear your news and I am sure that you will be very happy with your Jack Tar. I am being sent to the Highlands to the Big House for three months as Mrs Grainger believes that I will recover my senses there. The only reason that they are not dismissing me is that I have worked here since I was twelve and my mother and grandmother before me. So I am lucky. I will write when I am settled in my new home. But I am still dreaming and I am so shaken and nervous that I cannot even carry a cup of tea without spilling.

Your foolish friend
Mavis

CHAPTER TEN

Look at her garments
Clinging like cerements
While the wave constantly
Drips from her clothing;
Take her up instantly,
Loving, not loathing.

Thomas Hood
'Bridge of Sighs'

The afternoon was spent blamelessly listening to a lantern lecture on the Holy Land. As the lights came up, Phryne yawned. She loved lantern lectures but she felt short of sleep, which was silly. Dot had gone to enquire about Bridget of the local priest, and Phryne had an idea of what to do with the girl in due course. But she had been so

157

angry about what she had found in Rose Weston's commonplace book that she had quite exhausted herself and had slept neatly and unobtrusively through the Dead Sea and its amazing properties, through Hebron to the Mount of Olives and only came awake when Golgotha was announced. The Place of Skulls. How very appropriate. Didn't conquerors of the Attila the Hun style build pyramids of heads? I wonder how many heads you needed to make a good pyramid?

She came awake properly in time to join in the applause and gather the girls. St Kilda was *en fête* and that meant more than the usual number of pests, louts, petty criminals, pickpockets and robbers. It also included gangs of Nice Young Men from Good Homes who had heard that St Kilda was full of whores and attempted to prove it by propositioning every girl in sight. Phryne found them particularly trying.

'Miss Phryne?' asked Ruth, on her left side, 'You know we were talking about finding my father, well, I...'

They were driven into a huddle by a group of the Good Boys who had been forcibly repelled by some factory girls, who slapped and kicked and hooted at their dismay. Phryne relieved her feelings by giving the nearest Good Boy a hearty shove which almost knocked him over.

'Here, I say,' he protested, and came up into the glare of eyes as unemotional as a range finder and as cold as jade.

'Get out of my way,' said Phryne quietly.

He got out of her way. He even took his friends with him.

'Ruth, what were you saying?' asked Phryne. 'Come along, let's get around this corner and out of the main road.'

'It doesn't matter,' said Ruth, hanging her head. And not another word would she say, all the way home, though Jane nudged her impatiently. Phryne trailed the topics of fathers, missing fathers, dying declarations and the errors of youth before her like succulent tendrils of sandworm but Ruth, like a trout, would not bite.

They continued along the Esplanade toward Phryne's own house. Phryne began talking about Rose Weston, for lack of anything else to say.

'I think that she is probably somewhere in those camps,' she told Jane. 'But I can't imagine where and there is no way to search them without a regiment of soldiers.'

'And you haven't got a regiment,' Jane pointed out helpfully.

'Not at the moment, no. Nor enough proof to convince Jack Robinson to stage a raid. And it would probably be considered an overreaction to just toss in a torch and set them on fire.'

'I've analysed the things which the three fortune-tellers told me,' said Jane, to change the subject. Miss Phryne seemed upset at the fate of Rose Weston who was, in Jane's opinion, an idiot.

'Oh?' responded Phryne.

'The only one who said anything significant, that could not have been thought of by anyone who looked at me and saw that I was well-to-do, thirteen and female, was Madame Sosostris. She was interesting. She took my hand and told me I was clever at mathematics and chess, that I was going to be a doctor. She told me both my parents were dead. She said that I had a sister who was unhappy but she would find what she was seeking soon.'

'That is impressive,' said Phryne, instantly suspicious.

'Then she looked in the crystal ball,' continued Jane. 'The others did that too. But they said things like "I can see great clouds rolling" and "the ways of fate are inscrutable". Madame just rubbed the glass with a cloth and huffed on it as though she was cleaning her glasses. You know, as though she did it all the time, a little cross that it had got dirty so fast.'

'You're a good observer, Jane!' said Phryne, struck by this vivid image. 'A clever chocolate for you when we get home. What else did she say?'

'She looked in. I couldn't see anything but my own reflection upside down. Then she frowned and rubbed the glass again and said "Tell your mistress that the girl on the beach will die unless she gets to her by midnight. Tell her to walk the beach at midnight". Then she clutched at her temples and said to me, "That's all, girl, now go away". And I went. She was calling out to someone in the back of the tent for some aspirin as I left.'

'Curious,' said Phryne. 'Well, it can't hurt.'

Whether Madame Sosostris was in touch with the spirits or whether she was a cunning old baggage who thought, like everyone else, that stray girls were trouble and wanted to get rid of Rose, it was all one. Midnight would find Phryne on the beach.

'So I have to revise my opinion,' said Jane.

160

'Most fortune-telling is just watching people and telling them what they want to hear. But some of it is genuine.'

'A reasonable conclusion. Now, we're home, it's afternoon tea time and Dot should be back by now.'

'Miss Phryne? Are you going to rescue Biddy?' asked Ruth.

'I shall find somewhere else for her to go, yes. That house is not as bad as the one you were in – no, I take it back, it's cleaner, but just as mean and nasty. Biddy's got a family and a little sister and I'll bet I find that she's a good girl – is that the case, Dot?'

'I spoke to the priest at St Joan of Arc's,' said Dot, meeting Phryne at the gate. 'He says she comes to six-thirty mass several times a week, before she starts work. And always on Sunday. Her mother's got eight children. Her father works on the railways. He's not perfectly sober, Father O'Brian says.' Dot always got a little flushed talking to priests. This one had been old and Irish and not disposed to judge humans too harshly. 'But not a bad or neglectful man. Mrs Ryan has a job in a hotel. All the other children are at school except for little Mary, and that's why they jumped at a job where Bridget could take Mary with her. Mrs Ryan lost a baby in the care of a baby minder and she won't hear of Mary being minded. Miss, the priest asked me if Bridget was in moral danger in that house. I said I'd have to ask you. Is she?'

'I don't believe so, Dot. Not for the time being. Now, come along, ladies, a nice cup of tea is what we need. You would have liked the lantern show,

161

Dot. Would you like to go tonight? You could take Hugh with you if you're feeling nervous.'

'I'd like that,' said Dot. Even Dot's own mother, a censorious woman, could not object to a lantern show about the Holy Land. And she hadn't seen Hugh for a week.

'Good. I need to ring Lin. You have first go at the phone.'

Phryne toyed with the idea of taking Ruth into her parlour and making her tell Phryne what was on her mind, but gave it away. Forced confidences were not valuable. Ruth would tell her eventually.

The tea table was laid. Mr Butler waited until he heard Phryne coming downstairs after taking off her hat, and then he began pouring. There were small iced cakes. Jane brought the box of Haighs Superfine in which the clever chocolates, rewards for a clever question or answer, dwelt, and was allowed to choose one. She was in luck; it was her favourite, an orange cream.

Roused by the clatter of cups, James Murray woke and for a moment wondered where he was. In a lady's house, by the sound of the voices and the tinkle of teaspoons. He was warm and lying in a luxurious bed, perfectly free of leaks, water-stains, rats or lice. He was clean. He looked at the jazz-coloured curtains and the little pictures of street children all around the walls. Of course. Phryne Fisher had rescued him.

He dressed in his clean shirt – that Chinese laundry was quick and there wasn't a crease in it, they had even got the oil and tomato sauce stains out – and went in to see if anyone felt like giving him a cup. Preferably with tea in it.

They did. He sat down and drank and ate an iced cake.

'Do you have a family, Mr Murray?' asked Jane. James beamed. He could have kissed her. Just the question he hoped she would ask.

'Ah, there's my Maggie,' he said, digging in his pocket for his wallet and extracting a picture which he handed to Jane. 'She's waiting for me this moment, wondering where I am. But I'll be back with her soon.'

Jane examined the photograph of the strong featured woman and passed it to Phryne, who was sitting next to her. 'And children?' Jane asked.

'None,' he said sadly. 'But there's still time.'

Phryne understood. She was being warned off. She did not mind. This was a graceful way of doing it.

'That's a pity,' said Jane, reaching for her third cake. 'You're good at children. We like you. And you seem to like us.'

'Jane,' said Phryne. 'Remember what I said about making personal remarks?'

'But it's true,' said Jane, her invariable defence and reply. James Murray intervened.

'Aye, so it is, and I like you well. Do I not, my bonny bird?' he asked Ruth, and hugged her. She surprised him by returning his casual embrace with a swift, fierce hug. He buried his face for a second in her clean hair.

Ruth let go and left the table without permission. James looked up and felt Phryne's eyes upon him.

'She's a little upset,' explained Jane. 'About–'

'Jane,' said Phryne firmly, and Jane subsided into her cake. 'You have a concert tonight?' she asked James.

'Aye, at eight, in the town hall.'

'Are you likely to be home after midnight? I can give you a key.'

'Och, no, I've no taste for post concert parties. Too much weak tea and discussion about the definition of a folk song. I say it's a folk song if folk sing it. But that is never enough for them, because it would include "Daisy Daisy" and "My Old Kentucky Home". It's a minefield, this Folk Song Society stuff. I just stick to playing the fiddle and saying "och, aye" in the thickest Glasgow accent I can muster if anyone speaks to me. They think all Scotsmen have heavy accents. And a name beginning with Mac.'

'But you're not a Gael anyway,' protested Jane. 'You're a Viking.'

'Aye,' said James comfortably. 'But you wouldn't want to give a fellow away, would you, hinny? Not when there's a thumping good fee to be made.'

'And you're the best fiddler they're ever likely to hear,' said Phryne.

The afternoon passed uneventfully. Mr Johnson rang to find out the progress of Miss Fisher's investigations and she assured him that they were proceeding. And, she congratulated herself, she did it without the gritting of her teeth being at all audible.

The beach at midnight was a different place. Phryne had seen her household settled, made certain preparations, and was walking idly along

164

at the edge of the sea, where the sand was hardest. Lin Chung was walking beside her. They both wore dark clothing. Phryne was in her boy's clothes, with her cap pulled over her eyes.

Lin felt odd walking beside her. She really did look like a boy. She walked like a boy. Yet she was the object of his most profound desire. Underneath that rough serge was the body – and the passion – of a goddess. To cover his discomfort, he started to talk.

'So, we are doing this because a fortune-teller said so?' he asked.

'And because my old friend James told every gossip in the camp that tomorrow there would be a police raid.'

'This old friend,' Lin began.

'He was my lover once,' said Phryne, short-circuiting the question. 'When I was twenty, in Orkney. Now he is married to his Maggie and wants to go back to her. I just didn't want to see an old friend – and a wonderful musician – sleeping in the rain. Clear?'

'Clear,' said Lin. The way Phryne read his mind was disconcerting but it did make communication easy. 'I gather you don't think his scheme was a good idea?'

'No,' she said. 'I wouldn't have done that. It puts the girl in too much danger. She might be here of her own free will, you know. She was dining at Anatole's of her own free will with two of Bert's Bad Men. Who rejoice, by the way, in the names of Simonds and Mongrel. And I'm not the woman to take her back to her family, who sold her virginity, at the age of twelve, to Mr

Johnson for a great deal of money and stock market favours.'

Phryne, stuttering in outrage, needed to say this out loud. It seemed easier, in the darkness and the open, with the sleeping carnival on one side and the slapping sea on the other. She heard Lin's hiss of distaste.

'You know this because...?' asked Lin.

'I deciphered her diary,' said Phryne. 'And the cream of the joke is that Mr Johnson is paying me.'

'Ironic,' said Lin. 'Juvenalian. Not funny.'

'Quite. But I'm afraid that these two men might hurt her because she could tell on them. She's only thirteen, you know. She would have been easy to seduce. She doesn't value her body so she would give it away to whoever wanted it.'

'Or die in defending her honour,' said Lin. 'It can go either way for the ones who have been shamed. Except in China, where she would be expected to kill herself.'

'She hasn't anything to be ashamed of,' said Phryne.

'No, but I bet that isn't how she sees it. It's getting colder. How long do we need to patrol?'

'We'll turn when we reach those lights and come back,' said Phryne. 'For St Kilda dwellers, this is "the beach".'

'Running feet,' said Lin, slowing. 'And splashing. Here they come,' he said calmly.

He turned, his walking stick in hand. Phryne flanked him. In St Kilda it is never really dark. Two people were running, not toward Phryne and Lin now but towards the outcasts' camp.

166

One of them swore as he tripped, almost fell, and scrambled on. The other was wholly silent and somehow familiar. Both were lost to sight in an instant in the mess of canvas and lines.

'Oh God,' groaned Phryne, and was gone from beside him.

On the flat wet sand Phryne was as fleet as a deer and Lin laboured after her. He could not see what she was aiming for. Then he saw it. A bundle of wet garments carelessly left below the high tide mark. A bundle which Phryne was trying to drag out of the shallow water. As he came closer it developed arms and legs and a lolling head.

He grabbed the body under its armpits and Phryne took the feet and they hauled, sobbing with effort. The girl seemed to weigh as much as a fully grown whale. Sand slid and gritted under cold flesh and torn hair. Surely she was dead. She was the very definition of a dead weight.

He had reckoned without Phryne. She whispered, 'Move her arms! Up and down, above her head and down! Quickly!' Then she balled her fist and punched the rounded white breast which protruded from the torn dress.

'There's a faint pulse in this wrist,' said Lin.

Phryne listened at the slack mouth, took a deep breath, and breathed her own warm life into Rose Weston. The lips were corpse cold and salty under her own. The body flexed and shuddered as Lin moved the arms up and down as he had been told. Surely this was a waste of time. Surely the poor girl was beyond recall. But he kept dragging and releasing her arms, because Phryne was still trying. Water soaked his knees and seeped into his boots. He shivered with cold and the presence of death.

Then he felt the body convulse, and Phryne turned Rose's head to the side as she vomited water and sand, coughed, then breathed on her own. Once. Twice. A pause. Then she coughed and breathed again.

'Li Pen?' Lin called. The invaluable Li Pen, Lin's bodyguard, the only Shaolin monk in Australia who liked Vegemite, materialised with a blanket, wrapped Rose Weston and lifted her over his shoulder. He carried her without any effort, belly down and still spilling sea-water from her mouth. She was breathing in shuddering gasps but she was breathing.

'Where?' asked Li Pen. He was not surprised at the turn of events. The Jade Lady had said that tonight she would rescue this lost girl, and she had. The Jade Lady was invariably right. His master was fortunate that she only wanted to be his concubine. She was as formidable, in her way, as Lin's Dragon Lady grandmother. Li Pen was only sorry that he had not been able to catch those two miscreants who had fled into the camp. But he had been bidden to stay close to Lin Chung.

'Car,' said Phryne.

If anyone in the circus noticed two Chinese men and a boy carrying a blanket-wrapped girl out of their sacred precinct, they didn't feel it necessary to object.

'Hospital, or home?' asked Lin, helping Li Pen load Rose Weston into the back seat.

'I'll just drive for a while. How is she, Li Pen?'

'She has a bad wound on the back of her head,'

168

he said, drawing back the sandy blanket. 'She is bruised on all the parts I can see. Even her fingernails are broken. I do not like the thread of her pulse. Also, she is very cold.'

'If I take her home I'll have to hide her,' Phryne mused, allowing the great car to slide out into the silent street. 'If I take her to hospital there will be questions. And her family will be informed. She can't talk until she recovers and she'll need to swear to her diary for me to nail that old bastard, her grandfather and the kindly Mr Johnson. Home,' she decided, and found that her hands had already decided for her. The Hispano-Suiza, like a homing bird, had driven itself back to its own garage.

Li Pen carried the retching girl up the steps and into Phryne's house. Dot was awake. She had enjoyed a blameless evening at the Holy Land lantern slide show and had even allowed her young man to kiss her at the door. Hugh Collins kissed beautifully. Then somehow Dot couldn't sleep so she thought that she would sit up and wait for Miss Phryne, even though Dot considered that fortune-telling was contrary to the law of God, and unsound as well. Her crochet dropped from her hands as she jumped to her feet.

'You've got her?' she asked.

'In a bad way. Ring Jack Robinson, Dot, at the number he left. Tell him to bring a scene of the crime bag and the police surgeon. Lay her down here, Li Pen, if you please. Oh, Rose, you have been seeing life,' she commented.

Rose Weston had been comprehensively beaten. Her face was beginning to swell: eyes, cheekbones, jaw. Her arms were ringed with red finger-marks and as Phryne peeled more of the wet dress away, more bruises appeared, darkening now that Rose was warming back into life. Phryne sent Li Pen to the kitchen to make tea and fill hot water bottles and Lin to fetch several fluffy towels to wrap the girl under the blanket. The head wound started to bleed. Dot came back.

'He's on his way,' she said. 'Oh, Miss, that looks bad.'

'Head wounds always bleed a lot,' said Phryne. 'I'm more worried about her lungs and how cold she is. I wish I dared give her tea but she might have to have chloroform. Ah. Hot water bottles. Good.'

With the help of Li Pen and Lin, Phryne tucked the hot water bottles into the towels and wrapped Rose closely. Dot turned on the electric fire, a great convenience which gave instant heat. Rose and her wrappings began to steam. Phryne said with satisfaction, 'Now, we can sit down and have a drink, and Lin can dry his feet. Dot, break out the booze. Li Pen has made Chinese tea if you prefer, Lin dear.'

'Both,' said Lin. 'I was sure that she was dead, Phryne, when you hauled her out of the sea! You brought her back by sheer willpower. If she lives, she will owe you her life.'

'If she lives,' said Phryne, taking the small glass of green chartreuse which Dot handed her and sipping. It was not possible to gulp green chart-reuse if you ever wanted to have more than one functioning taste bud again. Dot poured herself a sherry. Lin drank Chinese tea and brandy alternately. Li Pen sank to the floor, removed Lin's shoes and socks and dried his feet. Thereafter he remained, cross-legged, on the floor with the teapot for company. He found western chairs uncomfortable. Dot thought he looked ever so exotic.

The room warmed until it was almost hot. The rest of the house was asleep. Phryne could hear Mr and Mrs Butler's snores, one genteel and one rather deeper. James Murray was sleeping like a mouse, and so were the two girls. Rose Weston breathed like a consumptive. Phryne nodded. Then she jerked awake as she heard footsteps on the porch.

She slipped out and opened the door before they could ring. She was so pleased to see Jack Robinson's unmemorable face that she could have hugged him.

'In here,' she told him, and conducted Jack and a solid older man with a doctor's bag into the parlour.

Everyone woke up.

'This is Doctor Page,' said Jack. 'And this is the victim?'

'We found her on the shore,' said Phryne. 'Below the high tide mark. We emptied out most of the water and brought her here. She's been beaten and there's a terrible bump on her head.'

The police surgeon looked at Jack Robinson, who gave him a nod. Well, if he was to examine a victim in a room which contained not one but two Chinese men and two competent looking women, it was Jack Robinson's funeral. Lin and Li Pen went into the other parlour as the police surgeon pulled the blanket and towels away from the mistreated body.

'Bad business,' Dr Page grunted. 'You did the right thing, Miss. Cold's a killer in these drowning cases. Been beaten with fists, I think,' he said, feeling over Rose Weston for broken bones. 'Heart sounds all right. Lungs are still fluidy. Bruising around the ribs, of course.' He took a spatula from his bag. 'Give me a little jar, Jack.' He scraped busily. 'Label that "sand from the victim's mouth", will you?' he said, and Robinson wrote busily.

The doctor took samples from every part of Rose Weston's body. Finally he probed the head wound, feeling for crepitus, the creaking of a broken bone, with sensitive fingers. Dot, who had been minded to object to his heartless handling, reminded herself that he usually dealt with dead people.

'Might be a small fracture,' he said, washing his hands in a bowl of water which Phryne had supplied. 'I'll clean it and put in some stitches. Then you need to keep her warm in a nice dark place – no sudden lights, no noises – and see how she is after a day or so. Wash all this sand off her and use arnica for the bruises. I'll give you some morphine, but you can't use it until she's awake and can walk and both pupils dilate the same. Morphine can kill in concussion. Just a light diet, aspirin and plenty of fluids. But you'll get your own doctor,' he added. 'Bit of a treat for me to work on a live body,' he added, patting Rose Weston on an unbruised space of shoulder. 'She'll do, I believe.'

Dot suddenly liked this red-faced, elderly person a lot better.

He cleaned and stitched the head wound neatly enough. Then he picked up his bag.

'Would you like some tea, or a drink?' asked Phryne.

The doctor put the bag down again.

'Whisky,' said Dr Page. 'A glass of whisky would be most acceptable. Poor girl! What happened to her?'

'That's what we have to find out,' said Jack Robinson. 'I know you said you'd find her, Miss Fisher, but I have to confess I didn't really believe you.'

'You should always believe her,' said Li Pen unexpectedly. He was lifting Rose Weston and her wrappings and hot water bottles and following Dot up to Phryne's bathroom. There the rush of water would not wake the household. They were used to Phryne having baths at all hours.

'Yes,' said Robinson. 'I suppose, after all this time, I should. You say that it was a fortune-teller who guided you there?'

'Either she was speaking to the spirits or she knew about the stray girl in the camp,' said Phryne. 'Rose might have been there of her own free will, but once the gossip was spread she was doomed. They had to get rid of her. Am I right to think that there was sperm in one of those samples?'

Dr Page, having long associated with hospital nurses and female police, was used to plain speaking women.

'I believe so. I shall know when I get it under a microscope.'

'She's not sixteen yet. She's a threat. And there

173

was the other thing as well. With her family. I do not believe that she meant to run away for good. She left ten pounds behind if she did.'

'Not possible, unless she was mental,' said Robinson.

'A little deranged by ill treatment, perhaps, but not that deranged,' Phryne told him. 'Two people were with the body but they ran away and we couldn't spare the time to catch them. Tell me, Doctor Page, did she fall off a ship and get washed ashore?'

'She's got the gooseskin hands,' he said. 'Been in the water an hour or so. At least. I haven't got any water from her lungs but the stuff in her mouth was definitely sea-sand. I reckon she was face down in the sand.'

'She was,' affirmed Phryne.

'Well, your two unknowns were either trying to help and got scared when they saw you coming, or they were...'

'Pressing her face down into the sand,' said Phryne. 'To suffocate. How very horrible.'

'Murder is like that, and this looks like an attempted murder. She wouldn't have been able to swim or even think with that great blow on the head. She might have fallen overboard, though, and hit her head on the way down. Then she might have floated or been washed ashore, and the two strangers might have been rescuers. It's all in the way you look at it,' said Dr Page. 'Now, Miss, I'll thank you for the whisky, and I'll take my leave. Jack?'

'I'll give you a lift,' said Robinson. 'Least I can do after dragging you out so late. Miss Fisher will

174

write me a statement about everything that happened on the beach. I'll call on you tomorrow, Miss Fisher. And – well done,' he said quietly. 'Sorry for doubting you.'

'Quite all right, Jack dear. After a few miles up and down that beach I was doubting myself.'

She let them out and closed the door. Then she sat herself across Lin Chung's lap. His arms closed around her. She rested her neat head on his chest.

'Shouldn't we go and help Li Pen and Dot?' he asked, holding her closer.

'They'll manage,' said Phryne drowsily. 'How very nice you smell, Lin dear. I have often noticed it.'

He kissed her on the top of the head.

'Thank you,' he said quietly.

Miss Anna Ross to Mr Rory McCrimmon

Rory dear husband for so I think of you. I cannot understand why Mama refused your proposal but I did not refuse it. I am yours as I said I was when you asked me. I shall try to creep out and speak to you at three this morning if you will wait for me at the corner of the street.

CHAPTER ELEVEN

Where youth grows pale, and spectre-thin, and dies

John Keats
'Ode to a Nightingale'

Morning found Phryne asleep with Lin Chung in her boudoir, Li Pen asleep on the floor of the second guest room, Rose Weston asleep in the bed of the second guest room, Dot in the chair in the second guest room and everyone else waking to greet the new morning in their usual fashion. Breakfast was served to James Murray, Dot and the girls in the dining room, to Lin and Miss Phryne in her own bedroom, and Li Pen was supplied with Vegemite toast in the kitchen. Dot did not dare disclose the presence of Rose Weston without Phryne's direct orders, so she mustered the household and took them all on a nice brisk walk to see the marching bands, despite their muttered objections.

Phryne saw them go from her high window. 'I shall have to buy Dot an especially nice present,' she remarked, turning to kiss Lin Chung with her coffee-flavoured mouth.

'Why?' asked Lin as he surfaced.

'Because she has taken the girls and James and even Molly firmly out of the house. And now we must get up and see how our patient is doing.'

'Li has been there all night. He knows a lot about injuries.'

'I'm sure he does,' said Phryne, removing a questing hand and getting pointedly out of bed. Lin sighed. Adventure had the worst effect on romance. On the other hand, adventure appeared to have an aphrodisiac effect on Phryne, and Lin was always happy to assist with assuaging her fevers.

He sat up to eat the rest of the stack of bible-leaf toast which Mrs Butler made so well. Very thin slices of rye bread, flash toasted and soaked in butter. Bliss. One just nibbled gently and – *voilà!* – somehow one had eaten all the toast. Rabbits must feel that way about lettuce, he thought. As he got up, Ember assumed his place on Phryne's moss-green sheets and settled down for a nice long nap, until Dot came to make the bed.

Musing gently, Lin took advantage of Phryne's absence to wash and dress. He had done this here often enough to have left a change of clothes in Phryne's wardrobe and to know where to find the towels. The house was very quiet.

Then, from downstairs, came a scream of pure terror.

Lin was out of the room before he realised that he had heard it. It was coming from the second bedroom. Li Pen came out.

'The young woman awoke and saw me,' he said, a little hurt. 'And she screamed.'

'Probably reads too much Sax Rohmer,' explained Lin sympathetically. 'I suggest you take a rest, Li Pen. Go and sit in the garden. I'd better keep out of the way, too. Ah, here comes the good

Mrs Butler. Come, Li Pen, and admire Camellia's garden. It is laid out on the best Buddhist principles.'

Phryne eased Rose Weston back onto her pillow, scolding gently: 'Yes, it was a Chinaman, and no, he isn't Fu Manchu, don't be so silly. He's a good friend of mine, and of yours, for he carried you when we rescued you last night. Now, have a drink of this nice barley water,' said Phryne, and administered it. Rose sipped, then seized the glass and drank thirstily. Phryne poured her another. 'You're all dried out,' she said. 'Too much sea-water in the system.'

'Sea-water?' asked Rose. She lifted a hand to push her hair away from her face and winced twice; once for the bruised hand, once for the bruised face.

'Yes. Now, look at me. Do you know who I am?'

'Miss Fisher,' said Rose.

'And what's your name?'

'Don't know,' said Rose through split lips.

'Ah. Do you hurt?'

'Everywhere,' said Rose. 'What happened to me? Where am I?'

'You were attacked and you're in my house and perfectly safe. No one shall know where you are. Li Pen and others will protect you.'

'Attacked?' said Rose, beginning to cry.

'Do you remember what happened?' asked Phryne.

'No,' said Rose. 'It's all dark.'

Mrs Butler came in with a tray. 'Have a little breakfast,' said Phryne. 'People come for miles to eat Mrs Butler's coddled egg. Don't try to remember. Your name, by the way, is Rose.'

'Rose,' said Rose uncertainly.

'And as soon as you can walk on your own, you shall have something for the pain. I'll be back later,' she promised, and went out. She found Li Pen and Lin in the garden, discussing philosophy.

'The yang of the bright sunny wall is balanced by the ying of the wet shaded fernery,' explained Li Pen. 'It is indeed a beautiful garden. Her use of bamboo to block out the strong winds is very clever. When the vines grow there will be a place to sit on the hottest day, while that side will always be warm, even in winter.'

'I haven't even begun to appreciate Camellia's talents,' admitted Lin. 'She wants to make a lotus pool. Great Uncle is delighted. He says that lotus flower tea is the greatest of all teas. Apparently you put the tea-leaves in the flower as it closes at night, and then take them out again when the sun rises and the flower opens again ... ah, Phryne. We are sorry to have shocked your patient.'

'She's a silly girl who reads too much Sax Rohmer,' said Phryne, confirming Lin's diagnosis. 'Also, she seems to have lost her memory.'

'That can happen with a sudden blow,' said Li Pen, mollified.

'Yes, but it strikes me as very convenient. Still, there is no rush. I will have to get someone to nurse her. I can't take Dot away from the girls. I've thought about Bridget but she's too identified with the Weston household. Perhaps Jack will have something to suggest. Now we need to improve the shining hour by writing out statements for our dear Detective Inspector Robinson. I've brought paper and pens; here is a nice place to recall such horrors. What was your impression, Li Pen? You saw it from a different angle. Were those two people trying to help Rose, or trying to harm her?'

'I really could not tell,' he said, after deep thought. 'It could have been either. They could have been trying to drag her further up the beach, or pressing her into the sand.'

'Drat. I can't decide either. So we'll write it as we saw it,' said Phryne, and sat down to do so.

When Jack Robinson arrived an hour later they had three well-written statements. Jack accepted tea and a paper of aspirins. He rubbed his eyes.

'Been a long night,' he said. 'Big fight in China-town over a fan-tan game.' He mentioned two family names, neither of which was Lin. 'Buggers fight with hatchets. Sorry, Mr Lin. There were arms and ears all over the shop and everyone was screaming. Then there was a robbery at the brewery, they came with shotguns and held up the night shift payroll. Not to mention the usual run of husbands strangling wives, whores rolling sailors and young bloods belting the living day-lights out of other young bloods and stealing their personal property. What a city! If the Sodom and Gomorrah police force was hiring, I'd be a shoo-in.'

'Tea,' said Phryne soothingly, and poured it out into a policeman-sized mug.

Detective Inspector Robinson added sugar and milk, imbibed, swallowed his aspirin, imbibed some more, then went on an intensely focused amble around the tiny garden, stroking the occasional leaf and sniffing flowers. Li Pen nodded. This was very proper behaviour for rebalancing the soul. He would have suggested an hour's meditation instead of the aspirin, but he knew that westerners preferred drugs. Lin and Phryne drank some more tea and watched, a little bemused. Robinson came back and Phryne refilled the mug.

'Those azaleas are going to be beaut,' was, however, his only comment.

'Detective Inspector, Camellia asked me if you would like to see her garden,' said Lin on impulse. He was rewarded by a genuine smile from the tired face.

'I'd like that,' said Jack Robinson. 'That's real kind of Mrs Lin. Just tell me when and where. Now,' he said, squaring his shoulders, 'let's see the statements.'

He read through them twice.

'How is the girl today?' he asked.

'Still alive and recovering, but short on memory,' Phryne told him. 'This may be true or it may be feigned, time will tell. I'm going to need a discreet nurse if I'm going to keep her here. Can you suggest anyone?'

'Know just the person,' said Jack. 'I'll send her along this afternoon if she's available. Name's Mrs Jackmann. Lily. Nice woman.'

'How do you know she's discreet?' asked Phryne.

'She worked for an abortionist for seven years,' said Jack. 'Never said a word. Not even to us. Nearly went to jail for her discretion. She's got a job lined up at the Queen Vic but she doesn't start for a couple of weeks and she can do with a little extra. I can pay her out of the "contingencies" fund, Miss Fisher.'

'Well, if the Queen Vic are willing to employ her she's fine for me,' said Phryne.

'She can live out,' said Jack Robinson. 'Got a husband. He's a mate of mine.'

'He's a policeman?' asked Phryne, amazed.

'Orchid grower,' said Robinson, and smiled again. 'Now, I'm off home to get some sleep. I'll be back tomorrow with the pathology report. Old Page was very impressed with you, Miss Fisher. Said you kept a cool head in a crisis.'

'Thank you,' said Phryne, and saw him out.

Li Pen and Lin also took their leave. Lin wondered how he was going to explain to the very shy Camellia that he had asked a policeman to see her garden. Phryne was wondering why a cool head in a crisis, a thing which most women possessed, was such a compliment, when a small barking missile collided with her ankles and Dot, James and one girl came home.

'Where's Ruth?' asked Phryne. 'Yes, yes, Molly, I'm glad to see you, too.'

'Said she'd like to follow the Salvos,' said Dot. 'She'll be back before lunch.'

'Good. Now, do come in. As you might have noticed, we have a guest. Her name is Rose Weston and no one is to know she is here, not the postman, the milkman, the friends at school, the idle pub acquaintances, anyone who calls asking for her, no one. She's been badly beaten and is in a state of shock. I've got a nurse coming this afternoon who will sit with her. Now, do I have your word, all of you? This is really important.'

'I swear,' said James immediately, fighting down the urge to salute.

'So do I,' said Jane.

'And me,' said Dot. 'On the bible, if you like. Poor girl! When Miss Phryne brought her in last night I didn't think she would live. And she cried all night, something pitiful. Now, Jane, you've got all that holiday homework to do, and I'm going to do my mending. You want to share the blue parlour?'

'Yes,' said Jane. Dot liked to mend, and she also liked the interesting facts which Jane unearthed and brought to her attention with as much charming assiduity as a dog with a bone or a ferret with a rabbit. Dot was learning a lot from Jane. Jane loved finding things to tell Dot.

Phryne had various small tasks to do which could not be put off any longer – bills to pay, accounts to clear, household sums to add. James Murray took his violin into the garden and limbered up his fingers. The Folk Song Society crowd might be argumentative but they were good judges of a fiddler. He had missed several notes in the reel last night and fudged several more, and did not mean to do so again. It was scales for him, and those tricky slides which the Irish fiddlers found so easy. He started playing softly, not wanting to disturb the house. After an hour he had everyone listening. He really was, Phryne decided, a fiddler who could make telephone poles dance.

Lunch came but Ruth did not. Mrs Lily Jackmann arrived. She was a jolly plump woman, younger than Phryne had imagined. Phryne explained Rose's condition.

'Let's have a look at those pupils, then,' the nurse responded. 'Got a flashlight?'

Phryne provided one. Rose murmured at the sudden light.

'Very nice. Identical. Come on, old thing, take my hand, and we'll walk you to the convenience,' said Lily, and Rose grasped her hand, moaning a little, then managed to stand and walk.

'Good. We'll soon have you comfortable,' said Lily cheerfully. 'What's your name, then?'

'Rose,' said the patient. 'My name is Rose.'

'One foot in front of the other, Rose,' urged Mrs Jackmann.

Feeling much better about her patient, Phryne went back to her bills, but her unease was growing. It was getting on for four, and Ruth had not returned. She had never stayed out late before. Still, it was a carnival, and there were a lot of things going on. But Ruth had been in a strange state of mind lately...

Unable to concentrate, Phryne took herself out for an exploring walk. She covered the foreshore, the main streets, the ice-cream shop and the town hall, but there was no Ruth to be seen. She had gone out wearing her lilac dress, sandals, a straw hat with a purple ribbon and her amethyst beads. Phryne strained her eyes for a gleam of purple, but saw none.

She went home cross. When Ruth returned she would have no other outings except school for three weeks. Six weeks.

Time went on and there was no sign of her.

When it got dark, Phryne really began to worry. Dinner was good but barely tasted and when it ended Ruth had still not returned.

Jane knew that she was for it when Phryne called her into the parlour. She had promised not to tell. But now it looked like there had been trouble and Ruth was missing and perhaps that meant she ought to break her promise? She bit the end of her plait.

'Jane,' said Phryne. 'Where has Ruth gone?'

'I – I don't know,' said Jane with perfect truth.

'But you know where she was going,' said Phryne, who had been born in Richmond, but it wasn't yesterday.

'She said... I promised,' said Jane miserably.

'I don't counsel anyone to break a promise,' said Phryne grimly. 'You must decide for yourself. Possibly you should not have made the promise in the first place.'

'No,' said Jane. 'I shouldn't have. But I did.'

'This has to do with her search for her father,' said Phryne.

Jane nodded.

'Did she think that she had found him?' asked Phryne.

Jane nodded again. James, passing the door, was moved to stop and listen. Like most musicians, while there was music he didn't notice much else, but the air in that room was crackling.

'What is his name?'

'Rory McCrimmon,' faltered Jane. 'He sent her notes. He left the roses. He's been asking her to come out for weeks.'

'And he's dead,' said James from the door.

Both faces turned to him, identically blank.

'If he's the Rory McCrimmon I knew when I was last in Australia, Phryne, then he's dead. As a doornail. I sent him back to Skye, dying of TB, and his mother showed me his grave when I went there on the way home. I played a lament for him. Rory McCrimmon is dead. And he says he's Ruth's father?'

'We went to see Ruth's mother,' explained Jane, shocked. 'She is dying too. Of TB. Ruth asked her for the name of her father. She gave us his name. Rory McCrimmon the piper.'

James staggered slightly and sat down in a chair. 'And this was – what, fourteen years ago? How many Rory McCrimmons were there, here in Australia, who could play the pipes? He was a very good piper. It must be my Rory he is impersonating. Because I am sure – certain sure – that he isn't the real Rory McCrimmon.'

'Then who could he be?' wailed Jane. 'And why does he want Ruth?'

'I don't know,' said James grimly. 'But I'm minded to find out.'

Phryne got up from her chair and grabbed his shoulder. It felt like wood under her hand.

'Don't rush off half cocked. You were in Australia with Rory McCrimmon – why?'

'We came out on a boat as sailors – precious little to live on in Skye or Orkney. Damn, we even made records for the Folk Song Society together, me and Rory and Neil, the drummer. Rory fell in love with his landlady's daughter, then he came down with consumption, the landlady refused the marriage, and I sent Rory home. I got a job on a cruise liner soon after. So the poor bride is still alive? What was her name, she was a sweet girl. Annie. That was it. Pretty Annie with her long brown hair. I thought she had died long since. And there was a babe? I never knew. I never knew.'

James seemed stunned.

Jane went to her room and brought back a sheaf of notes and letters. Now that her promise had somehow got broken, without her actually breaking it, she needed to help. Phryne turned them over, appalled. They were a subtle, clever seduction.

The first one just said 'Do you know who your father was?' The next one said 'I know where your father is', signed 'A friend'. The third said 'Why don't you want to see your father? Leave a light on and I'll come to your window.'

'We didn't leave a light on,' said Jane. 'But Ruth was really upset.'

'No rose is as fair as you' said the card which had come with the roses.

'Your father is missing you', said the next. 'He wants to see you and know you. Come out to the lane and I'll wait for you there.'

'He didn't mention any names,' said Jane. 'So we thought it was a trick. Then after we came back from the sanatorium, this one came.'

'Rory McCrimmon is your father and I am waiting for you by the lamp post.'

'Even then she didn't do anything because she was scared,' said Jane. 'Until this one. I haven't seen it before. He used to post them through our window.'

187

'Darling daughter I long to see you. Come to the town hall and wait by the first pillar at three in the afternoon. Your father, Rory.'

'She didn't think there could be any harm, if it was during the day,' pleaded Jane. 'He couldn't just pick her up and carry her away in front of all those people.'

'He didn't have to,' said Phryne. 'She would follow him like a lamb. This is very bad. We must think of what to do. Calmly. Go and get Dot, will you, Jane?'

'There will be something else that I have to tell, when the wee bird is found,' said James to Phryne as the door closed behind Jane.

Phryne gave him a look alight with intelligence and fury. She had already guessed what he was going to say.

'Yes,' said Phryne. 'But let us find her first. Stupid girl! I wish I'd burned those romances as soon as I saw them in her hands. Now some kidnapper has her, and what is the easiest method of kidnapping? Persuade the victim to kidnap herself. As if I didn't have enough to do! Oh God, here's Miss Jones, come to talk about appointing a new flower maiden. Go and tell Dot what's happened, James dear, and I'll be with you in a moment.'

Phryne gave Miss Jones her customary ten minutes and her tea as she strove to control her own emotions. She wasted no time in blaming herself for not making Ruth confide in her. She hadn't and there it was. Phryne had no use for guilt. It prevented sensible action.

Miss Jones said, 'I'm so sorry to disturb you,

Miss Fisher, but we need a new flower maiden.'

'Yes, it seems that we do,' said Phryne.

'I have retrieved the costume,' said Miss Jones. 'The family was not helpful. They do not seem to know where Rose is, or when she is expected back. So I had a thought – would you like one of your daughters to be on the float with you? Ruth, perhaps?'

'No,' said Phryne quickly. 'If I can't take both I won't take either. Who do you suggest?'

'I have a list of three,' said Miss Jones, settling down for a long discussion. Phryne wished her, politely, a long way away; in comfortable circumstances, but a long way away. She did not have time for discussions about flower maidens.

'Miss Jones, I have something of a domestic crisis on my hands. I have always relied on your judgment. Confidently. Who should it be?'

Miss Jones was very pleased. That Miss Fisher should rely on her judgment was very warming in a world which wasn't noticeably appreciative of her efforts.

'Oh, Jessica Adams,' she said. 'Quite the nicest girl, and also very close in size to poor Rose Weston.'

'Jessica it shall be,' proclaimed Phryne. She took delivery of a sheaf of tickets to various events and showed Miss Jones out into the windy darkness.

'Miss Jones, would you like me to arrange a taxi for you?'

'Oh no, thank you, I have my bicycle,' said Miss Jones, and went away.

Phryne closed the door. Now there was nothing to do but wait out the night.

189

The council of war next morning included Bert, Cec, Robinson, James Murray, Jane and Dot. Hugh Collins, Dot's intended, had come along on his day off to support Dot, who was very distressed.

'Thing is,' said Robinson, scratching an ear in embarrassment, 'until there's a demand there's not a lot we can do. Officially.'

'But we can help,' rumbled Hugh Collins. 'Unofficially.'

'What do you reckon this mongrel wants with our Ruthie?' demanded Bert.

'Probably money,' said Phryne. 'He wouldn't have gone to all that trouble if it was just...'

'Sin,' said Dot. The euphemism was gladly accepted.

'Yair, plenty of girls for sale if you want 'em,' said Bert. 'By the look of all them notes, he was going to a lot of trouble to get Ruthie herself. Not Janey. Ruthie.'

'Because he had a string,' said James flatly. 'That he could pull.'

'I'll pull his strings for him when I lay hands on him,' said Bert.

'What do we know?' asked Robinson. 'He says he's this Rory McCrimmon and you say he can't be.'

'That's right,' affirmed James.

'Then how does he know?' asked Phryne. 'Where did he get his information from?'

'He might have been listening outside the window,' said Dot. 'Ooh, that's a real nasty thought.'

'He might,' said Phryne. 'He might have found

out the name because the girls were talking about Ruth's mother's message. But how did he know which girl to target if he didn't know the name?'

'He might have known us back in the old days,' said Jane. 'He'd know that my parents were both dead. He might know old mother Andrews,' she added, shuddering.

'And there's one person here who knew about Rory McCrimmon,' said Robinson evenly. 'You, Mr Murray.'

'That's true,' said James slowly. 'You have the right of it. But it wasn't me. I'd never hurt Ruth. And I never heard the name until last night. Not since fourteen years ago. When I was here with Rory and Neil.'

He sat up suddenly. 'Oh, God in heaven,' he whispered. 'It cannot be him.'

'Who cannot?' demanded Phryne.

'When I got off the ship and pitched my tent in that camp,' said James very slowly, 'I thought I saw a man I knew. He was not in the same camp ground as me, and I never saw him again. But it would be like him,' he added to himself. 'It would be very like him, the sleekin' weasel of a man that he was.'

'James,' threatened Phryne, grabbing his wrist.

Dot bit her knuckle to suppress a scream of tension, and Hugh Collins took the mistreated hand and squeezed it. In front of his commanding officer, too, he thought defiantly. Jane held her breath. Phryne balled her fist.

'Surely it is him,' said James, seconds before Phryne knocked him cold. 'Neil McLeod was a cold, weaselly man. He is probably here. He

191

knew the whole tragedy of poor Rory Dubh and his Annie. He might even have known there was a child, though he never told me, the bastard. I know he's been trading around, between here and Malaya. He never went back to Skye, where he would not have been welcome.'

'All right. You saw him in another camp. Which one?' asked Robinson.

'The circus,' said James. 'I will find that Neil McLeod,' he said almost under his breath. 'And when I find him I will squeeze his neck until he tells me the truth.'

'Good plan,' said Phryne.

'Me and Cec,' suggested Bert, 'might be able to help.'

Cec stretched out both huge hands and cracked all of the knuckles at his disposal. James looked at him in some awe.

'Of course,' said Phryne. 'But don't kill him. Even our well-disposed Detective Inspector can't overlook murder. But a few bruises, a few broken bones...'

'If they happened in the act of apprehending the felon,' said Jack. 'Such things do happen,' he added. 'Quite a lot. But we wait for a ransom message,' he said.

'Leave Ruthie with that mongrel?' demanded Bert.

'I want Ruth back as much as you do,' said Robinson, defending his point. 'But I also want to lock her kidnapper up for life, and to do that I need some proof. Shouldn't be too long. This bloke's an expert at finding the right moment. He'll leave us to stew for a day and a night, but not long enough for Miss Fisher here to go to the police. Look, I'll make you a deal,' he offered.

'Yair?' snarled Bert, who did not do deals with cops as a matter of principle.

'Wait until the second post comes in. Ought to be about now. I'd put good money on the demand being in that delivery.'

'Five bob,' said Bert.

'Done,' said Robinson.

Time passed. Phryne went to visit Rose Weston. She was sleeping. Breath puffed through swollen lips. She looked like a prize fighter after the fiftieth bare-knuckle round. Lily Jackmann looked up from the magazine she was reading.

'Best thing for her,' she observed. 'Her body's taken a terrible battering. But she's a healthy creature, she's already healing well. A few days' rest and she'll be fine. Better that she sleeps through it.'

'Have you everything you need?' asked Phryne.

'Oh yes, Miss Fisher, the patient and I are eating like kings. Your Mrs Butler is a great cook. That was Jack Robinson I heard in the passageway, wasn't it? Say hello from me and thank him for a nice quiet job.'

'Has she said anything?'

'She talks a lot in her sleep,' said Lily. 'Morphine does that. But she doesn't talk a lot to me. Of course, her mouth hurts.'

'Write down what she says, would you? She's a victim of a very serious assault.'

'As you like,' said Lily affably. 'But I'd say,' she added, 'that someone tried quite hard to kill her.'

Phryne supplied Mrs Jackmann with a notebook and pencil and was in the hall when the postman rattled the knocker. With a superhuman effort, she went back into the parlour and waited until Mr Butler brought her the mail on a silver tray. Household rituals must not be wantonly abandoned.

There were various letters and a small parcel. Phryne slit it open with her paper knife.

Out fell a string of clear purple glass beads. The note said 'Fifty pounds in the left hand manger in the camels' stable at noon and you shall have your Ruth again'. It was signed 'Rory'.

'The bastard,' snarled Bert.

There was general agreement.

'You owe me five bob,' said Robinson.

Mr Rory McCrimmon to Miss Anna Ross

If it takes a thousand years I will wait for you.

CHAPTER TWELVE

All this it knows, but will not tell
To those that cannot question well
The Spirit that inhabits it

Percy B. Shelley
'To a Lady, With a Guitar'

Over Robinson's objections, Phryne drew five ten-pound notes out of her bank account and enclosed them in an envelope directed to Rory.

'Just in case we need to buy her,' she told the policeman. 'She'd be cheap at fifty pounds. Now, are we clear about the plan? I go to the camel stable and put the money in the left hand manger. You gentlemen are going to lurk. I'll just walk out of the stable and keep going. He'll have to pick it up fairly quickly.'

'Why?' asked James.

'Because otherwise the camels will eat it,' said Phryne. 'They aren't as omnivorous as goats but they generally feel that if it's in their manger, then it's food. You can't be too choosy if you live in a desert. Now remember, don't kill him. I want Ruth back and Jack Robinson wants the kidnapper in jail.'

'Yair,' muttered Bert, who felt that the man who had kidnapped Ruthie would look much, much better deceased. 'We got it.'

'Then off we go,' said Phryne.

The circus drowsed. Noon was warm around the tents. Most people seemed to be taking a siesta before the matinée. Even the guard dogs were asleep, noses on paws. Lions slept in their cages. Elephants slept, ears flapped over their eyes to keep out the glare. Phryne walked through the circus without challenge and found the camel stall by remembering that camels and horses do not get on well. The other side of the camp from the horse pickets would have the camels.

The stable was a big tent, high enough for the long necked, and it was mercifully devoid of camels. Phryne had no utter objection to camels as a species but she could not like them. A creature whose only motive in life was to lure a human close enough to spit a pound of semi-digested grass in their eye had a certain Juvenalian frankness but was not comfortable company.

There were three mangers. Phryne assumed that the left hand one was judged from the viewpoint of someone facing into the building and slipped her envelope into the hay. Her followers went to ground.

'Phryne, what on earth are you doing in here?' someone asked from the door. It was Dulcie Fanshawe. Her hair was redder than before, and wet, and she was rubbing it with a stained towel.

'Just wandering,' said Phryne.

'I looked out of my window and there you were,' said Dulcie, clearly intending to stay. 'I didn't know that you liked camels.'

'I don't,' said Phryne. 'Come along, Dulcie, I'll shout you a drink.'

'I'm not fit to be seen,' said Dulcie, sitting down on a bale of straw and showing alarming signs of settling down for the day. 'But a nice chinwag would be good. The trouble with dyeing your hair is that you can't stop dyeing it and this henna stains everything if you aren't careful with it.'

Phryne was aware of Hugh, Bert, Cec and James Murray trying not to breathe from their assorted hiding places.

'A cup of tea,' said Phryne desperately. 'No one in the circus is going to care what you look like. Come along, old dear,' she said, taking Dulcie by the elbow and steering her out of the tent. 'I don't have leave to be in here, you know. People are touchy about their camels.' She led Dulcie out of the stable and let the flap fall behind them. 'Your caravan, then?'

'No,' said Dulcie. 'I need to sit in the sun until my hair dries. I'll get Sam to go for a bottle for us, if you've got the gelt.'

'Gelt I have,' said Phryne.

Sam was a small, shrewd boy, clearly used to such errands. Phryne sent him for a bottle of the good gin and a bottle of Indian tonic water and asked him to scrounge a couple of glasses. Dulcie sat down on an overturned tub and spread her wet hair over her shoulders. They sat in silence until Sam should return. Phryne thought that Dulcie was looking older, more tired, despite the Jezebel courage of her hair. Then the boy came back with the doings. He left, suitably rewarded. Phryne made herself a drink, ear cocked for a disturbance in the camel stable.

'Chin chin,' said Dulcie, mixing herself a very large gin with a splash of tonic and sucking it down with pleasure.

Neil McLeod was sure that he had made no sound at all as he slipped into the camel stable and walked very gingerly across the straw-strewn floor. He reached into the left hand manger and found the envelope without making any noise that even a mouse would hear. He slit the envelope open with a tarry thumbnail and drew out five ten-pound notes. He stood gloating over his fortune and was turning to go when a flat Scots voice said, 'You blackguard,' quite quietly. Neil chuckled.

'Is it you, then, old friend? I thought I saw you in the outcasts' camp. Still playing that old fiddle, eh?'

'You knew,' accused James Murray. 'You knew about Annie's bairn and you never told me.'

'Did I not? Must have slipped my mind.' The tone was insolent.

'And now you're selling her for fifty pounds,' said James. His face was still.

'She's worth it to her mistress,' said Neil. 'Tell you what, for a clansman I'll give you ten to go away and say nought. Fair offer, Jamie?'

'I'm no clansman of yours,' said James, and struck, grabbing Neil McLeod by the throat and half lifting his feet off the ground.

'Where's Ruthie?' roared Bert, arising from a pile and shedding straw.

'What's this? You betrayed me?' demanded Neil, half choking.

'Betrayal? You talk about betrayal? You tell us where Ruth is,' said James, 'and I might not kill you. Mind, I'm making no promises.'

'Nah, mate, chokin's all right for bastards, but it ain't gonna make no impression on a bloody bastard,' explained Bert. In exposition, he punched Neil hard in the stomach. All the wind in him came out in a rush and he doubled over, retching.

'You may be right,' said James, doing the same.

'Then you gotta shame 'em, because bloody bastards ain't got no balls,' said Bert. He lifted Neil's sweating face and slapped him, open handed, across the cheek. 'Give us our girl back right now,' he roared. 'Or Cec is gonna tear you to bits. He's not nice like me and he's very fond

198

of little Ruthie!'

Cec stretched to his full height and patted Neil gently on the shoulder, as if range-finding for a blow. All the defiance drained out of Neil Mc-Leod. 'I'll take you there,' he said.

'Did I mention,' said Bert, 'what we're gonna do to you if you've so much as laid a finger on her?'

Bert occupied the time it took to walk through the circus to the horse lines in telling Neil, in careful, merciless, biological detail. By the time they arrived at the riggers' tents, Neil was white and only able to stand because James and Cec were holding him up.

'In there,' he gestured.

Bert dived into the tent and they heard his roar of fury. He came out with a handful of cut ropes.

'She's not there,' he said.

'Are you being clever, Neil?' asked James. 'Because if you want any mercy, cleverness is not going to get it, and you are sorely in need of mercy at present. Where is the girl?'

Cec picked Neil up by his shoulders so that he was looking straight into Cec's face. What he saw there did not reassure him. Hebridean ancestors of his had seen eyes like that seconds before a horde destroyed the village. Cec only needed a winged helmet and an axe to be a Viking.

'Tell,' said Cec. Neil babbled.

'I left her here, sleeping. Just a mickey, nothing harmful. She was upset and wanting to go home. So I sent her to sleep. It was only going to be for a little while, I knew Miss Fisher would pay. I tied her hands and feet in case she came round. Those are my ropes and my knots – Jamie, you know my knots! Someone has taken her!'

'Who?' asked Cec.

'I don't know!' wailed Neil McLeod.

Cec threw him away, disgusted. He flew through the air with the greatest of ease, hit the side of a tent and slid down into a sitting position. Hugh Collins plucked the envelope from his shirt and addressed his unconscious capture.

'Neil McLeod, also known as Rory McCrimmon, I am arresting you for the crime of kidnapping. You have the right to remain silent, which is what you are doing. Pick him up, if you wouldn't mind,' said Hugh to Cec. 'Jack Robinson isn't going to be happy about this.'

'You reckon he told us the truth?' asked Bert of James, who had the cut ropes in his hands.

'Yes. These are sailor's knots and the rope has been cut – no sailor cuts a bit of good rope. She might have escaped,' he said. 'She's a stout-hearted girl.'

Bert brightened. 'So she might – she's clever, our Ruthie. She might even have beaten us home. Let's get this bloody bastard into a nice safe cell before me feelings get the better of me.'

'And mine too. He called me a clansman. I'm no clansman of his,' snarled James Murray.

They left the circus. Phryne and Dulcie saw the procession pass.

'Now that's a thing you don't see every day,' said Dulcie, a little fuzzily. It was her third gin. Neil lolled over Cec's shoulder. Bert walked behind Cec, carrying his hat. Hugh and James flanked them.

'No, most unusual,' replied Phryne.

'Do you think we ought to tell anyone? That man looks hurt.'

'Not our business,' said Phryne. 'Well, I must leave you, Dulcie. You keep the rest of the bottle,' she said. 'And don't get up. Your hair isn't dry. See you later,' breezed Phryne, and ran to catch up with the men as they neared the street.

'Neil?' she asked.

'Neil,' said Hugh Collins.

'But where's Ruth?' demanded Phryne.

'Been there. Not there now,' said Hugh Collins dejectedly. He did so like rescues and this one had fallen very flat.

'Someone else stole her?' asked Phryne.

'Or maybe she escaped,' said Bert. 'The ropes was cut.'

'A cheering thought,' said Phryne. 'Let's get Mr McLeod out of my reach, shall we? There's a thing the soldiers taught me with a long thin knife which I've always wanted to try on a suitable subject.'

Neil McLeod gave a moan and fainted.

Jack Robinson was pleased at the capture of one blackmailer and downcast at the continuing absence of Ruth.

'She'd come home if she freed herself,' said Phryne. 'Wouldn't she, Jane?'

'Yes, I'm almost sure she would,' said Jane uncertainly. 'Or she might be so upset that she had been made a fool of that she'd hide somewhere. She has made an awful hash out of all this. It's a mess,' said Jane sadly. 'I'm so sorry,' she said to

Phryne. 'I should have told you. I shouldn't have promised to keep that secret.'

Phryne hugged her and removed the ragged end of Jane's pigtail from her adoptive daughter's mouth. 'It's all right, Jane, I am not blaming you – really. Don't you blame yourself either. You aren't your sister's keeper. Guilt is a useless emotion and not to be indulged in. No. I am blaming Neil McLeod and it is rather a pity that Jack took him away so quickly. He might have had more to tell us, if properly persuaded.' She shut her excellent teeth with a snap.

'No,' said Robinson. 'I've met that type before. He spilled everything he knew after the first entirely unavoidable blow sustained in arresting him. He did resist arrest, didn't he, Collins?'

'Like anything, sir,' replied Hugh without the flicker of an eyelash. He stood to attention and saluted, which looked odd with him out of uniform. Dot, who did not usually giggle, giggled.

'Well, she's either free and hiding or she's captive again,' said Jack. 'If she's hiding she'll come home when she gets hungry – that's what my kids always did.'

'So what do you suggest?' asked Phryne, aching to be doing something.

'Wait till tonight before we start looking for her,' said Robinson. 'Meanwhile, we've got the problem of Rose Weston and what actually happened to her.'

'What did the pathologist say?' asked Phryne.

'Sand in her mouth was sea-sand and it did seem that her face was pressed into the beach, she's got little scratches all over her face. But then, she'd

202

been in the water at least an hour to get what they call gooseskin – you know, when you've been in the bath too long,' said Robinson, who shared Miss Fisher's view that almost all human ills could be healed by a long, hot, heavily soaped bath. 'She's got rings of bruises round her ankles and wrists, someone might have held her down in the water.

'Or grabbed her to throw her off a boat. She can swim, so she might have swum ashore and someone else hit her on the head.'

'Six of one,' murmured Phryne

'And half a dozen of the other,' finished James.

'Yer pays yer money and yer takes yer choice,' muttered Bert. 'Well, I reckon we need to find Simonds and Mongrel. They were on the spot and they might have been hiding her or maybe they snatched her in the first place.'

'And they'd be happy to beat her to death if they thought she was a threat? Or do you think they might have been paid to kill her? Would they do it?' asked Phryne.

'For a zac and a glass of beer,' affirmed Bert. 'Bad bastards, them two.'

'Too right,' said Cec.

'What are you thinking?' James Murray asked Phryne.

'She was a continuing threat to our good Mr Johnson and nice Grandfather Weston,' said Phryne slowly. 'She knew things which they couldn't allow anyone else to find out. And she was unstable. She might babble. If those two knew that she was associating with Mongrel and Simonds, a few pounds in the right hand and that gets rid of Rose and her dangerous knowledge.'

'Why did he employ you, then?' asked Robinson.

'Oh well, he could expect me to fail, he could be doing it to look good to the police, or maybe Johnson wants her back and Grandpapa is ordering her death. He is perfectly capable of it,' said Phryne. 'A really horrible old bastard.'

'Hmm,' said Robinson. 'All right. I'll order a general search for those two. I won't put Ruth on the missing list before she has a chance to come home on her own. We need to do a rummage through the criminal classes,' he said to Hugh. 'And I'll take my leave before you start discussing anything which, as a serving member of the Victoria Police in good standing, I shouldn't hear.'

'Take this,' said Phryne. 'This is Rose's diary. I've copied it out – here's the transcript. I'd like it in a safe place. They might burgle the house for it.'

Robinson flicked through the pages. The spidery beige writing hurt his eyes. Phryne's transcript was written in black ink in her decided, educated hand. The first line that caught his eye was 'spent the night with Johnson. Oh, the horror. How can Grandpa do this? Johnson says he loves me.'

He gave a grunt of disgust, took both the script and the book, and left.

'Now,' said Phryne. 'Where do we start?'

They mapped out a campaign over a few drinks. Dot took notes. Mr Butler provided his considering cocktail. Mrs Butler provided sandwiches.

'Thing is,' said Bert, 'there ain't that many criminals in Melbourne. I know,' he said, raising a hand to still a protest from Hugh Collins, 'there's a lot of crime. But most of it is strictly amateur, like strangling your missus because you can't stand her nagging, or crowning your old man with a skillet because you can't take another beating or you've heard him tell you about the cricket once too often. Most crime's in the family, so to speak. Right?' he demanded, and Hugh Collins, veteran of a thousand domestic brawls, nodded. He fingered the small circular scar on his forehead which he had sustained from a sauce bottle when, as a young and enthusiastic constable, he had tried to intervene in a picnic which had turned into a brawl. He still felt vaguely aggrieved at the woman who had dealt it.

'Then there's the small fry,' continued Bert, pausing for a refreshing swig of beer. 'Shoplifters, petty thieves, people who bought it from a bloke at the pub and they can't remember what he looked like, Officer, people who meant to return that radio to the shop and people who were on the way to the police station with that wallet they found when they was caught. Right?'

Hugh nodded again.

'The main graft in town is in whores, sly grog and in SP and betting,' said Bert. 'Sorry, Miss Dot. I mean ladies of the night, of course.'

'I know what whores are,' said Dot. 'They're in the bible. Go on, Mr Bert.'

'Er ... right. That's where all the big money is. Now Cec and me can't get onto the high class blokes. We ain't high class.'

'But I am,' said Phryne. 'Tell me who, Bert dear, and I shall interview them.'

205

'There's really only three,' said Bert, 'since I don't reckon we need to look too far afield. Rose Weston lived in Brighton, so does this Johnson, and the action's happened in St Kilda. The city's divided into ... I dunno what to call 'em...'

'Fiefdoms?' asked James. 'Clans?'

'Spheres of influence?' asked Jane.

'Yair,' said Bert. 'Everyone has his own patch, right? It's only when someone gets too big for their boots that there's trouble between them, see? And everything's been quiet since Squizzy and Snowy passed on. Now gambling round here belongs to Mr Walker.'

'The Ace of Clubs?' said Phryne. 'The man with the boat?'

'Yair. That's the place to be if you want to talk to Mr Walker. But you be careful, my girl,' warned Bert. 'He's a powerful man. All the SPs and pub gamblers pay a percentage to Mr Walker, and he makes sure that there's no trouble. I didn't hardly like to say it with Robinson here, everyone knows he's straight as a die, he's not a bad bloke for a cop, but there's some cops making a good living looking the other way in St Kilda. Not naming no names, mind.'

'So, Mr Walker is mine. I'll visit his game to-night. You'll have to teach me to play baccarat, though,' she said.

'Take all of a minute,' grunted Bert. 'Baccarat ain't a difficult game. If it wasn't for the side bets you could die of boredom watching it. He don't allow unescorted ladies, though. Who you gonna take with you?'

'Lin,' said Phryne. 'He looks gorgeous in evening dress.'

'Yair, good. Everyone knows the Chinese are mad gamblers. Sorry,' he said.

'As long as it is what everyone knows,' said Phryne. 'No offence taken. Could Rose have gone overboard from his boat, do you think?'

'Could have,' said Bert. 'And if she did he'd know all about it.'

'All right. Who else?'

'I reckon that's enough for one night,' said Bert, 'Me and Cec are going to make a bit of a noise in a few pubs, drop a word into a few ears. Stir the pot a bit.'

'You'll need some drinking money,' said Phryne and handed over a note. 'Don't argue, Bert dear, I've saved fifty pounds' ransom today. Hugh, I want you to find out all you can about Mr Johnson. There's those secret police files, aren't there, on all the prominent citizens of Melbourne? The ones no one is supposed to know about?'

'No one's supposed to know about them,' said Hugh, astonished.

'Take notes. After that I want you to go to the office of a fetid little rag called the *"Hawklet"*,' said Phryne. 'They'll be somewhere in Little Lon. Suggest to them that you will give them first refusal on a really impressive scandal. They love scandals. The reason I can't tell you their present address is that they got another libel writ and closed. Again. They always reopen a couple of doors down. Pretty soon they will be running out of Little Lon and will have to start again at the top.'

'How do you know about the *"Hawklet"*?' asked

Bert, a little shocked.

'I make it my afternoon reading every time I can get a copy,' said Phryne promptly. 'What they don't know about the seamy side of the city you could put in a wineglass. They must know something about Johnson, and they may know something about Grandpapa Weston. Squeeze them, Hugh dear. If you don't get anything from them try the *"Age"* and the *"Argus"* archives.'

'All right,' said Hugh.

'What can we do?' asked Dot.

'I'm afraid that you've got the job of trawling the circus for Ruth. Call out for her quietly and look into every tent and building that you can. It has to be a really unobtrusive search, you understand? James, you might like to take your fiddle. She loves your playing. You might be able to coax her out if she's hiding, or alert her if she's captive. Dress like it's a holiday and carry a basket. Eat toffee apples. Drift.'

'Yes,' said Dot, 'we can do that. What do we do if we find that she's captive? Tied up, say, in a caravan?'

'If it looks too hard for you to handle alone, then go get Dulcie and ask her to bring an elephant. That ought to suppress any resistance.'

'Very well,' agreed James. 'I'll get my fiddle.'

'And I'll bring a basket,' said Dot. 'Jane, you need the old straw hat, not the new one. Back before dark,' said Dot.

They all left. Bert and Cec to selected pubs. Dot, Jane and James to the circus. Hugh to the archives and then the *'Hawklet'*. Phryne went to see how Rose Weston was.

'No change,' reported Lily Jackmann. 'She's been talking and I've been writing it down but it's all nonsense.'

Phryne read 'no no don't want to don't want to please don't hurt me' and felt that whatever happened to Mr Johnson and Mr Weston, it could not be bad enough.

'But it's doing her good,' said Mrs Jackmann. 'Talking. I reckon she's never said all this stuff before. It's just bubbling up. Better out than in,' said Mrs Jackmann briskly. 'Her temp's going down and her blood pressure's better and there's not as many noises in her lungs.'

Sigmund Freud would have agreed with her, Phryne thought. Much better out than in.

She phoned Lin and secured his escort for the evening. Her part in this campaign would come much later. The gambling boat didn't leave until eleven-thirty. That meant a strenuous night in prospect, and she needed to prepare. She took herself up to her boudoir and sat down at the window to clean and load her gun. Better safe, to use another aphorism, than sorry. The mechanism slid and closed under her handling, a perfect, shiny, deadly little toy for a lady.

Then, like the cat Ember, Phryne decided that a nap was just what she needed. She shed her clothes, put on a silk nightgown in a soothing milky shade and slid down into her bed. Ember grumbled a little and moved aside to allow her feet past. It was amazing how one small, relatively slim cat could occupy a whole bed, Phryne thought drowsily.

Then she plucked all her worries off, visualising

them as pocket-sized Notre Dame gargoyles, and hurled them beyond the imagined perimeter she had set up around her bed. She fancied that she could hear their howls of baffled rage as they clawed to get back in to annoy her and could not get past the border.

It was a technique taught to her by a very toothsome ceremonial magician in London, and it never failed. Phryne could not afford guilt or remorse. She was going to need all of her skills to rescue Ruth and find out what had happened to Rose Weston, and bring her attackers to a nasty legal end. Or illegal would be just as good. Phryne was not worried about that. She was concerned with justice, not law.

She fell asleep as neatly and completely as Ember.

Mr James Murray to Mr Aaron Murray
2 April 1913

Dear father, my longing for home increases as I contemplate this strong sunlight and mop my brow in the heat. My friend Rory's matrimonial plans have been interrupted. The good Mrs Ross refused his perfectly honourable proposal – why, I can't imagine, unless she objects to him on account of his being a sailor and poor – and now he meets his bonny birdie at the street corner in the dead of night. He caught a cold doing it, he coughs all night, and I am very sorry for him. He truly loves this girl and she truly loves him. And she is a good, sensible, well-skilled girl whom any Island mother would be pleased to see her son bringing home. In the words of the song, she can certainly make a griddle cake, and Irish stew, and singing hinnies too.

We've had to move to another boarding house. The food is not good and the presence of poor Rory moping about like a sick spaniel does not increase its cheer. I can't really leave him, Father, but we've a couple of months yet before I take my berth on the P and O. Neil has a job sewing sails in the port and we have been making gramophone records of the old songs. They all want me to be Scotch, not understanding that Orkney was settled by Vikings, so I call myself Hamish, a small joke at the expense of those who do not understand the Gaelic. Cruel, I know, but I am tired of being myself and here, so why not be Hamish McGregor? He might be a happier man.

With many good wishes,
Your loving son, James

CHAPTER THIRTEEN

Postern of Fate, the Desert Gate, Disaster's Cavern, Fort of Fear
The Portal of Baghdad am I, the Doorway of Diarbekir.

James Elroy Flecker
'Gates of Damascus'

'How's tricks?' asked Bert. 'Still got the old SP down the lane?'

211

'Yair,' said the barman at the Esplanade, after a brief pause for identification of the questioner. 'Bert, yair, I remember you. And Cec. G'day. Ain't seen you for a donkey's age. What's the news on the wharf strike?'

'Goin' from bad to worse.' Bert leaned confidingly on the bar which, at the Espy, was longer than some skittle alleys. 'Me and Cec've got a cab.'

'Might be a good idea,' said the barman, wiping the mahogany surface. He loved the Espy's bar and hated the way careless drinkers kept spilling beer on it, which took off the polish.

'But right now I'm looking for Simonds and Mongrel,' said Bert.

'What's a decent man like you want with scum like them?' asked the barman, caressing the surface briefly.

Bert shrugged. 'Got a message for 'em,' he said.

'They're banned,' said the barman. 'Boss got shut of 'em last week. I hope it's a strong message,' he added with a grin which exposed his four remaining teeth, two top, two bottom. Although as he had proved in a recent altercation, the Espy barman could still bite.

'Strong enough,' said Bert. 'Any idea where they'd have gone?'

'Try the Flora,' advised the barman. 'Get deloused after,' he added.

'Oh, jeez,' said Bert, 'the bloody Flora.'

'Too right,' said Cec.

Bert finished his beer moodily. When he found them two, he vowed silently, he'd make them pay for forcing him to go into the Flora.

Jane hadn't known that one could actually eat too much Turkey lolly, or too many ice creams, toffee apples, sherbert bombs or suspicious green sweets from a penny lucky dip. She was beginning to feel that she needed to find a convenient bush to be sick under, and they hadn't covered half the ground yet.

Dot bustled along, poking into every corner with an expression of half-witted good will which was very convincing. She had almost been clawed by a surprised lion, who was taking an afternoon nap, and a camel had spat at her and missed, neither of which events had damped her enthusiasm or curbed her activity. James sat in the middle of the riggers' camp, playing the fiddle so sweetly that Jane could not imagine it not drawing Ruth if she was there. Somewhere she had heard that the McCrimmons of Skye could pipe seals out of the sea. James Murray could fiddle whales out of the ocean and Jane expected them at any moment. She could easily envisage the huge grey heads turning to triangulate on the sound, and the vast bodies sliding through the deep blue.

Imagination was keeping Jane's mind off her stomach, which was a good thing.

Hugh Collins located the office of the *'Hawklet'* only because of a scrawled piece of paper in the window. Underneath in the cellar he could hear the thud of the press. They must have to take it apart and move it and reassemble it every time they get into trouble, he thought. That's a lot of work.

The police files which didn't exist and no one knew about had yielded a fair amount of very guarded information. Mr Johnson was a prominent exporter, mainly of fruit. In summary, he sent bananas to New Zealand and received cheese and wool in return. New Zealand, of course, made very good cheese, and Queensland grew very good bananas, passionfruit, guavas, alligator pears, mangoes, custard apples and pineapples. All of which Mr Johnson supplied through a network of growers and packers. He had a lot of interests in transport, which made sense. He was unmarried, which for a man of his age – forty-five – was unusual. There had been two separate complaints about him from underage girls, but the complainant had always refused to testify and the matters had not been proceeded with.

Mr Weston was described as retired and miserly. He had committed an assault with an umbrella on a woman collecting for the Home for Unmarried Mothers. He had been bound over to keep the peace. He owned shares in several of Mr Johnson's companies and – Hugh had found this odd – had divested himself of his house and most of his assets, putting them in his daughter's name several years earlier. Almost as if he expected some unpleasant and expensive discovery. Johnson's companies were, as far as the files knew, unblemished, though the same could not be said of their bananas. Hugh wondered what the 'Hawklet' was going to be able to tell him.

The door opened to his knocking. A shrewish face looked out, said, 'You're a cop!' and tried to slam the door. Hugh had had the forethought to insert a size eleven foot in a size twelve police issue boot into the gap and the door bounced off the metal toecap.

'Oh, all right,' said the shrewish man. 'No wonder they call you flatfoots! Give me the writ and go away.'

'No writ,' said Hugh easily. 'Got a bit of information for you, if you care to have it.'

'Police corruption?' breathed the shrewish man. He was about five feet tall, with longish dark hair that straggled into his collar, crooked teeth, and bright, feverish eyes. Hugh winced.

'Horrible deeds in high life,' he replied. 'I reckoned it was right up your street.' Hugh surveyed Little Lon, a sink of iniquity even at two in the afternoon.

'Come in. My name's Prayse, that's p-r-a-y-s-e, and I've heard all the jokes so don't bother. Horrible deeds, eh?'

'Extremely horrible,' said Hugh.

He looked for somewhere to sit down. The small room was crowded with furniture, books, long strips of paper and a very elderly and smelly bulldog in a basket. Every surface was smudged with ink and covered with a light veil of cigarette ash.

'Tell me,' said Mr Prayse, lighting another gasper.

'Johnson,' said Hugh, trailing his coat. 'And Weston.'

'Johnson,' mused Mr Prayse, 'and Weston. Always suspected some sort of deal between them. Just move some of the books and have a seat. Tea?' he asked, producing a battered kettle from the hob on which it had been steaming.

'No thanks,' said Hugh. He shifted a directory and sat down. Prayse poured out a cup as black as ink. It probably was ink. What else do printers drink?

'Weston. He's a miser. Never wants to let anything or anyone out of his hands. And yet his granddaughter is missing, right?'

'Right,' said Hugh, giving away his first card.

'Have something to do with Johnson?'

'Perhaps,' said Hugh warily. 'What I want to know is, what did Johnson have on Weston?'

'Oh, that old scandal? Everyone's forgotten about it,' said Prayse. 'If that's all you've got you just needed to read the *"Hawklet"*. Now go away and don't waste my time.'

Hugh put five shillings down on the desk, next to the overflowing ashtray. 'Let me buy half an hour of your time,' he said, 'while you tell me all about this scandal that everyone's forgotten.'

'For five bob,' said Mr Prayse, scraping the coins into his hand with alacrity, 'you could have the paper as well. Let's see. Yes. Two years ago Weston had shares in a company which were leaping up in value so fast that the chalkies were getting altitude sickness. Silver River Oil, it was. Californian. The market has fads, you know, fashions, and Silver River Oil was booming. Then all of a sudden it crashed without trace because a report came through that said it didn't have any oil. None at all. It had been a puff from the beginning. With me so far?'

Hugh nodded.

'Well, Weston sold out, just before the prices hit the floor. Made a mint. And Johnson's was the office through which the report came. Johnson didn't have any shares in Silver River Oil. He's not a fool. But Weston would have been ruined if he hadn't sold when he did.'

'Didn't anyone investigate it?' asked Hugh. 'Surely someone noticed.'

'Johnson stuck to the story that the report had never been out of his hands for a moment and Weston said it was a whim. We gave that a headline, "Gold-edged whim". But there's no legs in that old tale, so what have you got for me?'

'Nothing for the moment. But keep your eyes on Weston and Johnson. They're heading for a smash,' said Hugh, and got up.

'Can I have your name?' asked Mr Prayse, pencil poised.

'No,' said Hugh politely, and let himself out.

Even the air in Little Lonsdale Street, not locally considered choice, smelt good to Hugh, and he strode off towards Russell Street with a sense of a job well done.

Mr Prayse swore, said, 'Well, what about that?' and lit another cigarette.

The bulldog snored. The presses rumbled. Another issue of the 'Hawklet' was coming to astonish the world.

At five o'clock Dot gave up. 'She isn't here,' she said. 'You would have drawn her or we would have found her by now. We've searched this camp end to end.'

James stored his fiddle and bow and sat flexing his fingers, absently rubbing some life back into them.

'Where can she be, then, the little bird?' he asked helplessly.

'If she isn't here, at least we know that,' said Dot firmly. 'Now Jane just needs to go and be sick, and we can go home. My Hugh should be back and he'll have found something out.'

Jane was duly sick under a convenient bush. James, Dot and Jane walked back to the road. They had failed. But there had been beautiful music, Jane thought, much relieved.

Somehow, for no sensible or logical reason, that made it better.

The Flora was a hissing and a byword wherever anyone discussed pubs. It had been so for more than eighty years. Rumour had it that it was established as a government plot to poison Fenian diggers coming home from the goldfields with a strike. Elderly shearers, having retired their shears and stone, sat back in country pubs when there were complaints about their own local and said, 'At least it isn't like the Flora.' Hardened wharfies, offered a drink at the Flora as an essential link in a twenty-four hour pub-crawl, had decided that sobriety was their best bet at this point. Police officers entered the Flora only in pairs and only when they really, really had no option, even if that option was (1) resignation from the force or (2) explaining their actions to their sergeant.

It was, of course, dark. And, naturally, it smelt of old drains and beer spilled ten years earlier. And things which Bert didn't want to specify even to himself. The other drinkers were invisible in the gloom. They moved and muttered. They didn't like strangers in the Flora. Not that they got many. Any unwary idiot driven by thirst through the front door would surely have been put off by the barman, who appeared to have been dead for some years. Living humans usually have more flesh. And hair. And expression.

Bert laid a shilling on the bar in a pool of what was at least identifiable as spilled ale, and the aged barman creaked, 'What d'you want?'

'Beer,' said Bert. He had to buy it, but no power on earth could make him drink it. 'You seen Mongrel and Simonds?'

The invisible audience heaved and murmured.

'Why'd you want 'em?' growled the mummified barman.

'I owe 'em some money,' said Bert.

There was a pause composed of blank astonishment. Someone laughed.

'They're barred,' said the aged corpse. 'They started a fight. Last fight they'll start here, Boss said. Yesterday, it was.'

'Any idea where they'd have gone? There's a bob in it,' he added invitingly to the shadows.

'Nah,' said the barman. 'Don't know anything,' he added.

Bert took the horse-piss beer in one hand and turned around to survey the darkness. It seemed to throb gently. They were listening.

'Anyone know where Mongrel and Simonds are? They'll be dark on yer if yer do 'em out of their five bob.'

He had calculated the amount carefully. Five bob was a good sum, but not a fortune. Bert didn't feel like being robbed on the way out.

219

'They might'a gone to the Railway,' said an anonymous voice. 'They ain't banned there yet. They can'ta spent all that coin yet.'

'They had money?' asked Bert skeptically.

'That's what started the fight,' said the unseen voice.

'I'll just leave the bob on the bar, shall I?' asked Bert, and he walked backwards out of the Flora, Cec covering his exit.

'They must be bad bastards, them two,' said Cec.

'Why?' asked Bert, happy to be out in the nice clean St Kilda afternoon on the way to the Railway Arms, a respectable pub.

'I never heard of *anyone* being banned from the Flora,' said Cec.

'Too right,' said Bert.

Five-thirty saw all of the investigators back at Phryne's. She came down the stairs in a red house gown and smiled at them.

'Choose your poison, gentlemen and ladies, and let's exchange information,' she said. Bert and Cec chose tea, to her surprise.

'I never want to drink beer again–' Bert caught himself. 'At least until tomorrow.'

'But we did find out things,' said Cec.

'We didn't find Ruth,' said Dot sadly.

'But I found out about an old scandal involving Mr Weston and Mr Johnson,' said Hugh Collins proudly.

'Good. We'll do this in order and Dot, if she will, will make notes. Bert dear, you look a little tired. What have you found out?'

'We hunted 'em through several pubs,' said Bert, drinking tea with relish. It was just as he liked it, sweet, milky, and very strong. 'Finally found their last port of call, which was the Railway. They were rich,' he said significantly. 'Barman said they had pounds and pounds. Looks like you might have been right, Miss,' he told Phryne. 'Where are rabbits like Mongrel and Simonds going to get pounds and pounds? They ain't got the ... er ... well, they ain't got them, to be big time robbers. You don't find that kind of money on the street.'

'So they were spending some of their fee from murdering Rose Weston,' said Phryne.

'Looks like,' said Bert.

'But you didn't catch up with them,' said Phryne.

'Nah. Gone to ground.'

'Damn. What about you, Hugh?'

'I got a lot,' said Hugh modestly. 'I read those files that aren't supposed to be there and I talked to the editor of the *"Hawklet"*. Strange bird. Thought I was there to give him a writ.'

'So, what did you learn?' prompted Dot.

Hugh gave a summary of the scandal about the Silver River Oil shares, the odd whim of Mr Weston and the sworn oath of Mr Johnson that the report had never left his hands. Dot beamed at him proudly.

'Well, there's the motive for selling Rose,' commented Phryne. 'Weston was buying Johnson's silence. Well done, Hugh dear! Now, Dot, I gather you and James and Jane didn't find any trace of Ruth at the carnival?'

Dot shook her head. 'No sign at all,' she said. 'That elephant lady was very kind to us, showed us around the circus. She tried to make me feel better by telling me she was sure Ruth would turn up all right.'

'And I never want to eat Turkey lolly again,' said Jane, echoing Bert. 'At least, not until tomorrow.'

'Well, we look elsewhere,' said Phryne. 'Now, we can have dinner, then Lin and I are going to see the lantern show called the "Golden Journey to Samarkand", which I promised to attend. I have to meet my new flower maiden Jessica Adams and the others there. Then I'll come back to change for the midnight boat trip. And now, excuse me, I have to learn how to play baccarat.'

'Told you,' said Bert, shuffling a deck of cards which Mr Butler had brought on his silver salver. 'Work of a moment. Imagine that I'm dealing out of a boot with six decks of cards in it. Two players. One is the bank. On Mr Walker's boat, the bank is the house.'

'Why did I think that?' asked Phryne.

'Two cards each,' said Bert, dealing them. 'Aim is to get nine. If either card is a nine – a natural – or an eight, you have to turn it up. On a six or a seven you have to stand. On less than five you have to call for another card, which he deals face up. Bank has to draw to a point under three, stand with a point above six, and can do either of them if the mug has a four at the third card or a nine with the third card. See?'

'Court cards equal...?' asked Phryne.

'Nix,' said Bert.

They played ten rounds of baccarat. Phryne won once, with a natural in her first drawing, and after that the odds fluctuated. Basically, the house won. This was not uncommon. What was the point of having a house if it didn't win?

'And the interest in this game is...?' she asked, yawning delicately behind her hand.

'The side betting,' said Bert. 'This is a simple form of chemmy, where the bank passes from player to player.'

'Oh. Well, thanks a lot, Bert dear. See you on the beach at eleven-fifteen?'

'Yair,' said Bert. 'We'll be there. I'll get the password for tonight. And remember to bring your card.'

'Right,' said Phryne.

Dinner was, as usual, excellent. Mrs Butler, knowing that there was trouble in the house, had decided that soothing, easy to eat food was just the thing to slide past a lump in the throat. Nothing sharp, no pastry, no fried food. So she had cooked a nourishing chicken soup, a white ragout of veal with celery, and a selection of her justly famous sorbets: mango, pineapple and lemon. There was a savoury of Welsh rarebit and a strengthening pot of coffee. Phryne ate well but refused wine. She was going to need all her wits about her.

'We who with songs beguile your pilgrimage
'And swear that Beauty lives though lilies die,
'We poets of the proud old lineage
'Who sing to find your hearts, we know not
    why–'

223

Phryne leaned back in the hard seat of the church hall. Here was a voice which should have been on the Shakespearean stage, a rich, full, evocative voice. Professor Merckens, who was reading, must have been in his late sixties. He was tall, inclining to a corporation, with a shining bald dome and glasses. He was wearing full evening dress, in which he looked very comfortable.

The lantern slides were being worked by a girl in a belly-dancer's costume who jingled faintly as she moved. Her long black hair had been dressed with jasmine-scented oil which almost overcame the scent of tea-urns boiling, old hymn books and settled chalk dust, the standard scent of all church halls. The audience stopped coughing and rustling sweet papers and settled down like birds.

'What shall we tell you? Tales, marvellous tales
'Of ships and stars and isles where good men
　　rest,
'Where nevermore the rose of sunset pales
'And winds and shadows fall toward the West.'

The first slide clicked into place. There, in sepia, was the Great Gate of Baghdad, with camels and horses and small boys in nightshirts driving mules. And the beautiful voice went on:

'And how beguile you? Death has no repose
'Warmer and deeper than that Orient sand
'Which hides the beauty and bright faith of
　　those
'Who made the golden journey to Samarkand.
'Away! For we are ready to a man!
'Our camels sniff the evening and are glad.
'Lead on, O master of the caravan:
'Lead on the Merchant-Princes of Baghdad.'

The lantern slide clicked onto a map. 'You see here the Golden Road,' said the professor. 'It travels all the way across Persia and Turkestan to the cities of Bokhara and Samarkand, ancient seats of luxury and learning before the khanates were conquered by the Tsar in the late nineteenth century. It is 1500 miles long, and they were indeed very brave, who travelled it in caravans when the roads were beset with bandits. The weather was also a fierce enemy. The road follows the river Diyala through the mountains, which are high and cold, even in April.'

Phryne looked at the lantern slide of high mountains. They looked extremely forbidding. Especially if one was relying on a camel to climb them.

'From Baquaba to As-Sadiyah.'

Click. Baquaba, a low collection of tents and hovels covered in snow.

'From Bijar to Resht.'

Click. Bijar, a bigger town, with a turreted fort and a backing of snow-covered ridges. Then a lantern slide of Resht, a blessing, the high mountains behind it, and a place where there was grass and, yes, more sand, but at least it was flat.

'After climbing high, through snow all the way, where the camels' legs are wrapped in felt to save them from frostbite, it must have been wonderful to come down to sea level again. Even in the winter, sea level is warmer than snow-capped peaks.'

Click. The sea, presumably the Caspian. It looked like any other sea, but it would surely have been a sight for snow-blind eyes, wearied by days of dragging protesting camels – and if Phryne knew camels, they would have been protesting bitterly – ten miles a day through mountain passes haunted by wolves, bears and tigers.

'Behind are the Elburz mountains, and now the journey becomes easier. Time to take inventory, perhaps. What had the merchants of Baghdad to sell?

'Have we not Indian carpets dark as wine,
'Turbans and sashes, gowns and bows and
        veils,
'And broideries of intricate designs,
'And printed hangings in enormous bales?

'The caravan crosses the seashore at the edge of the Caspian for many miles. Perhaps there are bandits, but the guards are well trained and well armed. Some are even Pathans, feared tribesmen of Afghanistan, whose oath is their bond – if they can be made to take it. The trading cargo is very valuable.

'We have rose candy, we have spikenard,
'Mastic and terebinth and oil and spice
'And such sweet jams meticulously jarred
'As God's own Prophet eats in paradise.

'Travelling with the caravan there are other religions and other races. There are performers, dancers, musicians, widows, orphaned children; anyone who can pay the caravan master's fee. The Jews are there too:

'And we have manuscripts in peacock styles
'By Ali of Damascus: we have swords,
'Engraved with storks and apes and crocodiles.
'And heavy beaten necklaces, for Lords.'

Click. Lantern slide of a group of Jewish mer-

226

chants, wearing intricately knotted headdresses and long robes. Unlike other pictures of Jews that Phryne had seen, these stared levelly into the camera and were not abashed. She remembered Simon Abrahams and the Zion fantasy. She would warrant that these grave, robed merchants could tell Simon a thing or two about survival in the desert.

'Then upwards again, as the year is moving into summer. To Babul, Sari, Gurghan and then to the pass into Western Turkestan at Arkhabad.'

Click. Not as high as the other pass, perhaps, but dashed uncomfortable. And snowy. And the town that surrounded it was the picture of Oriental disarray.

'Then into kindly meadows, where the camels chew, and the master of the caravan asks about his strangest travellers:

'Who are ye in rags and rotten shoes,
'You dirty-bearded, blocking up the way?
'And they reply
'We are the Pilgrims, master: we shall go
'Always a little further: it may be
'Beyond that last blue mountain barred with
        snow
'Across that angry or that glimmering sea,
'White on a throne or guarded in a cave
'There lives a prophet who can understand
'Why men were born: but surely we are brave,
'Who make the golden journey to Samarkand.'

Phryne blinked tears from her eyes. Who was this poet? Ah, yes. She glanced down to squint at her program. James Elroy Flecker, a young Englishman who had been a diplomat and had

227

fallen in love with the East. That much was clear. Had written this book and a play, *Hassan*. And had died – another one, so young – in 1915, at thirty, of tuberculosis. Damn.

'Sweet to ride forth at evening from the wells
'When shadows pass gigantic on the sand,
'And softly through the silence beat the bells
'Along the golden road to Samarkand.

'Due east the caravan can see the high mountains, but they do not need to urge their failing camels that way. The land is flat and green and full of grain.

'We travel not for trafficking alone
'By hotter winds our fiery hearts are fanned:
'For lust of knowing what should not be known
'We make the golden journey to Samarkand.'

Click. A stone city, with wall and turrets all complete; a great gate; camels and merchants and a high frieze of mountains behind. Samarkand.

'Journey's end. Here they would sell their cargo and buy what Samarkand is most famous for: manuscripts, medicines and carpets. In Bokhara and Samarkand are made the most exquisite colours, the choicest dyes, and the elaborate and delicate patterns. One Bokhara rug of a good size would pay for the whole journey. But all journeys end at last.'

With a sad gesture, the professor recited the last two verses from memory:

'When those long caravans that cross the plain
'With dauntless feet and sound of silver bells
'Put forth no more for glory or for gain
'Take no more solace from the palm-girt wells.
'When the great markets by the sea shut fast

228

'All that calm Sunday that goes on and on:
'When even lovers find their peace at last
'And Earth is but a star, that once had shone.'

There was a pause, then wild applause. The lights came up. The belly-dancing girl shook a few bells as she bowed. Professor Merckens took her hand and bowed again.

'That was so sad!' declared soft-hearted Joannie, blowing her nose.

'It was true,' said Diane, 'and very interesting. Especially about the things they were selling. I would love to see one of those Bokhara carpets.'

'It was beautiful,' whispered Jessica Adams, the new flower maiden, mopping her face unaffectedly.

'It would be wonderful set to music,' said Marie. 'Like Mussorgsky, the Great Gates of Kiev, you know – the "Pictures from an Exhibition". Get a good tenor, a Russian maybe, to chant the verses, and run the music behind the voice.'

'You need to do it,' said Phryne. 'I'm just going to congratulate the professor. Are you coming?'

Phryne collected her maidens and slid to the front of the mob around the tea-urns. Professor Merckens turned at her touch on his arm and smiled.

'That was a wonderful reading,' she told him. 'Thank you very much.'

'Delighted,' he said. 'Miss Fisher?'

'Have we met?'

'No, but I am a great reader of "Table Talk".'

'Here are my flower maidens,' said Phryne. 'Miss Smythe, Miss Adams, Miss Pridham, Miss Bernhoff.'

'A lovely posy for a lovely lady,' said the professor affably. 'Do you want some of this ghastly tea?'

'No,' said Phryne.

'But I think you might find this agreeable,' he said, nodding at the belly-dancer. She bowed gracefully, tinkling her little bells and held out a round brass tray on which were small glasses in intricate wire holders. Phryne took one and sipped. Her mouth loved the taste. It was very sweet but strongly flavoured.

'Mint tea?' she gasped. 'I thought I had tasted mint tea before. This is marvellous.'

'This one is made by crushing and steeping the mint for hours with sugar, which extracts the volatile oils,' he said. Phryne nodded to the girls and they tasted it as well. Mint tea, unlike champagne, met with general approval. The jingling girl then offered a tray of Oriental sweets. Phryne chose a piece of what she had known as an insipid and gluey sweet called Turkish Delight. This was entirely different. She seemed to have a mouthful of rose petals and honey. The old man explained.

'Not made with gelatin, but with the gum of the mastic tree – the merchants of Baghdad were selling mastic. Mine comes from the Greek island of Syros, where I hope to retire very soon. They probably do make the best rahat loukoum in the world, though they say so themselves.'

'Thank you very much,' said Phryne. 'I will remember your sweets – and your voice.'

Professor Merckens bowed and passed on to another urgent congratulator. His show had definitely been a hit. Phryne gathered her maidens out the front, where their parents were to pick them up. Marie was pushed to the forefront of the group by Joannie and Diane.

'Miss Fisher, has there been any word of Rose?' she asked. 'Stop shoving!' she added to Diane behind her.

'No word,' said Phryne. 'But the police are looking for her.'

'I hope she's all right,' said Joannie. 'Do you think she is?'

'She'll be all right,' said Diane. 'She can swim. Come on, Joannie, there's your father's car, and – oh! There's Derek!'

'Yes, he's coming home to supper with us,' said Joannie, and the two of them hurried away. An astonished Phryne could not catch them as they vanished into the crowd. She can swim? What had Diane meant by that?

'Miss Fisher? It was awfully nice of you to choose me,' said Jessica Adams timidly.

'No, it was nice of you to agree to be a last-minute replacement,' said Phryne. 'Has Madame fitted the dress yet?'

'Yes, and it's lovely. But what if Rose comes back? The others are talking as if she won't but what if she does?'

'Even if she comes back, she won't take your place,' soothed Phryne. 'Is this your father? Good evening, Mr Adams. Might I compliment you on your lovely daughter? See you on Saturday morning, Miss Adams. Don't you worry now.'

Phryne packed the girl into her father's dark green Vanguard – nice car – and turned a considering eye on Marie Bernhoff.

'Did you hear what Diane said?' she asked.

'Yes,' said the girl uneasily.

'And do you know what she meant by it?' asked Phryne.

There was a moment of extreme tension.

'Oh, it's too silly,' Marie burst out of her taciturnity. 'Why do perfectly reasonable girls go mad when they meet a halfway pretty boy? Diane and that Derek were playing some kind of trick on Rose, that's all I know. Diane knew where Rose was going when she ran away and they sent her a note. And it had to do with the beach. That's why she said something about swimming. It was a cruel trick, I could tell, Diane was feeling wicked about it, which is why she can't stop talking about it. Hinting. And I,' said Marie furiously, 'am going home to sketch out the beginning of my Samarkand Suite and I don't want to talk about it anymore!'

Thereupon she burst into tears just as her dark, flirtatious father approached and took off his hat. He was a small, magnetic man with the dark brown eyes of a very able sheepdog.

'Tears, daughter?' he asked mildly. 'Miss Fisher, have you been tormenting my offspring?'

'No,' said Phryne. 'I'd diagnose it as artistic temperament. She heard some very moving poetry and wants to make a suite out of it.'

'Ah,' said the dark man with real understanding. He picked up his daughter's hand and drew it through his crooked elbow. 'A nice walk,' he said, 'in the fresh air. Then we shall talk about the scope of the music, and what you want to say.'

'It's all about love and death,' choked Marie, groping for her handkerchief.

'Then you shall write music suitable for love and death,' he said equably.

Phryne watched them walk away. The things we do for love, she thought. Like ruin ourselves, kill ourselves, kill other people. What a race, the human race. Dulcie might be right in her view that the only thing which would really improve the world for the animal kingdom of which she was so fond was to get rid of all of us.

Miss Anna Ross to Mr Rory McCrimmon

I'll come to you at midnight. Mama is out at a church social and will be back late. I will be your wife, husband mine. Then she can't deny us. Anna.

CHAPTER FOURTEEN

The dragon-green, the luminous, the serpent-haunted
   sea,
The snow-besprinkled wine of earth, the white-and-
   blue-flower foaming sea.

James Elroy Flecker
'Gates of Damascus'

Eleven-fifteen found Phryne and Lin on the pier, watching for the lights of a small boat. Bert was worried, and when Bert was worried, he had a tendency to nag.

'Now, you got the card?' he asked.

Phryne held it up.

'And the password tonight is "swordfish". You got it?'

'I've got it.'

'You look beaut,' said Bert, momentarily distracted.

Phryne twirled briefly. Dot, when presented with the twin desiderata, viz, a dress which would look very expensive, elaborate and upper class, and one in which Miss Fisher could, if necessary, swim, had come up with a novel solution. Phryne wore daring but not impossible slinky black silk evening pyjama trousers with a loose silk singlet and a beautiful flowing claret-coloured sequinned wrap which could be jettisoned if push came – so to speak – to shove. The lights approached. The Ace of Clubs was coming in.

'Good luck,' said Bert, and faded into the background.

The Ace of Clubs was a stocky, strong little boat in a very high state of polish. She rocked alongside the pier as a gangplank was laid out for the feet of the well-heeled, and Phryne and Lin stepped into line. A large sailor was checking cards and bending a huge head forward to listen to the password before allowing anyone onto the gangplank.

'Swordfish,' whispered Phryne into the great ear, feeling like an extra in a Hollywood film, and she was allowed to move past the monumental matelot and onto the deck. It was wood, holystoned almost white.

She surveyed the gamblers. Curious. She knew several of them. A barrister famed for his ferocious cross-examination, nicknamed 'the beast'. He was escorting a giggly lady in cerise who had already dined rather too well. There were two society ladies famed for the scantiness of their attire and the youth of their attendants. A couple of young men, just out of school, Phryne decided, who were finding this all exceptionally exciting and were drawling and smoking gaspers to cover their emotion. A famously wealthy squatter. A famously poverty-stricken author. A group of gentlemen who looked more horsy than salty. Mr Walker's clientele, of course, would self-select for the rich and silly. And a fine collection was present this night.

The air was full of expensive scents and the jingle of jewellery almost covered the rumble of the engines. The Ace of Clubs, Bert had explained, was a steam yacht, which gave her plenty of available horsepower in the event of a sudden maritime emergency, like a school of whales or policemen, or an attack by pirates or tax inspectors. She was indeed a shipshape and Bristol fashion boat, every line coiled and every rope's end brailed or spliced. The crew were unobtrusive but seemed chosen for heft.

The Ace of Clubs pulled out into the bay and began to turn, screws rumbling, for the trip across to Williamstown. The ladies and gentlemen were ushered inside.

The original crew's quarters had been transformed. There was carpet on the floor, a selection of blackwood furniture which made Lin whistle soundlessly, a large table and a lot of comfortable chairs, and even a chandelier. The walls were white and the extra decorations were gold and it was opulent and just a little stagey, as though it was a film set rather than a real room.

Presumably behind all this there must be the usual offices, and to judge by the quality of the hors d'oeuvres and the quantity of the champagne, a scullery and a kitchen. The attendant dealer was dressed in a spanking white naval uniform, with peaked cap.

'A nice touch,' said Phryne to Lin. 'Who inspires confidence like the navy? I never asked you, Lin dear. Do you gamble?'

'A little,' he admitted. 'But on games of skill, not chance. I do like bridge,' he admitted. 'I'm teaching Camellia. I know you don't play cards,' he said defensively.

'I'm sure that she will be a much better pupil than me. In fact, Jo Jo the Dog Faced Boy would be a better pupil than me. Well, I suppose I shall have to waste some money,' sighed Phryne.

She was conducted to a seat on the other side of the table to the naval dealer and the game began.

Baccarat, thought Phryne, as she turned over a three and a five, was the most boring game ever invented. Eight. The dealer had a jack, which counted for nothing, and a king, which also counted for nothing. He dealt himself a ten and Phryne won. Two more cards: a king and a ten. Phryne lost. Two more cards: an ace and a ten. Phryne lost.

This went on for about ten minutes, after which

she stood and gracefully yielded her chair to an eager young gentleman with more money than sense.

'Five pounds poorer,' she mourned to Lin.

'Five pounds richer,' he smiled at her. 'I bet that you'd win the first round.'

'Let's have a chat with the captain, eh?' said Phryne. 'Now that we're even.'

She laid a confiding hand on the huge forearm of one of the sailors. 'Can you ask Mr Walker if he would spare me a word? Miss Phryne Fisher. He might have heard of me.'

That Mr Walker had heard of Miss Fisher was evident. She and Lin were ushered into the captain's cabin and the door shut with some speed. A large sailor leaned against it.

Mr Walker was sitting in an armchair. He was beautifully dressed in a handmade cashmere suit which had not been tailored in Melbourne. He was a slick, hard-faced man with a chin on which one could break rocks, and thin red lips. His eyes were as compassionate and kind as chips of flint.

'The Hon. Miss Fisher,' he said in an even, icy tone. 'The society detective. Do sit down. I'm sure that we can clear up any little misunderstanding. One way or the other,' he added, looking meaningfully at the sailor, who was patting his breast pocket. The air was heavy with menace. Phryne shattered the mood as she stepped forward and shook Mr Walker's astonished hand.

'Mr Walker, how nice to meet you. The thing to do in these situations,' Phryne said, 'is not to get caught up in cinema expectations. It doesn't have to go like that. We just write another script, one in which I get what I want and no one gets shot. I am investigating an attempted murder and I am not in the least interested in your gambling activities, though I must say you do run a very nice, tight little ship. It must cost a fortune in brass polish alone. I have recently taken advice,' she said delicately, 'which indicates that you know all about gambling, which does not interest me at all. But I am vitally interested in whether a girl went overboard from your boat on Tuesday night. Now, I cannot imagine a businessman like yourself allowing such a fuss as a suicide attempt. It might have been an accident. But I need to know. And when I am fully informed, I will go away, and I promise not to darken the doorway of any of your establishments again.'

She paused. Mr Walker shook his head, puzzled.

'This would be Tuesday night,' he said slowly.

'Yes. Rose Weston, a rather unstable girl, was found on the beach about an hour after midnight. Been in the water for some time. Hit over the head.'

'I heard about it,' he said. Then he reached a decision. The flinty eyes softened to something like quartz. 'Very well, Miss Fisher. You may talk to any of my crew, and I will take you all over my boat. I will also give you a lift back to St Kilda. And after that, we are quits. Right?'

'Right,' agreed Phryne. She was pleased that she had not had to disclose the presence of her little gun, in the purse on her lap, aimed squarely at Mr Walker's well-tailored middle. She rose. Mr Walker opened the door for her.

The steam yacht was a very nice little boat,

Phryne decided after an hour's tour. The engines were in peak condition, kept so by a greasy man and a greasier boy, both of whom had been below and hadn't seen anything. The kitchen was run by an excitable Swiss, who had informed *Ihre Altesse, gnadige frau* that nothing untoward had happened on his side of the ship on Tuesday night except for the terrible discovery that he was down to his last crate of the Pol Roger.

The sailors who were not on guard duty were engaged in sailing the boat and in drinking a nice cuppa. They were sitting on the after deck, out of sight of the punters. They scrambled to their feet as Mr Walker led Phryne and Lin up the companionway.

'Boys,' said Mr Walker, 'I want you to tell this lady anything she wants to know. Then take her back to the main saloon.'

'Anything, boss?' quavered a red-capped sailor.

'Anything. Just answer her questions,' snarled Mr Walker, reverting to type, and left. There was general relaxation and also general puzzlement. Phryne, in the half-light, twinkled and glittered.

'What do you want to know, Miss?' asked the sailor in the red cap.

'Tuesday,' said Phryne. 'On the way out of St Kilda. Anyone go overboard from this boat?'

'No,' said Red-cap. 'We've got Tom for that, anyway. Some of the mugs lose their shirts and want to jump. Tom retrieves 'em.'

Tom grinned modestly. He was dressed in an airy costume of blue bathers and a fleecy dressing gown.

'I was a diver in the navy,' he told Phryne.

'Couldn't find a job when I got out. This is a good one. Anyone goes overboard, we ring down to stop engines and reverse, and I go in with the life preserver. Then we empty them out and dry them and send them home. Mr Walker doesn't like scandals. I've dragged in a few over the years but Tuesday was quiet.'

'All right. A quiet night. Did anyone see anything, hear anything, unusual in another boat?'

The crew looked at each other. Heads shook.

'Nah,' said a huge Maori. 'There was more noise than normal because of the carnival. More people around, too. Boss thought takin's would be down, but they ain't. One mug punter born every minute. What gave you the idea that we had anything to do with this murder? This is a well-run boat, this is.'

'I know that when the cops turn up they'll find that everyone is blamelessly playing bridge,' said Phryne. 'But isn't it rather expensive, throwing all those firearms into the sea?'

The big man grinned. 'They don't go in the water,' he said. 'They go in the safe in the captain's office. We're all members of a small arms club,' he said. 'We all got pistol licences. Proper, legal licences.'

'And you were all on the way home from a pigeon shooting contest?' guessed Phryne. 'And put the guns in the safe to make sure that there were no accidents?'

'That's how it is, lady, we take our bible oath,' affirmed Red-cap.

'That's very clever,' said Phryne, genuinely impressed.

'So why did you think we had anything to do with your murder?' asked Red-cap.

'You're the only boat going this way this late, apart from the big ocean liners,' said Phryne.

'And it's a long way down from them big buggers,' said Tom. 'She'd likely be dead when she hit the water, like falling off a building. Water's hard as concrete when you hit from a height. I should know,' he added. 'I dived off the bridge of a sinking ship off the Dardenelles and if I hadn't had my hands above my head, I would've been a goner. Lots of blokes were.'

'Exactly,' said Phryne. 'Did anyone notice any small boats about?'

'Small like a rowboat?' asked Red-cap. 'There were a few around. Fishermen. They're as mad as punters. I didn't see one with a girl in it, though.' He leered briefly.

'Have any of you seen a nasty pair called Simonds and Mongrel around on the beach? Last Tuesday night, for example?'

Red-cap drew in a censorious breath. 'You don't want to have anything to do with scum like them,' he protested. 'We don't either.'

'Nevertheless,' said Phryne gently, 'they were seen around the pubs flashing large sums of money.'

'Were they?' asked Red-cap. 'Well, well.' He did not elaborate. He looked around at the rest of the crew. They all shook their heads. 'No,' he told Phryne. 'We didn't see 'em. And if we had, we'd have run 'em off, because the boss don't like Simonds and Mongrel.'

'Heard they got banned from the Flora,' said

the diver.

'Don't be a donkey,' said Red-cap. 'No one gets banned from the Flora.'

'It's true nonetheless,' Phryne affirmed. 'I have it on very good authority. Thank you for your time, gentlemen,' she added, distributing coins. 'And I'm so glad I don't have to swim home.'

The crew laughed politely.

'You must have impressed the boss something cruel,' Tom told her. 'We ain't never been told to answer questions before. Just come this way, Miss. Boss wants you to go back into the main saloon, and Hans'll bring you a drink.'

Settled in a spindle-legged chair with a glass of the Pol Roger, Phryne sighed.

'Do you believe them?' asked Lin.

'Yes,' said Phryne. 'I had such a nice little theory about this boat. But one must never cling to theories. Unless Rose was out in a rowboat with a fisherman, which sounds unlikely, she didn't go into the sea from a ship. Which takes us right back to those thugs, and the seashore itself. And the strange involvement of that very pretty boy and the dark girl who was clinging to him – Diane. Apparently they knew where Rose was and decoyed her out onto the beach where whatever happened to her happened. Never mind,' she said, raising her glass. 'There is still champagne.'

Phryne slept well. She woke at seven with the conviction that Mongrel and Simonds had got into the house during the night and were garrotting her. However, she found, she was merely suffering from Lin embracing her from one side and Ember lying curled on the bedclothes on the other side.

She loosened the sheet from across her throat, removed Ember from his stranglehold position and listened to the house wake up. Jane by herself in her room, bereft of Ruth. Where was the girl? Mrs Jackmann coming in to get her patient ready for the day. Mr Butler vacuuming the breakfast room with his patent suction cleaner. Mrs Butler in the kitchen, clattering pots. James tuning his fiddle. Molly barking to announce a caller, or possibly a bird or an innocent aeroplane. Friday. What had she to do on Friday?

Confront Diane the flower maiden, that's what. How was she to extract the girl from her family? There was no chance that Diane would talk with Mama in hearing distance. Perhaps it would be easier to operate on the weaker of the partnership, the young man Derek. Girls with a serious case of love could be difficult. They would allow themselves to be burned at the stake rather than betray Him. But boys – Phryne knew a little about boys. Boys could be seduced.

She caught sight of her own slow smile in the mirror, the red lips curving, the green eyes merciless. Salome, she thought. Or Herodias, at least. My, my, Miss Fisher, how very dangerous you look.

Now to get Derek's address. And today, Phryne recalled, Bert had promised to introduce her to the man in charge of prostitution in St Kilda. That ought to be interesting. It was going to be a busy day, and she ought to get started right away.

Lin moved an arm and asked sleepily, 'Phryne?' His hand travelled slowly down her shoulder to her breast, leaving sparkles of sensation in its wake. 'Is it morning yet?'

'No,' said Phryne, slipping down beside him again. 'Not yet.'

Phryne saw Lin off with a kiss to return to his wife and her garden. Marie Bernhoff provided Derek's address. She told Phryne that she had already sketched the shape of her Samarkand Suite and even her father was impressed. Diane, when telephoned, was visiting Joannie and not available. Derek, when telephoned, was also at Joannie's house and Phryne had no mind to call him there. Shelving the seduction for the moment, she visited the patient. Rose was looking better. The swelling had begun to go down and she had a face again, not a carnival mask. That said, she was not ready for a close-up with Mr de Mille. Movie stars tended to have fewer broken ribs.

'Hello, Rose,' said Phryne. 'How are you? You're looking better.'

'Feel a bit better,' muttered Rose, careful of the split lip.

'Good. You won't be going near your family again, you know,' said Phryne chattily. 'So I want you to think about where you would like to go. When you are better.'

'They'll come and take me back,' wailed Rose suddenly. Her split lip broke again and spilled blood all down her nightgown. Mrs Jackmann mopped and tutted.

'No, they won't,' said Phryne.

She sounded so sure that Rose stopped wailing. 'How do you know?' she demanded.

'Because they will be in jail,' Phryne told her. 'Detective Inspector Robinson has your diary. All you have to do is swear that it is true. Then down go Grandpapa and Johnson and all. Did your mother know about it?'

'No,' said Rose. 'Or Dad. I just ... couldn't talk to Dad. Not after...'

'Quite,' said Phryne. 'Now, you just rest and leave it to me.'

'Don't have a choice, do I?' said Rose, and almost chuckled. Phryne raised an eyebrow. The girl had bottom, after all.

'For the moment, no,' she agreed. 'By the way, here is your capital.' She laid the purse on Rose's lap. Both hands came down to clutch it, to check that the money was inside. Then she hid the purse under the bed clothes.

'That was the price of my virtue,' said Rose blankly.

'Get better and you can spend it,' Phryne ordered, and left the room.

Bert and Cec were waiting for her in the parlour. They looked worried.

'You sure that you want to do this, Miss?' asked Bert. 'Me and Cec can go and see him.'

'Wouldn't miss it for worlds,' Phryne assured him. 'I am having a lot of success mixing with the local crime czars – isn't that what the American films call them?'

'So far,' said Bert. 'Mr Walker asked around about you this morning. Just to make sure that the story was kosher.'

'Well, it was,' said Phryne. 'Mr Walker is not a man one would fib to, not if one expected to live a full, rich and satisfying life.'

'Yair,' said Bert. 'Also, he's looking for Simonds and Mongrel. Did you happen to mention them, careless like?'

'I might have,' said Phryne. 'I hope I find them first. I would like to hear what they have to say,' she added.

Bert pursed his lips. 'Have to be fast,' he opined. 'You driving?' he added with well-concealed fear as Phryne led the way to the big car purring in the street. Mr Butler, living up to his billing as a chauffeur, had already started it and left it running warmly. Phryne got in and so, with some trepidation, did Bert and Cec.

'Which way?' asked Phryne, allowing the big car to take up first gear.

'Straight down past the George,' said Bert, hanging on to his hat.

Phryne was aware that there were such things as speed limits, but had never allowed the fact to cramp her style. The Hispano-Suiza was built for speed, and she didn't want it to mope. They zoomed past the George in a fine flurry of pedestrians who yelled and shook their fists, and then slowed so that Bert could instruct Phryne in the protocols of the establishment she was about to visit.

'This is the high class brothel,' said Bert. 'The highest we got in Melbourne. It's run by an old French biddy of a Madame, very starchy and correct. She's got a stable of fifteen girls and a lot of muscle to back them up. You be careful, Miss.'

'French, eh? They know how to run a house of ill-repute. They're legal in France. But you were talking about a "him". The brothel doesn't belong to Madame, then?' asked Phryne.

'No, it's actually the professor, and he's a powerful man. He's like Mr Walker. No one takes him on.'

'Fine. Is this the place?'

'Yair,' conceded Bert. 'We'll come with you.'

'You will wait in the car,' instructed Phryne. 'If I am not back in one hour, take it and get Jack Robinson. Don't argue. You are my insurance.'

'All right,' said Bert.

The building was a well-maintained old two-storey house, Federation style, with cornucopias and gargoyles. There was nothing to announce its avocation except a small brass plate, like a doctor's, beside the door. It just said 'The University. Please Ring and Enter.'

Phryne rang and pushed the door. It was locked. She rang again.

'I'm sorry, Miss,' said a magisterial butler who finally answered. He looked down a considerable length of nose at Phryne. 'We don't buy anything at the door or contribute to charities by collection.'

Phryne had been outfaced by experts and the butler, though impressive, did not come close to inspiring the awe generated by such giants amongst their profession as her father's Mr Harker or La Princesse Du Salles' M'sieur Gaston. She produced her own card, gave it to the butler and said sweetly, 'I am sure that the professor would not like to keep me waiting on the doorstep.'

247

Butlers are as susceptible to a title as other people, and this one gave in quickly. 'Of course not, Miss Fisher, do come in,' he said, showing her through a lofty hall and into a very well appointed parlour.

The theme was Chinese and it was all exquisite: paintings, porcelain, carpets and furniture. The brothel business was doing well, it seemed. Phryne was inspecting a jade bowl of perfect green, flawless, without any carving or mark, so thin that light fell through it and glowed like early spring, when the door opened and a parlourmaid came in.

She was as perfect as the jade bowl in her way: black dress, cap and apron all complete. Not only a parlourmaid but a French parlourmaid, with the correct 'follow-me-lads' ribbons on her cap. Phryne grinned.

'The professor is expecting you,' she announced. 'This way, Miss Fisher.'

Phryne followed biddably. She was shown into a large library. A fire crackled in the hearth. The air was full of the scent of old books mixed with a faint aroma of sandalwood. Tea was laid out on a linen-draped table. A man rose from a leather armchair by the fire and placed his pipe on a brass tray.

'Well, well,' said Miss Fisher, astonished. 'We meet again.'

Miss Anna Ross to Miss Mavis Sutherland
19 May 1913

Mama refused Mr McCrimmon's proposal, Mavis. I don't know why. When I burst into tears and de-

manded that she tell me she just shut her mouth with a snap and said 'He is not a good risk.' When I told her I loved him she said that I'd recover and find a better man, but there isn't a better man, Mavis, not for me. If I can't have Rory I will die a maid. I'll become one of those bitter old women who wear jangly things at their waists and grudge their boarders a spoonful of sugar to their tea. But Rory still loves me and I have a plan which will make Mother come around. I haven't been well latterly. I caught a cold and now I am running a fever. It isn't unpleasant except that the weather is very hot. But how are you? Are the dreams gone, now that you are out of London?

I very much hope that I will come to Britain and that I will see you again, your distracted but loving friend, Anna.

CHAPTER FIFTEEN

Have you not girls and garlands in your homes?

James Elroy Flecker
The Golden Journey to Samarkand

'Miss Fisher,' said Professor Merckens. 'How very nice of you, to come and cheer an old man's solitude. Do sit down. Tea? Chinese or Indian? And will you smoke?'

'I will,' said Phryne, sitting down and groping for a cigarette. 'Indian tea, if you please, milk and one lump of sugar. Professor Merckens, dear,

249

you are a Napoleon of crime! How very enter-
prising of you!'

'Spare my blushes,' he said, picking up the pipe
again and settling back into his chair. A curiously
coloured cat slipped across the room and swarmed
up, taking a balanced seat on the professor's shoulder. It had eyes the colour of sapphires and it
stared straight at Phryne, who stared back.
Eventually Phryne and the cat broke their gaze
simultaneously and the cat turned her head away,
refusing to notice Phryne again.

'What a very beautiful creature,' said Phryne.
'I've never seen a cat like that before.'

The cat had a wheat-coloured body and four
stockings in dark brown, and dark ears like a
polecat. There the resemblance ended. It was a
sinuous, sensuous, and at the moment censorious
cat who patently did not approve of Phryne. The
professor reached up a hand and slid his stroking
fingers under the cat's jaw. It began to purr.

'She is Thai Thai, a Siamese cat,' he told
Phryne. 'A present from visiting royalty. There,
my precious,' he soothed. Thai Thai pointedly
removed her face from his touch and scolded
him in a high, many-vowelled yowl. 'Oh dear me,
yes,' he said. 'How could I have forgotten?'

He poured a little milk into a saucer and placed
it on a silk tablemat on the floor. Thai Thai leapt
neatly down and crouched next to it, folding each
paw under and putting her ears back like a kitten
before her curled tongue touched a drop of the
sacred fluid. Phryne felt that she was witnessing
a devotional rite.

'I don't know where she learned such language.

The gutters of Siam, I assume, though she was born in the palace. She was brought up on goat's milk,' explained the professor. 'I prefer it myself. But she does appreciate the extra cream in cow's milk. Now, perhaps I can indulge in a brief apologia pro vita mea while you drink your tea.'

'And before I expire of curiosity,' said Phryne, taking up her cup. It was, of course, very good tea. And petits fours which she could have sworn came from Anatole's to have with it.

'Well, you see, I was always lazy,' said the professor, puffing gently at his pipe. 'I excelled in some subjects, because they came easily to me. Languages, for instance. I drifted along through school, won a scholarship to Cambridge. My parents, on the contrary, were hard working chapel folk. My brothers and sisters were all virtuous persons, married early and worked themselves into early graves, most of them. But I was – well, disinclined to make an effort. I liked sleep, and good food, and amusing company, and the theatre, and books. That sort of philosophy requires money, and I didn't have any. I was quite a skilled gambler, but after I was caught cheating I had to leave my clubs. I went, as is often the case with the exiled, to Paris. There I was reduced to abject poverty, both by some unwise investments and some very bad company indeed. There my future wife Marie found me, sitting on a doorstep, weeping quietly for the harshness of my fate, though it was all my own fault entirely. More tea?'

'No,' said Phryne, stubbing out her cigarette and lighting another. 'Do go on.'

'Marie was a *fille du joie* at a house in the Place

251

L'Opera. Are you familiar with Paris?'

'Certainly,' said Phryne. The cat Thai Thai completed her milk ritual and returned to her perch on the professor's shoulder, curling her tail neatly around her for balance. They made a pretty picture. She was reminded strangely of Dr Nikola.

'So she took me to her house, and Madame suggested that I could teach English to the girls and earn my keep. I did so. As you are aware, prostitution is an avocation in France, a legal job. Of course one has to register with the police and there is a lot of corruption, especially in places like Montmartre, pah, but Marie's house was a good solid bourgeois operation. She was happy enough there. So was I.

'Then the strangest thing happened – you might think that it was Meant. My brother Charlie died and left me this house. Really, it was providential. My Marie, though very desirable to me, was getting a little too old for the trade, and we had saved up enough between us to come to Australia and establish ourselves rather sumptuously.'

'Indeed,' said Phryne, 'the business must be going very well. That jade bowl, now; my friend is Chinese and recently brought back many things from the mainland, and even he doesn't have anything as beautiful.'

'Lin Chung,' said the professor, stroking Thai Thai. 'Eldest son of the Lin family of Little Bourke Street. Recently married to Camellia, and there lies a tale. She is not the Camellia he thinks she is.'

'You are very well informed,' said Phryne, not betraying the fact that Camellia herself had told

Lin that she was not the Camellia he had expected.

'Knowledge is power,' said the professor. 'That is how I have managed to gain, and indeed hold, my present exalted position. After a few years in this profession, Miss Fisher, one knows something about everyone.'

'Mr Johnson?' asked Phryne.

'I do not cater for such tastes,' said the professor calmly. 'He frequents another place of business.'

'Mr Weston?'

'A miser. He has no interest in sins of the flesh. Reputed to have sold his daughter to Johnson for his help in a share market fraud.'

'Detective Inspector Robinson,' challenged Phryne. The professor laughed.

'Likes orchids,' he said.

'Aha,' said Phryne. 'I am sure that you know all about me,' she said. 'And you are welcome. My life is an open, if rather highly coloured, book. And I'm sure that you know I have no intention of trying to interfere with anything you are doing in your own business – I am not suicidal and you have a fearsome reputation. In fact, Professor, I need some help,' said Phryne.

'A missing girl?' he asked wearily.

'Two. One is Rose Weston and the other is my own adopted daughter Ruth. I want them back. If I have to tear the town apart to find them, I will,' she said, showing her teeth. Thai Thai rose to her paws and hissed at Phryne, objecting to her tone.

'I believe you,' said the professor. 'And it is an earnest of my own trust in you that I will not tell anyone else that you have Rose Weston safe in your own house. I do have some information about Rose, though. Two low criminals called Simonds and ... er ... Mongrel attempted to sell her to a house of joy in Fitzroy. My colleague in the same position telephoned me and asked for my advice, and I told him on no account to allow this deal to go through as the girl was from a prominent family and undue publicity could not be avoided in the event of this purchase being approved. Also – forgive me – that she was promiscuous and hysterical and would not prove to be a worthwhile investment.'

'No more than the truth,' agreed Phryne.

'The girl, my colleague said, appeared to have been drugged. The two criminals removed her from the brothel and took her away. They did not make the same offer again, or I would have heard of it. Such things are not common,' said the professor severely. 'We do not white slave. The girls enter the profession voluntarily. I have a waiting list of young women who want to join my establishment. Here they receive suitable health care, instructions in various methods of retaining their vigour, good food, good accommodation, paid holidays and when they wish to leave us, a small party and a dowry. They may keep one of their children while they are here and after they leave they may have as many as they please. Run on French lines a brothel is just another place of business, with no need for emotional scenes. I do not like emotional scenes,' said the professor, and Phryne got a sudden intimation of why he was so feared. He did not have the gun-in-pocket aggression of Mr Walker but he was master of more secrets than a cabinet minister. How on earth had he found out about Camellia? And Rose Weston? The professor was a very dangerous man. But compared to the cold, insecurity and squalor of Fitzroy Street late on a Friday night, his house must seem like a palace to a working girl. Medical care. Dowries.

She suppressed a start of surprise as Thai Thai, leaving the professor's shoulder, landed as lightly as a leaf on the arm of her chair. The dark ears were forward, the eyes focused, and a gloved paw was laid delicately on Phryne's hand. Phryne caressed the silky coat and was rewarded with a pleasant remark in Siamese. Thai Thai began an elaborate wash, with whuffling noises.

'She has the softest fur,' said Phryne.

'That is a mark of considerable honour,' said the professor. 'I knew you were quality, Miss Fisher.'

'Do call me Phryne,' she said, watching the cat. Thai Thai's self adoration made Ember look modest.

'Phryne, thank you, my own name is Jeremiah. I shall institute enquiries about Ruth. You have a photograph of her?'

Phryne laid it on the table.

'She is thirteen? Yes. And she went missing on Wednesday, in the street outside the town hall. Thence decoyed to the circus and left tied up in a tent; the ropes being cut by the time her kidnapper came back. And he is now in police custody. Just so. I should have an answer for you by tonight,' he said. 'I will telephone.'

'I am very much obliged,' said Phryne. 'And perhaps you and Madame Marie will do me the honour of dining with me after this is all over?'

'You wish to further our acquaintance?' asked the professor, taken aback.

'Certainly,' said Phryne. 'Now I really must go. My minders will be getting nervous. I've been away for almost an hour.'

'You are a cautious woman with whom it is a pleasure to do business,' the professor told her. 'And I am delighted to accept your prospective invitation. See Miss Fisher out, Fifi.'

Of course, thought Phryne as she was escorted out of the University. What other name could the parlourmaid in a brothel ever have?

She was laughing about it as she jumped into the big car. Bert threw his chewed cigarette end into the gutter.

'You cut it fine,' he said. 'We was about to go for the jacks.'

'No need,' said Phryne. 'We got on swimmingly and he's going to ring me tonight. Now, can I drop you gentlemen anywhere? I am going home,' she said.

'We'll walk,' said Bert hastily, hopping out of the car. 'Me and Cec have a few people still to see.'

Phryne thought of calling him a coward, and refrained. One didn't say things like that to a pair of Anzacs. And perhaps her driving style was a little flamboyant. But that's what all those cylinders were for, she told herself as she pressed the self starter and heard the engine roar.

Phryne finally managed to catch the young man

Derek at his own house, before four. He was delighted by the idea of a tête à-tête at five with the delectable Miss Fisher. From his practised compliments, Phryne considered that he had been courted by older women before. That would make her surprise attack more shocking.

She assembled her household and told them that she was going to have an interview with Derek in her own rooms, that she didn't want to hear a squeak from anyone, and that Hugh Collins would oblige her by entering her large wardrobe with his notebook, pencil and flashlight. She suggested to him that now was the time to visit the amenities should he feel that might be necessary.

He did. Dot ascended to the boudoir to help Phryne find a suitable boy-seducing gown.

'How far do you mean to go with this?' she asked, thinking not so much of Phryne's virtue but of her own intended's modesty.

'As far as I need to,' said Phryne grimly. 'Make sure that Mrs Jackmann shuts the guest room door, won't you? It would be very bad if the little toad finds out that Rose is here, and bad for Rose, too. She is just beginning to emerge from her "amnesia". What about this one?' she asked, holding up a sheer length of blue silk with a shimmering muslin overlay. The neckline plunged, as did the back.

'Bit obvious.' Dot bit her lip.

'Don't worry, Hugh won't be able to see me,' Phryne assured her. 'Get into the wardrobe and check, if you like.'

'No,' said Dot, embarrassed.

'Boys like obvious,' Phryne told her. 'Men

prefer subtle but boys only stop thinking about sex when they are thinking about food. Or football. The adolescent male is a strange and horrible creature unless, of course, one's tastes run the same way.'

'And yours do?' asked Dot, swallowing her jealousy.

'Not anymore. When I was an adolescent they did. Hot, so to speak, to the hand but they are so fleeting.' Phryne looked momentarily sad.

Dot, thanking her patron saint that she didn't actually know what Miss Phryne was talking about, laid out a milk-coloured nightdress and negligee.

'If you're going to be obvious,' she suggested, 'why not be real obvious?'

Phryne gave her a hug.

'Good idea. Now, I've just time to bathe and change. Keep the others out of the way, especially James. You may explain to him what is happening if you think he ought to know. You let the boy in, Dot dear, bring him here, and leave him to me.'

Mr Rory McCrimmon to Miss Anna Ross

It's no good, Anna. I cannot marry you. It would not be fair. And now it seems that I cannot wait for you either, my bonny bird. I sail home on Wednesday. James has arranged it. Rory

CHAPTER SIXTEEN

'Oh Sister, Sister, let me live
And all that's mine I'll truly give.'
'Your own true love I'll have, and more,
But thou shalt never come ashore.'

Anon
'The Cruel Sister'

When Derek was ushered into Miss Fisher's boudoir the lights were low and a vision of loveliness was half sitting, half lying on a sofa before a small bright fire. There was a black cat curled at the foot of her sofa. She was draped in milky white fabric which entirely failed to hide the contours of her body underneath.

He swallowed dryly. Miss Fisher waved him to approach, and he sank down on the fur rug in front of the fire. Everything scented, he noticed; the fire was made of some aromatic wood, there was a scented sleeve over the low electric light, and Miss Fisher herself exuded some faint, attractive, Oriental perfume.

'How kind of you to visit,' she murmured, so that he had to lean close to hear her, 'when you must have so many calls on your time.'

'For anyone as beautiful as you I would always make time,' he said, a reply straight from the last Theda Bara movie he had seen.

259

'Sweet boy,' said Phryne. She trailed a hand over his face and felt him shiver. He really was transcendently beautiful, she thought. It would be diverting to really seduce him. But she was right about adolescent boys. Hot to the hand and over in a moment. Seducing him would probably muddle the chain of evidence she was trying to construct. Damn. 'All the girls are after you, I observed,' she said.

'Just Joannie and Diane,' he replied defensively. 'And they're...'

'Good girls?' drawled Phryne. 'Ah, I have never been a good girl.'

She allowed him to lean close enough to kiss her red lips. For a beginner, he did rather well. She wondered how Hugh in her wardrobe was managing with the sounds he could undoubtedly hear. Phryne had not lied to Dot. Hugh could not see her from the wardrobe. Phryne indulged herself with the young man's mouth for a full minute. Then she gently pushed him away.

'You must have fun with the girls, though they are good girls,' she hinted.

'Just a few practical jokes,' he said. 'Kiss me again,' he requested. Phryne kissed him again.

'Tell me,' ordered Phryne. 'Divert me. I get so bored,' she said untruthfully but within the Elinor Glyn genre.

'Well, there was Rose,' he said doubtfully. 'But that didn't work. We were meant to meet her at midnight,' he told Phryne. 'But she wasn't there. And then Diane found her, face down in the sand. So it didn't work as a joke.'

'And what did you do then with Diane?' asked

Phryne arching her back. The sight took the young man's breath away.

'We ran away,' he said artlessly. 'Someone was coming and we ran into the carnival. And then she let me kiss her,' he said. 'In the dark, among the tents. It was exciting. But not as exciting as you, Miss Fisher.'

'But Rose has been missing for days. How did you know where to find her to make your assignation, clever boy?' Her fingers toyed with his shirt buttons.

'I knew,' said the boy proudly. 'The men she associated with, they know me. I know them. She's a tart, that Rose.'

'My dear boy, where did you find such bad playmates?' asked Phryne, kissing him again. But there were things which kissing was not going to elicit from the boy.

'Oh, just around,' he said airily. The fingers which had strayed amongst his buttons now had him firmly by the collar. Phryne sat up, shedding her languor, and shook him.

'Unless you want to spend the night in the cells, dear boy, you'd better tell me how you know such creatures as Mongrel and Simonds,' she said firmly.

'I don't have to tell you anything!' he protested.

'No, you don't. However, you are already guilty of attempted murder, so anything else you say has to be an improvement. Didn't you notice that Rose was unconscious? She was lying face down in the sand below the high tide mark – didn't you notice that? I bet Diane did.'

'She got me into this,' said the young man,

slumping against Phryne's silk-clad knee.

'Tell me all about it,' purred Phryne. In the wardrobe, Hugh licked his pencil.

'How do you mean, attempted murder?' His eyes were blue and piteous in his angelic face.

'Well, put it to yourself, dear boy. If you leave someone in a situation where they can't move and, as it might be, the tide is creeping up as it does every night – and you can even feel the difference between high tide and beyond the tide, the sand is softer, you don't need a light – then you've left them in peril of death and if they die, it is your fault.'

'I didn't know she was unconscious,' protested the boy. 'Diane said she was drunk. It was dark. I didn't know.'

'Of course not,' soothed Phryne. 'What was Diane's stake in this?'

'She wants me to marry her,' said the boy miserably. 'I've got to marry money. Diane's all right, I suppose. And she really wants me. And she's got oodles of money. Her father has, I mean. The reason I know Simonds is he's my cousin. You can ruin me now, I don't care anymore. I grew up in North Brighton,' he confessed brokenly, as if admitting to leprosy in the family.

'I grew up in Richmond and my mother was a Mrs Mopps and my father was a waster,' Phryne told him. 'It is in ourselves, and not in our stars, that we are underlings, Derek. Pull yourself together. How were you going to hide your North Brighton lineage from the nobs, then?'

'Oh, Dad is dead, and Mother lives in a little house in St Kilda, the right street, so it's all right,' he said sulkily. 'But Mum told me herself that I only had one thing to sell and I'd better get the best price for it. I'm not clever. I'm never going to be a doctor or an engineer. So I have to marry money and Diane really wants me.'

'And Rose said she could take you away from Diane any time she wished,' Phryne remembered.

'She wanted me,' said Derek. 'She could have had me, too. She was fast. But that doesn't mean anything. Rose was a tart. Simonds said that she ... that she did all sorts of things for him. Then he got tired of her and tried to sell her, and then...'

'Then he must have decided to kill her,' said Phryne. 'Did you know Rose's family at all?'

'No,' said the pretty boy. 'Just that they haven't got any money. Diane used to laugh at the clothes they made Rose wear.'

'Do you know where Simonds and Mongrel are now?'

'No,' said Derek. 'I only see them sometimes. Really,' he added.

'All right,' said Phryne. 'You can go. But I want you to think about this – do you want to marry a woman capable of murder? For when your looks fade, beautiful boy,' she kissed him again, 'how long do you think you'll live?'

Dot led the startled, thoughtful boy down the stairs and past the guest rooms. Just as the front door was being opened by Mr Butler, Rose looked out of her sickroom, said 'Oh!' and recoiled.

The boy gave no sign that he had seen her, and Dot let him go. She returned to the boudoir and found Phryne pulling on her ordinary clothes. Hugh was still in the wardrobe with the door firmly shut.

'Just stay there for a tick, Hugh dear, and I can let you out,' Phryne was saying. 'Dot, can you get this dratted back fastening? Thanks.'

Phyrne buttoned the jumper suit and slipped on her shoes. 'Oh, it is very tiring behaving like an odalisque. Really,' she said to Dot's unbelieving frown. 'Now we have a lot more information and can piece the whole story together, even if Rose doesn't want to tell us. You can let Hugh out of the wardrobe now,' Phryne told Dot. 'He'll be a bit cramped but I bet he has all his notes.'

'I have,' said Hugh, red faced from confinement. He gave Dot an affectionate pat on the cheek. 'That little hound takes the cake,' he added. 'Did you hear him blame it all on the girl?'

'A natural gigolo,' Phryne commented. 'But I don't know if there is a legal case against them. I'd love to lock them up until their hair turned grey but I'm afraid that...'

'Detective Inspector Robinson will know,' said Hugh. 'Can we spring for a cup of tea for me?' he asked Dot, rumpling his hair. 'All that being shut in wardrobes is thirsty work.'

'Of course,' said Dot, as embarrassed as if she had ever doubted her Hugh. 'Come downstairs.'

'Yes, we need a conference before dinner,' said Phryne. 'Has James come back?'

'Yes, Miss, just in. I told him you were using Mata Hari methods to get a confession and he just laughed. The boy's gone. But he might have seen Rose. She popped open her door just as he was passing.'

'That's not good,' said Phryne. 'Did he react?'

'No, Miss, just looked downcast and miserable.'

'He has a lot to be downcast about,' said Phryne vengefully. 'Maybe it's nothing. To think I have to have that Diane on my float on Saturday! The things that get done in the name of love stagger the imagination, they really do.'

'Miss Fisher!' Rose's urgent whisper caught Phryne as she was passing the guest room.

'Rose?' Rose grasped Phryne's arm to steady herself.

'That was Derek! I remember! Diane, he was with Diane on the beach, and I thought they were going to help me, the water was coming up, and I couldn't move on my own, and they left me. They left me!'

'Yes, they did. And then Lin, Li Pen and I came and dragged you from the water. But you were pretty much out of it by then.'

'I only remember being lifted up, out of the water at last. And carried over someone's shoulder. Then everything suddenly hurt a lot.'

'I bet it did,' said Phryne. 'Would you like to sit up for a while?'

'No,' said Rose, trying not to weep. 'I think I'd better go back to bed.'

'Probably a good idea. But don't be cast down,' Phryne told her, lowering the girl back into her bed. 'There were people who didn't save you, agreed. And there were people who tried to kill you. But there were also people who saved you. And the world mostly works out like that. Here comes Mrs Jackmann with your chicken soup. Drink up and don't despair. There's no sense in it.'

She returned to the blue parlour. Jane was cutting bright pink ribbon into precise lengths and James was telling a story to sweeten her labour. Phryne sat down to listen to it. 'Once there were two fiddlers,' he said. 'One was Evan, the best on the island. The other was his best friend James, a good enough fiddler, always asked if Evan wasn't around, but never when Evan was. They were walking one night, very late, home from a dance, past the fairy mounds on the left of the Stromness road, when Evan said, "I can see a light". "Where?" said James, who couldn't see anything and just wanted to get home. "I'll just take a wee look", said Evan. He walked towards the mound, and vanished clean away. James called and hunted in the darkness but could not find him anywhere. The next day he came back with other men of the village and they searched so close they would have found a lost bead; but they found no trace of Evan, his cap or his fiddle.'

'He'd just gone?' asked Dot, who loved stories.

'Gone clean away, like fog off glass,' said James. 'Well then, James was the only fiddler now, and he got asked to all the fairs and funerals and marriages and wakes. And his fiddling got better because he didn't have his envy of Evan to hold him back. He never married, though, convinced that no woman would want him, and that the local maidens were all longing for the return of Evan, which they were, but some would have made shift with James if he had asked, but he never asked.

266

'And then, twenty-five years to the day after Evan vanished, by chance James was walking past those same fairy mounds on the left of the Stromness road at night, very late, home from a dance, and Evan fell in beside him and said, as if he had never been away, "But Janet is the fairer", continuing the discussion they had been having about the girl whom Evan was minded to marry.

'"Dead these ten years," said James. "Of the TB. Evan, where have you been?"

'"I stepped through a little door into the land of the Faye," said Evan. "And I played all night for them. It must be getting very late, I said, and then the king gave me this bag of gold, and here you still are." He punched James playfully. "Such a good friend, waiting all night!"

'"Evan, I've waited twenty-five years," said James.

'Evan took some convincing. It was only when James took him to the grave of his intended, and then to the house of the young woman Janet, and he saw her children, her eldest daughter just like her, that he believed. But to Evan it still seemed that only one night had passed since he left James on the road.'

'How terrible! And what happened then?' asked Jane, who had finished snipping.

'Evan married the daughter of his Janet, and had children of his own and twenty-five years' gossip to catch up on. And James, well, a woman got tired of waiting for James to ask and asked him, and he married as well and was very happy. But no one in Stromness walks down the road on the side where the fairy mounds are, and if they

267

see a light, they say nothing and hurry home, for no bag of fairy gold is worth the loss of twenty-five years of the society of people.'

'That's a good story,' said Jane. 'Miss Phryne, I've cut all the ribbons for the nosegays. But ... have you any idea where Ruth is?'

'I shall know more soon,' said Phryne. 'You did a very good job, they are exactly the same length. Bundle them up. We are plotting.'

'Oh, good,' said Jane, stuffing the ribbons into a basket. 'I like plots.'

'One place Ruth may be,' said Phryne, 'is the Weston house.'

'You mean that they might have stolen Ruth because they think you might have Rose?' asked James.

'Yes. How they would know that I do not know. But they might. So we need to search the house, and for this we need Dot.'

'Me?' quavered Dot.

'You have all the qualifications. You are a loyal daughter of the church, the priest will vouch for you and therefore Biddy will trust you. I want you to get along to St Joan of Arc's for Mass tomorrow morning and get hold of the girl. We have left her there too long. That ends tomorrow. I have a very nice destination for her. Now, what I want you to do thereafter is this,' said Phryne.

The voices fell to a confidential murmur. Once, James laughed. When Phryne finished, Dot nodded firmly.

'I can do it,' she said.

'Dinner,' announced Mr Butler, and they went in.

Phryne was restless. The rest of the household had found things to do, but she did not seem to be able to settle. She was worried about Ruth. Perhaps the girl had run away, but perhaps she had not. And if she had not, if she had exchanged one captor for another, the second might not be an improvement. Rose's condition proved it. Phryne itched for action. A lover would have been nice, but Lin was taking most of his younger relatives to see the famous Chinese magician Loong Jack Sam – 'a marvel of Oriental artistry' – and his lovely assistants Mi Ma and Mi San at the Tivoli. Finally Phryne sat down and began to deal her favourite clock patience, only resorted to when she did not want to think. It absorbed the time until the phone rang.

She almost beat Mr Butler to the phone. She was lurking in the hall when she heard him say, 'If you will wait a moment, sir, I will ascertain if Miss Fisher is available.'

'Who is it?'

'A Professor Merckens, Miss Fisher.'

'Wonderful.' Phryne only restrained herself from snatching the receiver out of her butler's hands by the knowledge that he would be affronted. 'Professor? I mean, Jeremiah? This is Phryne Fisher.'

'Phryne,' said the wonderful voice. 'I have undertaken the enquiries. I have to tell you that no sign of such a girl as Ruth has been seen, even in the most ... basic of houses. And none of the street prostitutes have seen her. One cannot question them all, of course, but my agents are tolerably thorough.'

'Good, that's good news,' said Phryne a little breathlessly. 'Thank you very much. And Simonds and Mongrel?'

'Nothing,' said the professor. 'Though I did find out that Mr Walker is also looking for them. An admirable man, but very direct in his methods. If you want to talk to them it might be necessary to find them soon.'

'Quite,' said Phryne. 'While they are still breathing.'

'Yes,' said the professor.

Phryne thanked him effusively, repeated her invitation to dinner, and rang off. Good. The odds that Ruth was not captive were rising. Unless, of course, she was in durance vile in the Weston house, and that was a matter for tomorrow. When, come to think of it, she had to rise early. Not only was it a day to search someone else's house quite illegally, it was the day of the Lady Mayoress's Bazaar.

The day dawned far too bright and fair. Phryne yawned her way through dressing and gave herself an extra strong cup of Greek coffee, a cruel and unusual beverage which woke her up like nothing else could. Dot was awake, dressed, and characteristically cheerful. Dot liked dawn. Phryne only liked it from the other side. James was ambulant but silent.

Mr Butler drove them to St Joan of Arc's in Brighton, and Dot in her coat and hat went to the door. Six-thirty exactly, and early Mass was beginning.

'Mrs Butler said that you might like some more

270

coffee, Miss Fisher,' said Mr Butler, offering a thermos and a cup. Phryne grabbed and gulped. James refused and Mr Butler had already had, he said, as much coffee as was good for him. Phryne, who had never had as much coffee as was good for her, poured another cup and sipped luxuriously.

'Your wife, Mr Butler, is a woman of great qualities and I hope that you are very happy with her,' she said fervently.

'Thank you, Miss Fisher, I am, and I shall convey to her your good opinion,' replied Mr Butler. James stretched and yawned.

'It's a fair morning right enough,' he commented. 'But since I became a fiddler I've liked it less and less. I'll just have a brief nap, Phryne, if you don't mind.'

'By all means, I'll wake you if we need you.'

'There,' said Mr Butler. 'That would be the young person, I believe, Miss Fisher.'

Running as fast as the child on her hip would allow, a shabby girl with a too-large hat came galloping down the road. She dived into the church as if bears were after her.

'That was Biddy,' said Phryne contentedly.

Bert and Cec arrived, and Phryne and James removed themselves to the cab.

Biddy liked early Mass. It was always calm and quiet in the church and the elderly priest had a nice Irish voice. The Tridentine Latin flowed over her like a cool stream. Familiar, comforting. She had a lot to worry about. Since Miss Rose had gone the house was fraught and since Ethel the kitchen maid had escaped it was both filthy and hungry. Biddy could not order from the tradesmen because the old man would not allow her any money and she could not cook with the child Elijah around her ankles all the time. If she left him, even for a moment, he shrieked with temper and broke something. But Mother had to work and Biddy really needed this job. Also, they owed her three months' wages.

Father O'Brian approached her after he had said 'Ite, missa est.' He had a lady with him, a woman with plaited hair, a beige suit, and a hat very like a terracotta flower pot. Father O'Brian said, 'Here you are, Biddy. Biddy, this is Miss Williams. She has found you another job. You may take it. I've spoken to Miss Williams' priest and he approves too. So go along with Miss Williams, Biddy, and I'm sure that you will continue to be a good girl. God bless you,' he said, and went back into the church for breakfast.

Biddy bobbed her usual curtsey. Mary reached out towards the lady's mother of pearl rosary and crooned 'pretty beads!'

'Hello, Bridget,' said Miss Williams. 'We must go back to your house and collect your things.'

'Oh but, Miss, they'll be angry.' Biddy clasped little Mary closer. 'That old man won't let me leave!'

'He will,' smiled Miss Williams. 'Come along. Miss Fisher has sent the car for us.'

'Ooh, a car!' Biddy was fascinated. She had never travelled in a car before. She set Mary down on her feet and they looked at the shiny car, the reddest of all reds.

'Come along,' said Miss Williams, loading Mary and Biddy into the machine. 'The Weston house, please, Mr Butler.'

'Just as you say, Miss Williams,' said Mr Butler, awe inspiring in his livery and peaked cap. Just like a sea captain, Biddy thought. And the car moved without a jolt or jerk. So fast! Much faster than walking. Much faster than a galloping horse. It was marvellous. Biddy began to feel hopeful. Surely such masterful people as this would not be frightened of that terrible old man and his terrible house.

Now Miss Williams was talking to her. No, no one had come to the house lately, except two nasty men. One was a natural who drooled. The other was a nasty man. Biddy could not specify any more than that. And Mr Johnson, who looked at her strangely. Biddy always took the children into the kitchen when Mr Johnson came.

They reached the Weston house far too soon. A cab was parked outside.

'We'll leave little Mary in the car,' said Miss Williams. 'There might be words.'

Little Mary was fascinated with the mother of pearl rosary which Miss Williams allowed her to hold. Biddy, gathering her courage, led the lady around to the kitchen door, to which she had the key. She had not been given it. She had found it in a box of rusted metal objects and had cleaned it. When tried, it fitted. No one in the house knew that Biddy went to morning Mass three times a week.

Miss Williams left the kitchen door wide open. 'Go up and pack your things,' she said to Biddy. 'I will wait here and talk to Mrs Weston. It will be all right, Biddy.'

Biddy went, taking the stairs at a fast, silent run.

Bert, Cec, James and Phryne filed in through the open door. They were carrying such implements as might prove useful and they split up immediately. Phryne went down to the cellar. She had a heavy duty flashlight for illumination and a crowbar. Phryne liked crowbars. They made an admirable tool and anyone hit with one stayed hit. The cellar was filthy but empty except for two bottles of wine left in a spacious rack. She emerged and checked the coal cellar, in which were all of five shovelfuls of coal. Then she roamed the first floor, finding shut-up rooms full of moths and spiders, and once a fleeting rat, but no sign of human occupation.

That was her lot, and she rejoined Dot in the kitchen.

Bert, Cec and James took a section each and searched it. The door with fifteen locks on it was the old man's bedroom; James listened for long enough with his trained ear to be sure that there was only one set of lungs breathing in the room. Bert and Cec found wastes of dusty boards and flat walls where faded patches told that pictures had once hung, but nothing else. They were done and out in the garden before Biddy came down, dragging her box from step to step. The bumping noise woke Elijah and he started to scream, and his dog started to yap, which woke his mother and the old man.

All four of them arrived at the bottom of the stairs simultaneously. Dot was the only person in the kitchen. To Biddy's relief, she came forward and removed Mr Weston's clawed hand from the girl's arm. The child Elijah continued to scream and the dog continued to bark.

'Bridget has a new job,' Dot announced. 'She is leaving. Can she have her wages, please?'

'Presently.' The old man's eyes lit up. 'What has she got in that box? Some of our property? It must be searched.'

'You aren't actually allowed to do that,' said Dot. 'But we will allow it if you pay her properly. Come along,' she coaxed. 'You can't say that she hasn't earned it.'

'She's a wicked, ungrateful girl, after we gave her a good home. A Paddy straight out of the bogs, and probably a Catholic as well. She can come for her wages tomorrow, if she has the boldness to do it,' said Mrs Weston. 'Oh, do be quiet, 'Lije, do!'

'She isn't coming back here ever again,' said Dot. 'Wages. Then you can search her box. If you insist.'

'She can go to the devil,' snarled Mr Weston. He had made a lightning calculation that whatever was in the box wasn't worth three months' wages.

'Your own destination,' said Dot, disgusted. 'Come on, Biddy. You take one side of the box and I'll take the other.'

Biddy did as she was told. She only turned back for a moment, when the child screamed, 'Want Biddy!' at the top of his voice.

'Come along,' said Dot, and Biddy obeyed.

Outside she was surprised to meet three men and a lady she had seen before at the big car.

'Nothing,' said one of the men. 'And it would be a step forward in slum clearance to set a torch to the place, so it would.'

He almost sounded like an Irishman. He saw Biddy and smiled. Then he lifted the box without any effort and put it in the car.

'Come along, birdie,' he told her. 'You're well out of there.'

In his big house in Yarraville, which seemed smaller every day, Detective Inspector Robinson heard the doorbell ring as he was attempting to spoon cereal into an uncooperative two year old – one of the great lost causes of the world. He waited, then realised that his sister was feeding the baby and his wife was walking the four year old in the garden. He left the toddler to scream in his highchair and went to the door.

'Yes?' he asked.

'I've brought you a present,' said Phryne. 'Nice apron. Is the decoration cereal? This is Bridget and her little sister Mary. I'm lending you Dot for the day to get them settled in and buy her some new clothes and things. I'm responsible for her wages. She's been running a big household almost single handed. You'll find her very useful. Deal?'

Miss Fisher seemed to be in a hurry. Dot Williams had already had the child's box brought in. Biddy herself had followed the noise into the kitchen. The noise stopped suddenly. When Robinson got there he found that his screaming, kicking devil of a nephew was placidly eating cereal while the Irish girl told him that he was a fine boy, to be sure, and he didn't surely want to be making such a rumpus on such a fine day. He could hear himself speak for the first time in hours.

'Done,' he said. 'With thanks,' he added.

He laid out some porridge in bowls for Biddy, who looked like she hadn't had a square meal in all of her years, and her little sister. Mary was much better fed, probably because Biddy had given her food to Mary. He watched them eat for a while. One of the pleasures of the world is watching hungry children eat.

When he offered Biddy a cup of milk, she had asked gravely, 'How far down am I allowed to drink?' and Robinson, who was a kindly man, had had to turn away to hide his face. Biddy was likely to be fed to bursting in Robinson's house and even if there were ten times the children she would still be better off than in the Weston house.

Miss Anna Ross to Mr Rory McCrimmon

Rory, what is wrong? I have your cruel note dismissing me. What have I done to forfeit your love? I swear I never knew any man but you, never loved anyone but you. If you leave me I will die. Anna

CHAPTER SEVENTEEN

Cutpurses, cheaters, bawdy-house doorkeepers
Room for company at Bartholemew Fair
Punks, aye, and panderers, cashiered commanders,
Room for company, ill may they fare!

Anon
'Bartholemew Fair'

Pleased with her good deed, and tickled by im-
agining what the Westons would do without poor,
abused, starved and overworked Biddy, Phryne
had herself driven home for a nap and something
rather scented in the way of baths. James decided
to wander off on a Simonds-and-Mongrel hunt
with Bert and Cec, although it might just have
been an excuse for a drink in a place with no
excitable females in it. They seemed to have
become friends, which was nice.

Phryne drew herself a bath and strewed milk
powder into it. If it worked for Cleopatra, it
ought to work for her. She drowsed in the warm
water. How to understand misers? There were
things in the house, antiques, according to Cec,
that might have been fine if they had been cared
for. Now they were worthless. The house itself
was the last word in discomfort. There hadn't
even been a bath...

Phryne awoke with a start as she slid underwater. She leapt out, dried herself and dressed for a social occasion. Knowing what these bazaars were like, she chose a hat which clung closer than a brother, a handbag on a shoulder strap, and comfortable shoes. She collected Jane on the way out. Mr Butler was still chuckling at the cleverly contrived escape of Biddy. He hadn't liked leaving the poor child in that awful house. He should have known that his Miss Fisher would come through. He listened to the conversation in the back seat. Nice, comfortable, everyday conversation.

'Have you been to a bazaar before, Jane?'

'No,' said Jane. 'Just church ones.'

'This is the same, only bigger. If you get lost, head for the edge. They build a lot of stalls in the town hall, you see, and they get heavily decorated with paper flowers and things. Very confusing. Have you got your pocket money?'

'Yes. I wish...'

'That Ruth was here? So do I. But we know that she isn't in that Weston house and we also know that she hasn't ... er ... been left in a bad position. Have some extra coins,' said Phryne. 'Buy Ruth something which she might have bought for herself. Parcels are to be put in the car. Mr Butler is staying with us, which is noble of him, eh, Mr B?'

'After that trick this morning, Miss Fisher,' said Mr Butler, beaming, 'I'll follow you anywhere.'

'It was rather neat, eh? Two birds with one stone.'

'What did you do with Biddy, Miss Phryne?' asked Jane.

'Gave her to Jack Robinson, whose sister has just been left by her husband with a broken heart and three children,' said Phryne. 'The sister moved into Jack's house with the children and he's been going out of his mind. He needs the help and Biddy needs a home. It was a neat match. Now, we must listen carefully to the Lady Mayoress's speech, then it's every girl for herself. See you soon, Mr Butler.'

'Have fun, Miss Fisher,' he replied, sliding the great car around the side of the town hall and parking.

The town hall was bedecked with paper flowers, strung with paper streamers, and wreathed in paper ivy. Underneath this the floor space had been divided into booths, which displayed every sort of hand craft that the mind of woman had ever imagined, and some which indicated a worrying state of sanity in the inventor. There was a high-pitched hum of female voices, like a beehive in summer. Jane took Phryne's hand.

'It all looks very grand,' she observed.

'Might I point out all those old books over there?' Phryne saw Jane's eyes light up. 'Get Ruth's present first,' she advised. 'One thing I've learned about second-hand book stalls, the ones which you would buy are never the ones which other people buy. I think that is so nice of them. Well, well,' Phryne added, surveying the palpitating crowd. 'Everyone who is everyone is indeed here. Which includes us, of course. All of my flower maidens,' she said tonelessly. 'And Derek. How nice.'

'Is he a boy?' asked Jane. 'He's so pretty I

thought he was a girl and wondered at him wearing trousers. Gosh,' said Jane, staring openly.

'Not you, too,' said Phryne crossly. 'Handsome is as handsome does is particularly apposite in relation to that young man, Jane.'

'I don't want him,' said Jane, a little taken aback by the ferocity of Miss Phryne's tone. 'I was just looking.'

'That's what they all say. Come along, we'll struggle inside so we can hear the Lady Mayoress.'

In sidling and occasionally shoving their way inside, Phryne passed right in front of Diane Pridham. Beside her, Joannie laughed and flirted with Derek, who seemed rather unresponsive. Jessica Adams smiled excitedly. Marie Bernhoff was thinking about music and gave a vague wave, though she might have been conducting an imaginary orchestra. Diane gave Phryne a hundred watt glare.

'You lost him for me,' she hissed.

'No, actually, you did it yourself,' said Phryne amiably. 'You can't take a boyfriend along on a murder and not expect the relationship to show signs of strain. In any case this is not the place to discuss it. You'll be lucky if you don't go to jail, but don't blame me. The fault's entirely yours,' said Phryne, and seeing a clear space, sprinted for it, Jane at her heels. 'That's better,' she said. 'Room, at least, to breathe.'

'And there's the Lady Mayoress,' said Jane. 'And Miss Jones.'

The speech was mercifully brief. The Lady Mayoress thanked everyone involved – including, for the first time, Miss Jones, who blushed pink –

got in a few advertisements for the Lord Mayor's Fund and the Ladies' Fund, and was cheered. The assembled ladies were delighted. The last Lady Mayoress had quoted her own poetry and gone on for forty-five minutes. This one knew what it was to feel that, somewhere, a bargain waited with one's name on it.

Phryne did not share the popular view. Her method was to stroll along the more unfrequented aisles, buying whatever took her fancy from the stalls which looked sad or neglected. She then sent her purchases off to the next bazaar. It was a great convenience because she always had something to donate.

Jane was more careful and examined everything, even pokerwork cigarette boxes one-eighth of an inch too short for any mortal cigarette and lumpy cups made by lady potters, almost too solid to lift even without the coffee. Phryne was wondering irritably why anyone would paint perfectly good white china with designs of shepherdesses when she was bumped quite heavily. She staggered and turned. Her assailant was Diane Pridham.

'You'll be sorry,' she snarled, and battered her way through the crowd toward an exit, trampling on small children and pushing through groups of girls.

Phryne propped herself up beside the tea enclosure and lit a cigarette. This ought to make sharing the same float with Diane very interesting. Phryne might prove to be the first Queen of the Flowers to be assassinated in her own parade.

Jane had found the old books and could safely be left for a while. Phryne purchased a few armloads of assorted wares – lampshades made of shells, ashtrays made of gun casings, jazz-coloured garters, a charming stuffed dragon toy which was destined for Lin Chung, and a cigarette case made of mother of pearl scales, which was a find. It was the first thing she had ever found at a bazaar that she might actually keep. She found the perfect present for Dot: a picture made out of pressed autumn leaves in all her favourite shades. Ruth, if she ever came home, would be pleased with a gramophone recording from the Folk Song Society of Highland Dances, which included pipes played by Rory McCrimmon, drums by that snake Neil McLeod, and fiddle by Hamish McGregor. Phryne had all the things carried out of the crowded hall and into the street, to find Mr Butler – of all people – reading the telltale pink pages of what was either the *'Sporting Globe'* or – gasp – the *'Hawklet'*. Phryne hoped it was the *'Hawklet'*, so she could read it next. She glimpsed the masthead as he hastily folded it. Good. The *'Hawklet'* it was. Phryne dismissed her carriers with thanks.

'Lots of stuff, Mr Butler. Can you load it for me? Take care, that lampshade is wobbly.'

'Wobbly?' asked Mr Butler, steadying it. 'It's cock-eyed, if you ask me. Still, bazaars will be bazaars. Mrs B always comes home from them with some useless thing which has caught her fancy. I saw one of those flower girls of yours,' he added. 'She stormed out like she had a bee up ... like a very unhappy and angry person,' he said, hastily amending his language.

'The dark one?' asked Phryne, dropping her new cigarette case into Mr Butler's hand as he nodded. 'Take care of this, it's ducky. That was, I'm afraid, Diane Pridham. She is not one of my admirers at present. Nothing to be done about that. One of the reasons that she is so angry with me is that she did it all herself. Never mind. Can't be helped. Jane is likely to be back in about an hour with more books than she can carry. Let her loose where there are second-hand books and she's like a fox in a henhouse. I'd better go and help. See you soon, Mr Butler. Oh, and keep the paper for me? I always like to catch up with the *"Hawklet"*.'

Mr Butler agreed. He spread the paper out again. The banner headline read 'Johnson and Weston – new light on an old fraud'. His eyebrows rose. If what the *'Hawklet'* was alleging was true, then Rose Weston had better stay where she was, for about ten years. Or maybe twenty. Until the scandal died down.

Phryne went back into the town hall. Now that she had surveyed most of the booths, she knew where she might find useful things. She had presents to buy and purchased them without fear or favour, according to the taste of the intended recipient. Jane had bought Ruth's present, it was clear, because she was sitting on the floor beside the second-hand book stall, leafing through a stack of volumes taller than she was.

Miss Jones fluttered up to Phryne. 'Such a good turnout,' she said. 'Such lovely things.'

'Miss Jones,' said Phryne. 'I have bought you a present.'

She handed over a large bag. It had two straps, so that it could either be slung over a shoulder or carried in the hand. It had innumerable pockets and was big enough to hold a pad of foolscap paper and a lot of pencils. It was decorated to within an inch of its life with tassels, little silver bells, barbola gumnuts and silk blossoms. It was embroidered with gum blossoms and gumnut babies in pink silk. Tatting in three shades of olive decorated the edges. And the body of the bag was a bright shade of green.

Miss Jones, already overwhelmed by public recognition of her work, By the Lady Mayoress! From the Platform!, was freshly touched. 'Oh no, Miss Fisher, I couldn't,' she said, reaching out and touching the embroidery. So fine! And so much beautiful decoration. And the gumnut babies. So sweet. She had never owned such a beautiful, frivolous thing.

Phryne was not going to let Miss Jones get away with modestly declining a present. 'You can and you shall. The little bells make it hard to lose, ditto the colour, and it has a place for your glasses and all your notes. Really, you must take it, Miss Jones, or I shall be offended.'

'Well, very well, thank you,' said Miss Jones. Miss Fisher was a little frightening and she had said the last sentence with a straight face. 'Thank you. It's lovely. Now I really must...' and Miss Jones was gone, clutching her beautiful handbag to her bosom. Phryne felt suddenly disgusted with her own snobbish taste and decided to collect Jane and go home for a penitential reading and attempted translation of the poems of François Villon – always a good stretch for the mind and a sobering reflection on how much French she didn't know – and a nice calm evening. Dot would be home late, after she had settled Biddy into her new home. The Butlers were going to the movies, so dinner would be cold and could be taken late or early. James was performing at a concert and the only possible visitor was Detective Inspector Robinson, who was supposed to be coming for a consultation about what to do with Rose. And Robinson might easily find that domestic trials prevented him waiting on Miss Fisher, who seldom had them.

It took three people to carry Jane's books to the car. She was flushed, dusty, and delighted.

'I got all of the *Classical Encyclopaedia!*' she exclaimed as the great car started. 'And the *Cambridge Ancient History*. And a lot of Greek plays and a textbook on anatomy. *Gray's.* And some novels and some poetry and I bought this for you, Miss Phryne. With my love,' said Jane.

It was a slim, leather-clad volume entitled *The Golden Journey to Samarkand* by James Elroy Flecker,

'Lord, Jane, what a lovely thing, just what I wanted,' Phryne told her. 'You've got a good eye,' she said. 'It's a first edition. What did you get for Ruth?'

'Well, there were lots of romances, but I didn't think she'd fancy them anymore, so I got this.'

Phryne hefted the sober, heavy, blue book.

'*Scotland Described* by James McGregor. A good solid factual book, with plates. A good choice,' Phryne approved. 'I found a present for you but it's in the boot. Well, that gives you something to do when we get home. I'm going to do some translation. I've been swanning around fixing people's lives far too often than is good for me. I'll show it to you when it's finished,' said Phryne. 'It's called the "Ballad of the Hanged Men". You'll like it.'

'I'm sure I will,' said Jane.

They occupied the remains of the afternoon quietly. Phryne handed over her present, which was an ingenious clip for holding a book open without damaging it. Jane was delighted. Phryne chewed her pencil and stared out of the window, an essential part of any translator's working life. Jane catalogued her new books, dusted them, and ranged them in her bookcase. The overflow was stacked neatly on the floor.

James practised the fiddle and then dressed for his concert. Mr and Mrs Butler put on their hats and went to the movies. A cold collation was eaten and the leftovers carried out to the kitchen. Molly, foiled in her attempt to steal the ham, accepted a few scraps instead. Rose Weston, recovering, demanded a mirror and was told that she could have one tomorrow. The house was quiet.

Jack Robinson arrived at about eight and accepted a whisky and a chair.

'That Biddy is remarkable,' he said. 'The little kids just hang on her every word. Poor little creature, she's still cheerful, and she's never had a reason to be. My sister's plotting to get her to stay forever. And her little sister is a good-natured child. Thank you for your present, Miss Fisher. Miss Dot's taken care of a new wardrobe for both girls. They didn't even own a hairbrush between them. She's staying to supervise the early evening.

Now, what are we to do with your patient?' asked Jack Robinson.

As if in answer, the kitchen door swung open, and two men came into the parlour. One was an idiot, drooling and mouthing. The other was a small thin man, and he carried a sawn-off shotgun.

Mr Rory McCrimmon to Miss Anna Ross

It cannot be, Anna, I love you more than life itself and I must go. Do not wait for me. Find another husband. I will not see you again. I could not bear it. Your heart-broken Rory.

CHAPTER EIGHTEEN

I met Murder on the way

Percy B Shelley
'The Mask of Anarchy'

'Where's the girl?' demanded the man with the shotgun.

'Who are you?' asked Phryne, jumping up. 'No, actually, what I mean is, who the hell are you?'

'Allow me,' said Jack Robinson, getting to his feet. 'This is Mongrel,' he indicated the idiot. 'And this is Neville Simonds. You've heard a lot about him.'

'I certainly have,' said Phryne. She was moving

away from Jack Robinson as she spoke. The gun could have only one target at a time.

'You're the nobby slut who queered our pitch with Weston, ain't you?' asked Simonds. He hadn't been sleeping in a bed lately. There were leaves on his coat and in his hair.

'I don't know what you mean,' said Phryne. 'I was hired to find Rose Weston.'

'And I reckon you did,' sneered Simonds. 'I met my little cousin Derek and he told me you had her here. After I belted him a bit. Snivelling brat.'

Simonds was, Phryne could see, desperate. Walker's men were hunting him. The professor's were aware of him. The Westons had refused to pay. This situation was very dangerous. Much better to face a calm disciplined soldier, because he will only kill you if he has orders to kill you, than a sleepless madman with a sawn-off shotgun.

'Now, now, Simonds, simmer down,' said Robinson. 'We ain't told no one about you. We're still looking for that girl. And another one that's gone missing. Do you know anything about that?'

Mongrel had sighted the bottles on the drinks tray and had stumbled across the room to them. He stank like the drain in which he had probably slept. He knocked the stopper out of a decanter and drank as if it was cordial. Phryne was pleased. That was port. A good dose of that and Mongrel ought to be off to never-never land fairly smartly. But Mongrel was never the problem.

Simonds yelled, the gun barrel lashing wildly from side to side. 'Get me that girl or I'll shoot the lot of youse!'

If only no one comes in, thought Phryne. If only Rose doesn't come out, or Lily Jackmann – no, Lily goes home at five. If only Jane doesn't surface from all those books. He could kill me and Jack without moving. He's got two barrels and they're both loaded. Come on, brain, think.

'How did the deal go wrong?' she asked. 'Perhaps we can do something about that.'

'It's that old bastard Weston,' Simonds actually answered Phryne. 'Tells me, be nice to the girl, take her out, show her a good time, then get her to go away with you and sell her to a brothel, make her a tart, she'll be too ashamed to come home, no one will ever believe a word she says again, that's what he says. Ten quid, he says. So I did it. I was nice to her, she followed me like a lamb when I said come with us. Mongrel and me spend the two quid down-payment in the pub. I give her a mickey in case she cuts up rough. Then it all went wrong!'

His voice soared to a scream. 'No one would buy the bitch! No one! So what's a man to do with a stray girl? She kept asking questions. Kept wanting to go home. Then she got loose. Mongrel caught her by the edge of the sea. I thought he'd killed her. Thought I'd better finish the job. Thought I had. Then I go to the old bastard Weston and do you know what he said?' Simonds advanced on Phryne, saliva flying from his jaws. 'He says, no deal. He's heard that she's still alive. She can't be, not with the belting Mongrel give her.'

'Sounds like she's a goner, all right,' observed

Robinson. His reward was a wild swerve of the gun and the tightening of the finger on the trigger. Then it moved back to Phryne. For one moment she looked death in the face. She had done so before. The sensation did not improve on reacquaintance. ''Tis not as deep as a well or as wide as a church door but 'tis enough, 'twill serve,' as the dying Mercutio had said. Phryne stared into Simonds' empty eyes. Then the gun swung away again.

Mongrel, having emptied his decanter, collapsed on the floor. He gave a faint snore. He seemed harmless for the moment. But Simonds was working himself into a homicidal fury. Phryne backed away and got her fingers around the rim of a small table. She exchanged a glance with Jack Robinson. Usually, throwing things was a good tactic with a gunman. But in this confined space anyone in the room was going to be shredded when that shotgun went off.

Phryne spared a moment to wonder where Molly was. Had they killed her on the way in? It looked like her mistress would shortly be joining the poor puppy. Nothing ventured. She might at least die in her own defence. Then Simonds' finger slipped and the barrel swung up.

One barrel fired. The house was shocked into silence. From the insulted ceiling, plaster fell like rain. Mongrel turned in his sleep. Simonds stepped closer to Phryne.

'You give me the girl, now!' he screamed.

'Or what?' asked Phryne. Close up, she could see the bitten lips, the crazed eyes of unbearable stress. The stench of his fear wrapped around her like a filthy garment.

'I'll kill–'

There was a soggy thud. With a look of unutterable surprise, Simonds slumped forward, and Phryne caught the shotgun as it fell from his hands.

Behind him, now revealed, stood Ruth, holding Mrs Butler's long-handled heavy iron skillet and looking sheepish.

'Er...' she said. 'I'm sorry I ran away.'

'You're forgiven,' said Phryne, and sank down into her chair.

Miss Anna Ross to Mr James Murray

I believe you, Hamish. I wish it was not so. I will come to you in the early morning.

Anna McCrimmon

CHAPTER NINETEEN

Thou hast not many miles to tread, nor other foes than fleas to dread

James Elroy Flecker
'Gates of Damascus'

Dot came home to find that things had clearly been happening in her absence.

There was plaster dust all over the small

parlour, which Mr Butler was removing with his vacuum machine. In the blue parlour, Jane was hugging Ruth, yes, the prodigal Ruth, and Molly, all three entwined on the sofa and wolfing down a platter of leftovers which must have come from dinner. Phryne was pouring drinks with a liberal hand for James Murray, Detective Inspector Robinson, and herself. Rose Weston, wrapped in a red woollen dressing gown, was sitting in an armchair, smiling. Ember was not there and Dot was not surprised. It was no place for a decent cat. It reminded her of sermons she had heard on Babylonian orgies or the reason for the destruction of Sodom and Gomorrah.

'Come in, Dot dear,' called Phryne. 'It's all over. Ruth is home and Simonds and Mongrel are in jail – well, Mongrel is in jail and Simonds is in the Pentridge hospital with a very nasty bump on the head. Courtesy of Ruth.'

Mr Butler concluded his suctioning and admitted Bert and Cec. Bert grabbed Ruth and hugged her, and was heartily licked by Molly for his pains.

'Little Ruthie!' he said. 'We been looking all over for you! You all right?'

Ruth nodded and kissed Bert's grizzled cheek.

'And Simonds and Mongrel are in the Bluestone College,' said Robinson with great satisfaction. 'And if they ever get out again, I'll be one very surprised policeman.'

'Can't have that,' said Bert, accepting a beer.

'Too right,' said Cec, accepting a glass of raki.

'So what happened?' asked Bert. 'Where had they been all this time?'

'Sleeping rough,' said Phryne. 'Really rough. In the park rough. Leaves in the hair. Hungry, too. And very, very cross. Lord, Jack, I was so close to death tonight I could smell his breath.'

'Me too,' said Robinson. Mr Butler refilled his glass. He was profoundly thankful that all this had happened when he and Mrs B were blamelessly watching *'Desert Song'*.

'What I don't know is what you were all doing,' said Phryne. 'I was terrified that you might come out of your room, Rose.'

'I didn't do anything brave,' said Rose. 'I just put my blanket over my head and tried not to breathe. And hoped I'd die before Neville found me again.'

'And I was hanging on to Molly so that she wouldn't bark,' said Jane. 'I knew that you'd win, Miss Phryne, I didn't see how I could help.'

'And then just as I really did think that this was the end, and Jack and I were going to be splattered – well, never mind – Ruth arrived and belted Simonds a very pretty two-handed blow which knocked him out for the count,' said Phryne.

'I came in through the kitchen door,' said Ruth. 'I thought I'd sneak in and ask Jane if – if you wanted me back. Then I saw that the door was open, and then I heard the voices. So I went back and got the skillet. I hit him as hard as I could. And then – Miss Phryne caught the gun so it didn't go off when it hit the floor, and the place was full of policemen.'

'I sent them to bring in Johnson and old man Weston,' said Robinson. 'They're reopening that old fraud charge. As well as the others. And your mum is going to be rich, Miss Weston. The old miser transferred all his property to her a couple of years ago.'

'He never told her,' said Rose, astonished.

'He reckoned on getting it back, I suppose,' said Phryne. 'But, as it happens, he didn't. Have you thought about what you want to do, Rose?'

'I'd like to go back to school. I'll be better at it this time around.'

'They will have you back,' said Phryne. 'But the scandal will be immense. It won't be pleasant.'

'After what I've just been through,' said Rose, 'I can manage unpleasant.'

Phryne patted her with approval.

'Then,' Rose went on, 'when all the money stuff is cleared up and Mum has sold that awful old house, she can buy a little one, and hire some help, and not have to deal with Grandpapa. I might be able to go home. Perhaps. She's not too bad, my mother. Grandpapa drove her demented, and no one's been able to do anything with Elijah because Grandpa wouldn't allow him to be disciplined.'

'Good,' said Phryne. 'You'll be able to go back for final term. I'll put my lawyer Jilly onto the financial stuff. She's a shark. A nice shark, I mean. You'll like her.'

'Miss Fisher? Now that we are celebrating and all, can I have a glass of that champagne?' asked Rose.

'Of course,' said Phryne. 'Now, Ruth dear, I have to know. Where have you been?'

'I got away from Neil McLeod,' said Ruth.

'Well, I didn't precisely get away. I was freed. He gave me a drink of water that tasted funny and I got very sleepy. Then I can sort of remember that someone cut my wrists and ankles free and told me to walk, so I walked, and then they put me down on a bed in a caravan and went away. A lot of time went past. A big dog licked me. I thought I could hear Mr Murray playing the violin. Then I woke up properly and I was so ashamed. I had been fooled, really fooled. He wasn't my father. It was a dream. And instead of looking at it carefully I had gone all high-flown and romantic and run away. I felt like such an idiot. I wanted to come home but I didn't know if you'd want me back.'

'Yes,' said Phryne. 'So where were you?'

'With me,' said Dulcie. She had come in through the as yet unclosed back door and looked as abashed as a woman who rides elephants can. 'I overheard that snake McLeod talking about his little plot, and I thought, I can do myself a bit of good here, I am flat stony motherless broke and I have a big dog and three elephants to feed, so I'll snatch this ransom when it arrives, but first I have to free the hostage. So I did that and left her in my caravan with Bounce while I went back for the money. But you were there, Phryne, and I didn't have a chance. I knew that Ruth would take a while to wake up and I admit that I toyed with the idea of asking for another ransom, but you're my friend, Phryne, I really couldn't. So when the young woman woke I told her to go home and I've been telling her to go home ever since.'

'She has,' said Ruth. 'She said you were looking

for me all over the place and you really wanted me back.'

'So I did,' said Phryne. 'So I do.'

'Silly,' said Jane, kicking Ruth with her free bare foot. 'I told you so.'

'Dulcie,' said Phryne, taking a familiar envelope from her purse. 'Have forty pounds. I've already spent some of the ransom. Thank you for keeping Ruth safe. It's a loan, if you insist,' she said. 'Pay it back if you like.'

Dulcie clutched the envelope and mouthed 'thank you'.

'Now, we'd better all drink up and go to bed,' said Phryne, swigging her brandy. 'Because to-morrow I am going to be Queen of the Flowers.'

She went to bed, taking the brandy with her for the moments during the next week when she would see again the black maw of the shotgun swinging towards her, and smell the sweat of terror.

(Mrs) Dulcie Ross to (Mrs) Henrietta Walgett
15 January 1914

I am sending you my daughter Anna as per previous arrangements. Her husband is dead and the child, if it survives, will need to be immediately adopted into a good family. I cannot run a boarding house by myself. Please supply midwifery care at your usual standard and return the girl as soon as possible. Mrs Ross.

CHAPTER TWENTY

So maids be loyal when your love at sea
For a cloudy morning brings in a sunny day.

Anon
'The Dark-Eyed Sailor'

After the excitement of the night, it was soothing to sit on the floor of the blue parlour in the midst of the flower baskets and make nosegays for the flower maidens to throw. They were easy to make. Two sweet peas and a rosebud, a sprig of baby's breath, a twist of the pink ribbon and a fat bow. Jane had done her fifty and Ruth had made seventy-three when James Murray came to help her. He was good at knots and the work went very well. Jane was helping the flower maidens to dress. Jessica, Joannie and Marie were present, but Diane Pridham had not yet arrived.

James was singing under his breath. Gradually Ruth realised that he was singing to her. She had heard the song before and thought it very romantic. The maiden is challenged to forsake her old love, whose half-ring she is wearing. She refuses indignantly. Then the stranger produces his half of the ring.

'One half of the ring did young William show; she ran distracted with grief and woe. Crying William William there's much love in store, for

298

my dark eyed sailor has proved his love once more,' he sang.

'It was you, wasn't it?' asked Ruth, laying another nosegay in the basket.

'Aye, it was me,' he said gravely.

'I liked you as soon as you came into the house,' said Ruth. 'She remembered you, you know. But she remembered you as Hamish.'

'That's how she knew me,' he said. 'Hamish is the Gaelic form of James. One of them, at least. And I called myself Hamish McGregor for the Folk Song concerts.'

'Did you love her?' asked Ruth, her eyes on her nosegay.

'Aye, I did,' he said.

'Did she love you?' asked Ruth.

'I don't know. Perhaps. But she sent me away. If she could not have Rory, she did not want me. Rory was barren and dying. She was in despair. She lay with me to conceive so her mother would let her marry Rory. But I sent him home to die before she knew she was carrying and I never saw her again. I did not know about the bairn – about you – or I should have stayed if she wanted me or not. But it was my ring she gave you,' he said, breaking a thin line of tarred string which was around his neck. He put the pendant into her hand. Ruth pulled her mother's ring from her pocket. They matched. It was the same ring.

Ruth put both arms around James Murray's neck and embraced him tightly.

'My bird,' he said into her sweet-smelling hair. 'My dowie, my dove.'

He rocked her gently in his arms in the scent of

299

the flowers. Tears filled his eyes and spilled silently onto her plaits. Something inside James Murray which was old and cracked, softened and relaxed. He had not wept in twenty years. Ruth snuggled into his embrace. She was as warm as a puppy. After a while, she released herself.

'And you are going away,' she said.

'Aye, I was, at the end of the week. But I will do as you bid me to do, daughter. I have wronged you very cruelly.'

'No,' said Ruth. 'You haven't. I will stay here,' she said. 'And you will go home. We can write letters. Send pictures. I can get used to having a father and you can get used to having a daughter. Then, when I have finished school, you can travel. Or I can travel.'

'I would like to show you Orkney,' he said. 'I would like it fine.'

'So you shall,' said Ruth, picking up her nosegay again. 'Father.'

'You are very wise,' he said. 'Daughter.'

They went on making nosegays in perfect harmony. Jane, who had been listening through the open door and holding her breath, let it out again. Who would have thought that Ruth would be so sensible? She certainly had changed.

Three of the flower maidens were dressed. Phryne was ready. Her gown was magnificent. The underdress was of heavy morocain, so dark a red as to be almost black. The loose overdress was formed of rose petals, many-shaded from purple to maroon. Her hat embraced her sleek head, the stem and inner petals of the rose, lapping her throat, clear to show her fine profile. Madame Fleuri had surpassed herself.

In the kitchen at Anatole's, Anatole himself was putting the finishing touches to his menu for the celebration feast. The soup: *consommé printanier Imperatrice;* the fish: *sole à la Reine;* the meat: *selle d'agneau Duchesse;* dessert: *pêche Dame Blanche.* He had composed a menu entirely named after female royalty, and he was sure that the Queen of the Flowers would appreciate it. He mopped his brow and poured himself another small calvados to celebrate. Jean-Paul rather pointedly brought him a cup of black coffee.

The nosegays were ready and the minions were waiting to dress the float, which was the bed of an old truck.

'Oh, Miss Fisher!' yelled Maxwell Drake, designer of the float. He was dishevelled, out of breath, and horrified. 'It's awful!'

Phryne, who had spent the night reliving Simonds and his shotgun, was curt. 'Sit down, drink this, then tell me what is wrong,' she ordered.

Maxwell Drake gulped, choked, and said, 'The float! It's been wrecked! Someone took an axe to it and the flat bed is smashed. It's a wreck. And we found this on the top. Do you recognise it?'

Phryne recognised it all right. It was the ragged remains of a flower maiden costume, and Phryne was in no doubt as to who had destroyed the float. But she was not going to allow one nasty young woman's malice to ruin the parade which everyone had worked so hard to bring about. She had an idea.

She scribbled busily. 'Take this down to the

301

circus and put it into Dulcie Fanshawe's hand, no one else, right? Go!'

Maxwell sprang away and ran like the wind. Phryne doffed the outer garment of her costume, appearing in her shorter undergarment, and went into the street.

'There's been a change of plan,' she said to the assembled minions. 'Someone find some white-wash, make those big paper flowers into really huge wreaths, and buy me as many toffee apples as you can find. I need a dozen at least,' she ordered. To hear was to obey. Puzzled, the minions scattered.

It had been a pretty good parade, the denizens of St Kilda thought. Loads of marching bands, good oompah-pah, fine float from Mr Clapp of Eat More Fruit fame, with girls tossing apples into the crowd. Nice dancers, terrific horses, real loud Scottish pipe bands playing 'Scotland the Brave', files of marching soldiers and lifeguards and police. All very well and good. But where was she? Where was the Queen of the Flowers?

They had been expecting a float. That was the usual thing. But stepping elegantly down the middle of the Esplanade, as though they were taking part in a durbar before the regent, came three huge elephants. They were white, thus precious, and they were garlanded with flowers. Huge baskets hung at each side of the elephants, out of which three girls dressed as sweet peas were flinging nosegays. The scent swirled all around them.

And riding on Kali, her costume fluttering in the wind, a red-headed mahout in front of her, dripping with many-coloured petals, was the most beautiful flower of them all, smiling, waving, appearing like a goddess on a cloud of sweet perfume. She was very beautiful and very exotic. Professor Merckens, in the crowd, caught his breath. Kali raised her trunk and trumpeted as though to announce her advent and her power.

She was Phryne Fisher, Queen of the Flowers.

Mr James Murray to Mr Aaron Murray
15 January 1914

Dear father, I have taken the new cruise ship job and I will be home by midsummer. With a reasonable sum, enough to begin with, in fact. There is nothing for me here now that Rory has gone and Neil shipped off to Malaya. There never was much here for me, and now it has been taken away. I will see you soon, God and the trade winds willing. Your loving son, James.

BIBLIOGRAPHY

BOOKS

Barrow, Andrew, *Gossip*
Hamish Hamilton, London, 1978
Brennan, Niall (ed.), *The Melbourne University Students' Song Book*
University of Melbourne, 1946
Broome, Richard with Nick Jackamos,
Sideshow Alley Allen & Unwin, Sydney, 1998
Brown, George Mackay, *The Two Fiddlers*
Piccolo, London, 1979
An Orkney Tapestry Quartet, London, 1973
Buck, Percy C., *The Oxford Song Book*
Oxford University Press, London, 1931
Child, Francis James (ed.),
The English and Scottish Ballads (five volumes)
Dover Books, New York, 1965
Clayre, Alasdair, *100 Folk Songs and New Songs*
Wolfe, London, 1974
Darling, F. Fraser and J. Milton Boyd,
The Highlands and Islands
Fontana, London, 1964
Dower, Alan, *Deadline*
Hutchison, Melbourne, 1979
Escoffier, Auguste, translated by
Vyvyan Holland, *Ma Cuisine*
Mandarin, London, 1965

Flecker, James Elroy,
  The Golden Journey to Samarkand in *Hassan*
  Penguin Books, London, 1922
Healey, Tim, *The World's Greatest Trials*
  Hamlyn, London, 1990
Lawler, James R., *An Anthology of French Poetry*
  Oxford University Press, London, 1960
Lloyd, A.L., *Folk Song in England*
  Paladin, London, 1967
Lussier, Suzanne, *Art Deco Fashion*
  V&A publications, London, 2003
Mackie, J.D., *A History of Scotland*
  Penguin, London, 1964
Martin, A.E., *Common People*
  Wakefield Press, South Australia, 1994
Miller, Christian, *A Childhood in Scotland*
  John Murray, London, 1981
Parlett, David, *The Penguin Encyclopaedia of
  Card Games* Penguin, London, 1979
Wilson, Colin, *World Famous Murders*
  Robinson, London, 1993
Wilson, Colin and Patricia Pitman,
  The Encyclopaedia of Murder
  Pan, London, 1961

PUBLICATIONS
'Community Song Books', Allan and Co,
  Sydney, circa 1925
'Harmsworth's Home Doctor & Encyclopaedia
  of Good Health', The Fleetway House,
  London, 1924
'Pears Shilling Cyclopedia', Pears' Soaps,
  London, circa 1820
'The Home', Art in Australia Ltd, vol. 10, no. 6

The legal principle discussed in this book is to be found in *R v Hallett* [1969] SASR 141 (Supreme Court of South Australia).

AUTHOR'S NOTE

This is a work of fiction. I have researched it as carefully as I could. There are undoubtedly some small errors of fact and timing and one big anachronism, which was when I unilaterally moved the Flower Parade from 1929 to 1928. Please forgive me and do not feel moved to correct me. Anyone else is welcome to email me on kgreenwwod@netspace.net.au

MR BUTLER'S REFRESHING COCKTAIL
one measure of cherry brandy
one measure of gin
squeeze of lemon juice
splash of Cointreau
sugar syrup to taste

Shake all the ingredients together. To make a long drink, add soda water or bar quality lemonade. Garnish with a cherry.

THE DARK-EYED SAILOR
Anon

As I roved out one evening clear
It being the summer time to take the air
I spied a sailor and a lady gay
And I stood to listen to hear what they would say.

He said fair maiden why do you roam
when the day is spent and the night is come?
She heaved a sigh as the tears did run
For my dark eyed sailor, so young
  and far from home.

Tis seven long years since he left this land
A ring he took from off his lily white hand
One half of the ring is still here with me
And the other's rolling at the bottom of the sea.

He said you must wipe him out of your mind
Some other young man you will surely find
Love turns to sorrow and full cold does grow
Like a winter's morning, the hills are
  white with snow.

She said I'll never forsake my dear
Although we're parted this many a year
And Willy wasn't a rake like you

To induce a maiden to slight a jacket blue.

One half of the ring did young William show
She ran distracted with grief and woe
Crying William William there's much
  love in store
For my dark eyed sailor had proved
  his love once more.

And there is a tale from my younger days
This couple's married and no more grieved
So maids be loyal when your love's at sea
For a cloudy morning brings forth a sunny day.

We do hope that you have enjoyed reading this large print book.

Did you know that all of our titles are available for purchase?

We publish a wide range of high quality large print books including:
Romances, Mysteries, Classics
General Fiction
Non Fiction and Westerns

Special interest titles available in large print are:
The Little Oxford Dictionary
Music Book
Song Book
Hymn Book
Service Book

Also available from us courtesy of Oxford University Press:
Young Readers' Dictionary
(large print edition)
Young Readers' Thesaurus
(large print edition)

For further information or a free brochure, please contact us at:
Ulverscroft Large Print Books Ltd.,
The Green, Bradgate Road, Anstey,
Leicester, LE7 7FU, England.
Tel: (00 44) 0116 236 4325
Fax: (00 44) 0116 234 0205

Other titles published by Ulverscroft:

MURDER IN MONTPARNASSE

Kerry Greenwood

Seven Australian soldiers, carousing in Paris in 1918, unknowingly witness a murder and their presence has devastating consequences. Ten years later, two are dead — under very suspicious circumstances. Phryne's wharfie mates, Bert and Cec, appeal to her for help. They were part of this group of soldiers in 1918 and they fear for their lives and for those of the other three men. It's only as Phryne delves into the investigation that she, too, remembers being in Montparnasse on that very same day. Meanwhile, her lover, Lin Chung, is about to be married . . .